Joan Donaldson

Hearts of Mercy

Black Rose Writing | Texas

First printing

ISBN: 978-1-68433-091-1
PUBLISHED BY BLACK ROSE WRITING
www.blackrosewriting.com

Printed in the United States of America
Suggested Retail Price (SRP) $18.95

Hearts of Mercy is printed in Chaparral Pro

With gratitude, to Lisa, Robin, and Suzie

The pearl of justice is found in the heart of mercy.
Catherine of Sienna

HEARTS *of* MERCY

CHAPTER ONE

The last time I'd hiked to this lookout and gazed across these hills, Charlie's fingers had caressed my shoulder. His gentian blue eyes had scanned my face with longing before he kissed me good-by. Blast it all! Charlie's dratted letter ending our engagement felt like a porcupine slapping me with his tail, lodging his barbs into my heart. The harder I yanked at the quills, the more pain swept through me. I blew my nose, and stuffed his letter beneath a chunk of sandstone. Let his words rot.

I refused to give into silly ladylike vapors, swooning over my recalcitrant beau like some girls did after their fellows returned to England. Those gents weren't worth the powder to blow them to hell, but Charlie had been different from other foreigners. My Englishman had been eager to understand our ways, and had tried to buy land in the settlement. Then troubles came to Rugby and Charlie had fled north to apprentice in Michigan. How could he prefer living where folks didn't eat grits?

As my feet slapped the trail, I vowed to stay single, and weave coverlets until called to my heavenly home. Designing new patterns and weaving brought me more pleasure than a fickle man. I'd make my aunt's land prosper with a flock of sheep and a goat for milk, and would build rail fences to surround the pastures. Another quill bit me; I had reckoned on Charlie's hands to work with me. He would have split the rails while I stacked them, pausing now and then for a quick kiss.

When I reached the pike, men in slouch hats shouted to teams of oxen pulling wagons, filled with lumber. The scent of freshly cut pine boards trailed behind them, and the oxen's big hooves left half-moons in the dusty road. The settlers' English accents still jolted me; they had come to experience Mr. Hughes's utopia. We highlanders gossiped about how the English stopped at four o'clock, changed into starched collared-shirts, and sipped tea from thin china cups while eating tiny sandwiches. Come evening, they would swing a tennis racket or toss horseshoes, or their women played the piano and sang. Between hoeing corn, and scything hay, most ridge folk hadn't time for such foolishness. We went visiting on Sundays.

At first, I had hated how the foreigners had cut down our trees and built a town, with boardinghouses, a print shop, and a library. But then I had met Charlie who called *cumulus* and *nimbus* clouds by their names and praised my weavings. The settlement's grand Tabard Inn had burned last year, but a flock of carpenters now sawed and whacked nails as they constructed a new hotel. My Charlie should have been raising a hammer amongst them with his shoulders straining against a homespun shirt stitched by my hands. Despite the ruckus, I was grateful for the wealthy summer guests who spent their cash money for my coverlets at the Commissary. Money that was supposed to help Charlie and me on our farm.

I turned down a dusty side street, and marched toward the gray clapboard boardinghouse where my sister, Lizzie lived. Maroon gingerbread, like rolling waves, edged the house's gables and a rising sun expanded over the screen door. Mounds of red, white, and pink dianthus bloomed around the porch steps and scented the air. The screen door slapped shut behind me. I bumped into Mrs. Carroll who ran the place.

"Ah, Viney, your sister's in the parlor, with an elderly gentleman who's been waiting for you." With red, curly hair and blue eyes, Mrs. Carroll resembled a drawing in a book of Irish folk tales that I had found in Rugby's library. As soon as Mrs. Carroll spoke, folks realized she had come from across the Great Waters.

"Thank you, ma'am." I slipped into the room smothered in red velvet from the heavy curtains to the plush settees. Red roses decorated the rounded shade of the hanging kerosene lamp, and the prisms along the bottom of the shade jiggled as I walked to a rocking chair. Big pink and red cabbage roses splashed across the wallpaper, and a huge oriental rug covered the wide pine flooring. All that plush and roses made me stifle a sneeze.

Lizzie nodded toward a white-haired, bearded man sitting beside her. He wore patched trousers, a blue collarless shirt, and a fraying brown wool vest. Lizzie and the man stood up. "Viney, meet our daddy."

My mouth felt full of wool. Three days after our mama had died from birthing me, our father had run away, leaving our two aunts to raise my sister, my older brother, Jacob, and myself. Not once in nineteen years, had we received a letter, a few dollars, nor had a passing stranger delivered a word about this man. Our aunts had lectured us to forgive him, but I hadn't. Instead, I had spun my anger into thread, strung it on my loom, and whacked the beater against reconciliation. While I had wondered what sort of man my father was, I had named him a coward for abandoning us. Now, I certainly wasn't going to call this fellow, "daddy" and blubber about his return. But our aunts had taught us manners.

"Pleased to meet you, sir," I crossed the room. My belly twisted when I recognized the shape of his face matched mine. I had always thought my oval face and ash blond hair came from my mama. "How can we know you are telling us the truth?"

"Viney!" Lizzie frowned, and plopped down on the settee.

With shaking hands, the old man pulled a small Bible from his coat pocket and gave it to me. "Look at the first page, where your mama, God rest her soul, wrote in Lizzie's and Jacob's birth dates. Your Aunt Alta had to write in yours, 'cause of your mama dying."

Sliding onto the settee next to Lizzie, I recognized Aunt Alta's handwriting, and because of the weaving drafts our mother had lettered out, I knew that the other script was hers.

"After all these years." Lizzie said, as tears puddled in the corners of her eyes.

I stared at the gent. "How do we know you didn't steal this from our father?" I wanted to add, if'n you are our daddy, why couldn't *you* be bothered to write in my name? What if this man had found out about Aunt Alta dying, and had come to claim the farm she had deeded to me?

From the back of the Bible, he took a piece of linen paper and unfolded it. "What they gave me when the war ended. Saying that I fought for the South, God bless her. If'n you don't believe me, go talk to your brother. I spent last night with Jacob in our old cabin."

I glanced at the document and stood up. "Well, reckon we need to step out, and talk things over with Jacob."

"Yes," Lizzie wiped her eyes. "Let me fetch my bonnet. Please excuse us, sir. If you would like a cup of tea while you wait, I could speak to Mrs. Carroll. And she just baked shortbread, too."

The old feller sighed. "Thank you, daughter, that's right kind of you."

A few cumulus clouds floated over the mountains, and their shadows brushed the hills like black moths, as Lizzie and I headed across the ridge to where Jacob and Hazel lived. My sister had been old enough to fix a few memories about our father, so I reckoned that was why she was teary-eyed. Or perhaps it was because her intended had died of the fever last year, leaving her soul bruised. Slender, with black, curly hair and lavender eyes, Lizzie drew suitors like bears to a honey tree; men stumbled when they spied her curves. But she still pined for her Englishman, George, and avoided frolics and dances. Lizzie preferred working a few days for Mrs. Carroll and spent her free time, knitting fine lace, and reading novels.

"Lizzie, with all the ruckus about our supposed father, I couldn't tell you that Charlie broke off our engagement." I held my breath, hoping Lizzie would tongue-lash the scoundrel.

"I'm so sorry." Lizzie gave me a one-arm hug around my waist. "But men can be capricious, wait and see if Charlie changes his mind."

"Is that the best you can do?" My words trembled. I'd expected her to bawl with me and stamp her feet a little. My tears threatened to spill, but I swatted them away. I was weary of crying over him.

Lizzie paused, wrapped her arms around me, and kissed my forehead. For a moment we stood in silence, as a catbird chortled. Here was my sister who knew how to soothe my heart and offer hope when clouds surrounded me. I breathed in the scent of the rosewater she splashed about her face. Even if all the men in the world abandoned me, I had Lizzie, and for her, I would do almost anything. Oh, we scrapped and fussed at each other, but before the sun went down, we forgave each other.

"Truly, I'm sorry, losing a beau is hard. But ever since Charlie left, I wondered if things between you two would unravel. Perhaps you both need time to ponder your feelings. But having Daddy back is good news."

"If this man truly is our father... don't forget how he rejected us and didn't even bother to write." I wanted to curse, but Lizzie's look squashed the words.

When the woods cleared, I spied Mama's pink roses blooming near the porch, and inhaled their heavy scent. Brown-haired Hazel sat churning butter with her babe playing on an Ohio Star quilt. Another little one rounded her belly, pushing up her dark green calico dress and muslin apron. Jacob would soon have a flock of youn'uns to help him.

But as we climbed the porch steps, my mind flitted to sitting here in the twilight, with Charlie holding my hand. We had chattered about the farm we would have where Charlie would breed new varieties of apples, and I would raise sheep to mow the orchards. Now, I reckoned he planned to grow his apples in the north. At least I had my wooly friends.

"We knew you would come," Hazel said. "Jacob's expecting you. He's hoeing corn."

We headed toward the corn patch where I spied Jacob chopping weeds. My heart splintered. One year ago, Charlie had worked with me in the same field, until blisters rose on his soft palms, but by the end of summer, calluses had thickened his hands. Now, I would never see him again. Why had our father returned instead of Charlie?

"You're wanting to know what I think about Daddy." Jacob leaned on his hoe. "Let's sit under the big oak. Got a jug of water, there."

Lizzie and I settled on a log next to Jacob while he gulped, water dripping onto his beard. He poured a little on his head and swept back his brown hair as a rivulet trickled down the front of his sweat-stained shirt. Jacob wore a pair of britches from wool that I had woven.

"He showed you Mama's Bible, and his Confederate papers?" Jacob took another big gulp.

"Yes," I said. "But how do you know this man didn't take them from someone else?"

"He showed me the puckered line of skin on his shin, where shrapnel grazed his leg at Chancellorsville. I remember Daddy telling me stories about the battle and seeing the ugly scar. If you look at the back of the Bible, you'll see where I penned my name. I was so proud that I could write it, but Daddy tanned my hide for messing with the Good Book."

Lizzie wiped tears off her cheeks. "So he's telling the truth. Our daddy's come home. I wish Aunt Alta had lived long enough to see her prayers answered."

My stomach tumbled to my toes. "But why would he come back, now?"

How could Lizzie so easily welcome the man who had run away from us? Until he apologized to me, I wanted to spit at his feet.

"He's got the palsy, and figures he hasn't long to live. So he wants to make peace with us." Jacob ran his fingers through his hair. "It won't be easy, but I reckon our aunties would want us to do what's right. Even if you don't want to make amends with him, Viney, you should do it for them."

I jumped off the log and circled my siblings. "I'm done with men. Charlie just wrote and ended our engagement." Every inch of me felt as if I'd been thumped up and down in a butter churn until I'd clabbered. "And don't forget that this old gent didn't want you, too."

"I'm sorry to hear about Charlie," Jacob said. "Maybe you'll be gentler with the next fellar who comes courting."

I ignored him. "So what does our long-lost father want?" Whatever it was, I refused to give it.

"To know his children. Hazel and I offered for him to live with us. But he said this place, especially the cabin, held too many memories of Mama." Jacob unfolded his lithe frame and paced in a circle. At age twelve, he had taken over the farm and Aunt Alta had moved back to her sister's cabin. Plowing and chopping wood had sculpted Jacob's shoulders and powerful thighs.

"Appears that after leaving the ridge, Daddy wandered as far west as the Rocky Mountains. When he came back east, he felt too ashamed to come here, so he settled near a brother living in the Great Smoky Mountains. Daddy plans to return to Wears Cove, to the little cabin he built on our uncle's land."

"Sounds like a dandy idea. When does he leave?" Good, I'd only have to endure a few days of this carrying-on, celebrating the repentant father. Shouldn't the prodigal be a child and not the parent?

"Daddy wants you and Lizzie to go with him," Jacob said. "But he's afeard to ask you." Jacob picked at a scab on his thumb. "He needs someone to take care of him."

"What? He expects us to keep house and nurse him? That's the most addlepated idea." I threw a rock into the woods. "Why should we? Must be some other kin living in the cove who could move in with him."

"You don't have to go, Viney, and I won't fault you if'n you say no,"

Jacob said. "I wouldn't agree to uproot my family and move, but you and Lizzie are not wed."

"That's not fair! We both have plans..." I stuck out my foot to trip Jacob, but he dodged it.

Lizzie took a deep breath. "Burying George, set me to pondering about everything that's happened in my life, and what I want to do. Too many years have been wasted, we should share whatever time Daddy has left. After my cottage is built then I'll come to him."

Jacob put an arm around Lizzie. "Our aunties would be proud of how you've grown into a generous woman."

My brother might as well have said, "but I'm not proud of you, Viney, because you are acting like a self-centered child who has no place in her heart for her father."

"How can y'all expect me to head out with a stranger and move to a foreign place?" I studied their expressions. Why couldn't they understand the pain of losing Charlie? And now, they wanted to snatch me from my home and my weaving?

"Well, what's keeping you here?" Jacob stretched his arms in front of him, locked his fingers, and pulled, his way of expressing his frustrations.

"What about my weaving? My flock of sheep is growing. I need to put up hay, hoe the corn, fill in the chinking to the cabin, there's always something to do. And I'm hoping the visitors will buy stacks of coverlets. I've no desire to go gallivanting off." As I listed each fact, I broke a piece off a stick and flung the bit over my shoulder.

"I'll ask Mr. Hill to find a settler to care for your farm. Daddy told me that our Uncle John has a passel of daughters with looms and spinning wheels. Appears they even grow flax and weave linen. Besides, you should be thinking about helping your family and not about earning money."

"You might enjoy spending time with our cousins," Lizzie said. "You could learn some new weaving patterns. You know how everywhere I look, memories of George haunt me. You're going to see Charlie by every tree and porch swing, sometimes a new place helps ease grief. Please Viney, do this for me. You go for the summer, then I'll come in the fall."

"Oh, Laws." After her months of sorrow and grieving, Lizzie knew I wouldn't deny her request. And my sister was usually right about men and love. “Only ‘til the end of August. Then Lizzie can swap places.”

Jacob grinned. “What if you meet a sweetheart? You might not want to come back.”

I picked up his jug and doused him. “Maybe our girl cousins are single because there aren’t any good men in those mountains.”

CHAPTER TWO

Charlie Breckenridge thrust his hands in his pockets and walked away from the Traverse City, Post Office. Viney should have received his letter at least three weeks ago, and could have written back by now. He shouldn't have sent that letter. He should have known Viney would be furious and not answer him. Despite the pain of watching his friend, George die, Charlie should have stayed in Tennessee. He shouldn't have fled north to Michigan. The tap of his boots on the wooden walkway beat out, "he shouldn't have, he should have."

A sharp breeze off Traverse Bay blew down the street lined with shops, hotels, and saloons. Men drove wagons filled with crates of chickens, milk cans, and barrels. Huge stacks of logs lined sections of the wharf where men loaded them onto schooners. Charlie headed north on the road running along the east peninsula, a finger jutting out into the bay. Orchards covered the low hills with endless rows of apple and cherry trees.

Gulls cried, and sand sifted into his boots. The wind whipped Charlie's auburn hair around his face until he stuffed the wayward locks under his slouch hat. Sunshine shimmered on the waves rolling to the dunes. Charlie closed his eyes, and the sounds drew him back to his home in England, except in Michigan there was no taste of salt in the air or gorse hedges bordering the road. But if he had returned to Weymouth, he would have had to choose his father's plan to study law, and the only books Charlie read taught about farming.

He tramped up the lane leading to a two-story white clapboard house trimmed with green gingerbread. Behind the house stood a barn with a steeply pitched roof. A tall, blonde-haired girl wearing a spotless shirtwaist and a clean apron, emerged from the chicken coop. Charlotte held a filled egg basket, and she glided in her long skirt.

"Charlie! Home so soon?" Charlotte linked elbows with him, and they walked towards the house. "There wasn't any mail?"

"No, not for any of us." Charlie opened the door, watching the sway of Charlotte's hips.

"You did remember to buy that spool of thread?" She set the egg basket on the kitchen table, and kissed his cheek.

"Ah, no. I forgot." His brain had floundered, too preoccupied with thinking about Viney.

"You forgot it yesterday, too." Charlotte shook her head as she rinsed the eggs and stacked them in a bowl. "What were you thinking about?"

Viney. Rugby. Viney. The hills of Tennessee. Viney's teasing laugh. The mountain mist floating across the ridge in the cool morning. Viney's lips.

"Home. It's been a while." He couldn't tell his thoughts to Charlotte. She was the reason he had written Viney. Two weeks ago, when Mr. Burnett had moved next door and turned Charlotte's head, their relationship had tottered. Yet, if their new neighbor had weaseled into Charlotte's affections, then why had she kissed his cheek? Was Charlotte toying with him the way Viney had? But eventually love for him had filled Viney's heart.

"Yes, I'm sure you miss your family and farm. I've only been to England once, but it was a lovely place." Charlotte set the bowl of eggs on a pantry shelf. "Papa said you should milk a bit early tonight."

Charlie grabbed the tin bucket and headed out to the barn. Two Jersey cows mooed, sticking their pebbly noses through the gaps in the gate. Lifting the latch, Charlie allowed one cow to enter the bay of the barn. His hands gripped and squeezed; the milk foamed into the bucket. Resting his head against Clover's side, he longed to find himself in Viney's barn, or dancing with her after a work bee, or walking along the path to Wilson's Lookout while stealing kisses. But he was stuck at this farm for two more months.

During the fall and winter, when Charlotte had clung to his arm and covered her dance card with his name, Charlie had dreamed of marrying her. As an only child, one day, she would inherit this farm, but Mr. Burnett had become the novelty who explained the delights of Boston to Charlotte, and any other willing listener. Charlie tugged too hard, and Clover's tail swatted his cheek.

"Sorry, old girl." Charlie stripped Clover of the last drops of milk. Last

June, his hands had grown tired after ten minutes of milking, but farm work had strengthened his fingers and expanded his shoulders. By the end of the day, his beard bristled red and gold along his cheeks and chin. Charlie carried the milk to the house, handed the bucket to Charlotte, and headed to his room.

Tucked beneath the steep roof, the room sported a cot, his trunk, a table, and a chair. Charlie ducked his head, avoiding the roof joists, as he poured water into a basin and scrubbed his face. Cheesecloth covered the one small window looking out at the cherry orchard. Frost patterns had etched the window in January, and now heat radiated from the roof. Charlie longed to soar across the miles and land at Rugby. He had bunked in a tent erected on a wooden platform, and each night, the cool mountain air had floated between the trees as the whip-poor-wills called. If only he had stayed. If only he hadn't written that letter.

At the dinner table, Charlie pushed in Charlotte's chairs and took a seat opposite her father, Mr. Townsend who sat at the head of the table. A linen tablecloth, polished silver, and china graced the table. Lace curtains hung against cherry window trim and wainscoting circled the lower walls.

"Steak and kidney pie," Charlotte said, as she placed a steaming helping on his plate. "Your favorite."

"Yes." When Charlie first arrived, the fragrance evoked his mother's kitchen, but now, he yearned for cornbread and soup beans, and a dish of Viney's blackberry cobbler. After supper, he and Viney had sat on her front porch and watched the fireflies flickering as they rose and fell in their mating ritual. If Charlie had kept his promise, he and Viney would have been wed and living in their own cabin.

Between bites of asparagus and steak, Charlie wondered why Charlotte had drawn his attention. She was too sweet, too obedient, and too delicate, compared to Viney who had hid snakes at the Tabard to scare the visitors, threw peaches at snobbish Englishmen, and dragged her sister from a burning building. And yet, the way Charlotte looked at Mr. Burnett still irked him.

• • • • •

From between an apple tree's branches, Charlie watched Mr. Henry Burnett tie his horse's reins to the hitching post. Although it was a Wednesday evening, Mr. Burnett wore a black frock coat, top hat, black trousers and a white shirt with a black cravat. Thin and tall, he looked dressed for a funeral and not a Chautauqua lecture about Longfellow's literature. As Charlotte exited the house, her blonde hair gleamed beneath the brim of her straw hat tied on with lavender ribbons. She had pinned her mother's gold brooch at the neck of her cream-colored shirtwaist, tucked into a long navy skirt. Mr. Burnett offered Charlotte his pale hand, and assisted her into his buggy. He climbed in and the buggy's wheels rattled away towards town.

Eyeing the spacing of apples on the branch, Charlie picked off a cluster as he thinned the fruit. Last summer, he had performed this task in Mr. Hill's peaches while Viney kept house for Mrs. Hill. Now and then, Viney had helped him, wanting to learn about fruit farming. Charlie's calloused hands tossed a little green apple at a fence post. Even a month ago, Charlotte had crooned about his English accent, but now she shunned his scratchy fingers. Charlie lobbed the hard apples at two ewes grazing in the orchard. Somehow, he must claim enough courage to admit his mistakes and hop on the next train south.

But would Viney welcome him back?

CHAPTER THREE

Even though rain pattered against the train car, I claimed the window seat and watched Lizzie talking to a young gentleman and an older woman. Dressed in a black frock coat and top hat, the man must be a summer visitor, and not a new settler. As our train chugged out of Sedgemore, Lizzie escorted the pair to her buggy and drove off toward Rugby. Her last words to me had been a plea to forgive our father, to seek the good in him, and to make memories that I would cherish after he passed away. It was easy for her to preach forgiveness, seeing how Lizzie wasn't interrupting her summer plans and rolling away from home. Nor had her fiancé cast her aside. At the present, I hadn't many charitable thoughts towards men.

The locomotive rumbled east on the narrow tracks that curved around the sides of the mountain, and it chugged across iron bridges, strung high above rivers. I marveled at how the train roared past the fields and through villages, blowing its whistle, leaving clouds of smoke hovering above the tracks. But as the countryside blurred, I pondered how Charlie had sailed in a steamer across the Atlantic, and had ridden several trains in order to travel to Sedgemore, before walking the seven miles to Rugby. For a fellow so determined to live in Mr. Hughes's utopia, why had Charlie left?

Like my father fleeing the death of my mother, after George died, Charlie said too many painful remembrances resided in Rugby. I ran my fingers along the wooden arms of the seat, wishing Charlie's long legs were stretched out beside mine. If'n he had stayed, I would have held Charlie in my arms when he wept and baked him peach pies to cheer him. We would have created some happy memories to shove away the painful ones.

My father slept next to me, a withered potato with a few licks of white hair. If'n I hadn't seen my child in nineteen years, I'd ask questions so as to get acquainted. But I reckoned, he could feel my anger. He couldn't even look me in the eye, much less speak to me, and sought refuge in sleep. I set to knitting on a sock that was to have fit Charlie's foot, blaming him for getting me into this tangle. If we had wed, Charlie and I would be snuggling beneath my coverlets, partaking of the love I wanted to give and receive. Lizzie's rear end would have been warming this wooden seat.

After my father and I spent the night in Knoxville, a noisy city full of folks riding in buggies, and wagons rattling along past midnight, we hitched a ride with a teamster heading to Sevierville. I rode in the back of the buckboard while the two men chatted on the wagon seat. Thank goodness for the sacks of flour that protected my behind from the ruts and rocks littering the road. The team of mules splashed through creeks, and hugged the sides of hills as the road climbed higher and higher, and then dropped down again. My home looked puny compared to these great mountains with their smoky blue haze. Turkey buzzards floated on the downdrafts, and deer crashed off into the briar thickets. Once, we even drove through a tunnel of rhododendrons covered with white blossoms.

About mid-morning, we arrived in Sevierville, and found hogs rooting next to the general store, where two other wagons were parked. Across the dirt road, beneath five oak trees, sat an Old Primitive Baptist Church. Even though I was miles from home, the village reminded me of Sedgemore. How queer my ridge must of have looked to Charlie after living in a village with thatched cottages and cobblestone streets.

"I'll check and see if anyone from the cove has come to town," my father said. "Do you want something to eat? I could buy some cheese and soda crackers. And a few pickles." Because he was so stooped, his wrinkled face was level with mine. A bit of light shone in his eyes, and he attempted a tiny smile.

"No, thank you, mostly I need a drink. There's a well behind the church."

"All right, then." His shoulders slumped, and he shuffled into the store.

A nest of adders tangled inside me. My Aunt Alta would have clucked her tongue, telling me to be gentler to the man who was my father, and appreciate his kind offer. Truth was, I'd have enjoyed a bit of cheese, but not from him. I stepped over to the church.

Hauling up the bucket, I dipped a gourd, and drank until my body shivered from the flood of icy water. As I walked back to the wagon, the store's screen door banged, and a fine looking man stepped out with my father.

"Meet your cousin, James Walker. One of your Uncle John's sons," my father said. "He can drive us into the cove."

"Pleased to meet you, Cousin Viney." James held out his hand. "Right sweet of you to come take care of your daddy." His eyes scanned me from my boots to my bonnet, and I hoped he didn't find me lacking. For the flick of a bee's wing, I wished dust didn't cling to my dress, and that I had washed my face.

"Nice to make your acquaintance." I shook his large hand, feeling like a slug. If this hazel-eyed wonder with blond hair and broad shoulders knew that I hadn't wanted to come with my father, he wouldn't say such nice things. A tall drink of water, James stood a foot taller than me, dressed in a homespun linen shirt, and woolen trousers held up with black braces. Even the straw hat on his head was handmade from braided oat straw. While James loaded my trunk onto his wagon, I swiped my face with my apron and smoothed the wrinkles out of my dress.

When James' hands circled my waist, and he placed me onto the wagon seat, I wanted to jump off so he'd have to lift me again. As if sensing my wish, a hint of a smile raised the corners of his mouth, accentuating his cleft chin. The pleasant scent of boxwood drifted from his shirt; his womenfolk must drape their washing on those bushes.

James hopped up, settled in the middle of the seat, shook the reins, and clucked to his mule. When the road split, James tugged on the right rein, and the mule stepped onto a narrow trail threading through rising mountains. Hemlock roots wrapped around outcropping boulders and wide chestnut trees shaded our path; now and then, a spring trickled from between a cleft in the rocks.

"You're kin to the weaving sisters I heard tell about?" I pried my eyes away from the fine hair on James' strong wrists, and looked up at my cousin. "I weave, too." I liked the way his hair poked out from beneath his hat, forming little wings. Oh, Laws, how would it feel if his hair brushed my cheek?

"Yes, even my youngest sisters spin and weave. Get moving, Red." James's large hands relaxed a bit as the mule hastened its gait.

James didn't speak much except when my father asked him questions about Uncle John's health. Although James didn't seek to learn anything about me or his kin back in Rugby, I caught him glancing at me as the wagon rumbled along. See, Charlie, I wanted to say to him, other men find me pretty. Hopefully, my cousin would want to visit some evenings, so I would have to spend less time alone with my father. I would have to remember what Aunt Alta had taught me about baking pies.

My farm in the Cumberland Mountains was beautiful, but the many ridges of the Great Smoky Mountains rolled endlessly, and a few of the peaks stretched higher than the others. They set swallows swooping inside me. For the first time since reading Charlie's letter, I wanted to cut loose and swing a partner to the beat of a reel. Maybe Lizzie had been right, and a summer in these hazy blue mountains would be the tonic my heart needed.

The sun brushed the tops of the ridges, when our wagon rattled through a gap and into Wears Cove. Even though I had never seen the sea, I reckoned that one of those watery harbors would be like this broad valley sheltered by the mountains. But here, the shimmering waves rippled over fields of corn and oats, as the evening shadows of the mountains crept closer. A meadowlark sang a welcoming song from an oak tree, and a rabbit flung itself across the road, and into a blackberry thicket.

Smoke drifted from stone chimneys rising from the roofs of log cabins sitting near vegetable patches. Split rail fences surrounded log barns, and cows, mules, oxen, and sheep freckled the pastures. A few apple and pear trees grew near the fences, adorned with grapevines. A small sign nailed onto a post pointed to a road leading to a gristmill. James drove to a cabin set apart from the others at the base of the mountains. Despite the peace and beauty, I missed my farm.

"Here you go," he said. Our eyes met as he lifted me from the wagon, and my cheeks flushed. Appeared James liked what he saw.

"This is your Uncle Abe's place. Your pa's cabin sits near that little creek." James pointed toward a footpath. He carried my trunk onto Uncle Abe's porch, where a large man with gray streaks in his black hair opened the door. His body put me in mind of an old boar with black eyes, thick jowls, and legs and arms like tree branches. I doubted his lips knew how to smile. Several young boys tumbled after him.

"You must be Lavinia," Uncle Abe said. His palm swallowed my hand. "About time you come keep house for your pa. Thank you, James, for fetching them."

"You're welcome, sir," James said. "Best be off." He tipped his hat at me and climbed up. "My sisters said to come visit them." He slapped the reins and drove up a narrow road leading to the top of the mountain.

"Thank you," I called after him. Turning back to the house, I counted two girls and five boys. Two of the boys were twins. A blond-haired woman about my age, with an apron covering a huge belly came out and smiled at me.

"Meet my new woman, your Aunt Sayward. My wife, Nancy died a year ago," Uncle Abe said. "Sayward, quit gawking, Fix my brother a plate. You youn' uns, move." He swatted the older girl on the rear end. "Sissy, help your new ma."

The children scattered like ants before a boot. I followed my father into the cabin filled with a large rope bed with a trundle bed beneath it, a trestle table, benches, and a few chairs. I spied more pallets up in the loft. Aunt Sayward waddled to the hearth and lifted a kettle from a hook.

"Do you like rabbit stew? And corn pone?" She uncovered a plate holding sticks of corn bread.

"Sounds tasty," I said. "How can I help?" Aunt Sayward's feet and ankles were so swollen that I wanted to wait on her. Weariness had paled her face and dimmed her blue eyes, and her willowy arms looked even thinner compared to her belly. I picked up the plate of corn bread.

"Oh no, Miss Viney, Daddy told me to help." Sissy grabbed the plate and took it to the table where she laid out plates and cutlery.

Across the room, the boys gaped, nudging each other, whispering. Judging from the elbows jutting out of their sisters' sleeves, and the girls' skinny faces, the lads finished most of the food before the girls were allowed to sit and eat. Uncle Abe and my father leaned against the porch railing, talking. And in a corner were two unfinished splint baskets shaped like watermelons, waiting for their edges to be bound. Who was the basket maker in this family?

"Sissy, tell your pa that their supper's ready." Aunt Sayward brushed away the strands of hair slipping out of her bun.

"Send one of the twins. Please. Send Bobby Joe," Sissy picked up her little sister.

"Can't always do that, child." Aunt Sayward spoke to a small boy who skipped out the door. The lad tugged on his father's sleeve until Uncle Abe bent his head.

"Come, Jesse." Uncle Abe pointed to a seat. "Viney, sit next to your pa so you can help him."

I slapped my bottom on the bench, my lungs squeezing my heart. Uncle Abe took a seat opposite me, fixing his eyes on mine. Black hair furred his hands, reminding me of the huge Carolina wolf spiders that loved to lurk in the dark corners of a cabin.

"As long as you live on my land, you mind what I say, hear? No courting with the fellars. You're here to care for your daddy, not to find a husband. Church on Sunday mornings and evenings, and you'll attend the Wednesday prayer meetings. When Sayward's time comes, you can help. Sissy's too flighty to be worth much. And if'n you bring shame to my name, I'll lay my strap on you. I won't be having the White Caps coming after you or my family."

"Yes, sir." My fists clenched. Just try and take a strap to my backside, I wanted to say, and you will pay. I'd had my calves blistered by Mr. Lufty, a schoolteacher who hadn't lasted one term because of a trick I played on him. And who in tarnation were the White Caps?

"Good. Eat." Uncle Abe pushed back the bench a bit and stretched out his legs. "Sissy, fetch my pipe."

The poor girl ran to the hearth, carrying over the pipe, and a pouch. I crumbled corn pone into my stew and began to fill my belly, but my craw was already overflowing with disgust for my uncle.

• • • • •

That night, I slept on the same pallet with Sissy and one-year-old Hannah. Sissy's nightgown was as patched as her dress. If'n Lizzie were here, she would be measuring this girl for new undergarments, including a couple of petticoats edged with her hand-knit lace. Two days gone, and I sorely missed how my sister loved to fuss over her clothes and hair. Until Charlie began courting me, frocks and lace didn't mean much to me, but Lizzie had shown me the value in such frippery. Sometime in the dim gray-light of predawn, Hannah wet the bed, and Sissy almost rolled on top of me.

"Beg your pardon, Cousin Viney," she whispered. "Didn't mean to."

Sissy's cold feet moved closer to mine. Her curly, flaxen hair rippled across the pillow; sky blue eyes filled her small face. With her porcelain skin, Sissy had the delicate beauty that would bring boys tumbling about the cabin door. Lizzie would have delighted in drafting a pattern, choosing the perfect calico, and dressing Sissy in a dress with a bustle and a deep ruffle on the skirt.

"Just call me Viney. I'm only three or four years older than you." But after living midst the Englishmen and escaping from a burning building, I felt ancient compared to this scared girl. Appeared to me, she feared something even more threatening than her father.

"Can't do that around Daddy." A shiver rolled over Sissy, as she snuggled next to me.

"I reckon not. You must miss your mama."

"I do. My Mama Jo was Daddy's first wife and died birthing me a brother. A month later, Daddy married Nancy."

"Nancy was a kind mama?" Below us, one of the youngest boys said something to Aunt Sayward. The cabin door opened, and she took him to the privy.

"Yes, Mama Nancy loved to cook and garden, but having babies wore her out, especially birthing the twins. She died from the ague, three months after Hannah was born. Daddy said, if I had helped her more, she wouldn't have been so tuckered." Sissy stroked Hannah's hair.

Why would my uncle twist his daughter's mind? The menfolk on my ridge had sneered at the Englishmen's prissy women, but most didn't manipulate the truth against their wives and daughters. Oh, they wanted their womenfolk to obey them, but most fathers heaped love on their families.

"Daddy don't pay much mind to Hannah. Reckon he also blames her for Mama Nancy dying." Sissy kissed her little sister. "Just makes me love her more."

"But at least your pa didn't run off." Like most men, he had wed another woman to tend his home and had started making more babies. Aunt Sayward would bring a dozen children to this cabin.

"How old is Sayward?" The cabin door closed, and at the hearth, my aunt stirred the fire.

"Nineteen."

Same age as me; I wanted to gag. "Uncle Abe must be twenty years older than her." Why hadn't he married some older widow? No man that age would ever kiss me. A shadow of James' muscular shoulders, and the way he swung his legs slipped through my mind. "Sayward seems like a sweet mother, a good woman."

"Oh, she's good alright. She minds Daddy." Sissy trembled. "And you best do, too."

I gritted my teeth, knowing how my uncle was the sort of man who made everyone obey. "Your daddy mentioned the White Caps, who are they?"

Sissy's eyes darkened, her breathing quickened. "Men wearing white hoods over their faces; some even wear long white robes. If'n they hear that a woman is wanton or won't obey her pa, they warn her by leaving a hickory switch and a note. If she don't mend her ways, then they come and whip her. Sometimes they even beat her pa for not disciplining his daughter."

"Don't the fathers protect their daughters from those men? Why won't anyone stop them?" What was wrong with the folks in this valley?

"A few men have tried, but everyone's a-feared of the White Caps, because there are too many of them to fight. Last week, they left a switch at my friend's cabin with a note calling her a slut. Lydia's betrothed to her cousin Saul, but someone seen her kissing Ahab."

"Well, that wouldn't be proper, but whipping women isn't right either."

"Lyddie said, Ahab grabbed her when she was fetching home the cows. He knew when she'd be stepping by and waited for her, so he could force himself on her."

My skin crawled. Folks in the cove needed to ask more questions and take a whip to the White Caps. Thank goodness, I'd have left at the end of summer. Poking my feet out of the quilts, I reached for my dress.

CHAPTER FOUR

Uncle Abe took my father fishing while Sissy and I trudged over to my father's one-room log cabin. Sissy chattered about different families in the cove as she scrubbed the floor with sand. I washed the two windows, and the few bits of furniture. After kindling a fire and setting a pot of yellow-eyed beans to simmer, we hauled my pallet up to the tiny loft. I spread one of my indigo and cream coverlets over the narrow mattress, wanting to scold Charlie. If'n he weren't so double-minded, I would be waking every morning on my farm, with one of his arms around me. Instead, I flopped on my pallet and touched the ceiling with my palms, hoping there weren't any huge spiders lurking between the shingles. Just before Sissy departed, I asked her who was making the baskets.

"Sayward started them before her belly got big. Now, she's so worn out that they just sit there. Do you know how to weave baskets?"

"I do." During the first light of the morning, I had resolved to help my aunt by finishing those two, and come September, I'd take them to Rugby and sell them at the commissary. So Uncle Abe wouldn't fuss, I'd trade them for calico and muslin for new dresses and underclothing for his womenfolk. Not that I cared what my uncle thought, but I didn't want him to feel ashamed and reject my gift. When I sent the dry goods, I'd write a note thanking Sayward and Sissy for welcoming me to the cove. Lizzie would enjoy sewing new clothes for them.

• • • • •

Before sundown, my father plodded up the path, leaning on his cane. He hung his hat on a nail, and surveyed the cabin. "You done good. I like those daisies in that tin, cheers up the place. Cornbread smells good, too." He sank onto a chair. "Fishin' makes a body hungry."

Worthless Uncle Abe had frittered away the day while Aunt Sayward chopped wood, cared for a passel of youn' uns, and even hoed a bit in the garden. I lifted the lid off the Dutch oven, took out a pan of cornbread, It's toasty fragrance made my stomach growl. After setting a bowl of beans in front of my father, I stood back, waiting like Aunt Sayward.

"Fill a bowl and sit, child," my father said. "I'm not my brother."

"Thank goodness," I muttered, and drew up a chair as my father bowed his head.

"Thank you, Lord, for a clean cabin, a hot meal, and a daughter to care for me. Please watch over us. In our Lord's name, amen."

My father's hands shook as he crumbled cornbread into his beans and lifted a spoon. Now and then, the spoon tipped, and the beans fell back into the bowl. Slowly he chewed, mostly on one side because he had lost several teeth from his lower right jaw. Milk dribbled down his beard when he sipped from his mug.

I stirred my beans, watching the steam drifting from the bowl. Despite my hunger, my belly balked at the smell of food. Unless this bitterness bubbling inside me departed, it was going to be a tedious summer; only an apology from my father could drive my anger away.

"You're wondering why your uncle is so mean." My father dropped chunks of cornbread into another bowl. "Could you pour me some milk, please?"

"Yes, sir." I wanted to say, I'm also wondering why you ran off and left three little children. Why didn't you marry another wife and give us a mother? I filled his bowl with milk and chewed a bite of cornbread. The gritty meal silenced my tongue.

"The War Between the States changed your uncle. The violence, the hunger, the endless days of wondering when life would be normal, again. The hardships altered everyone. Being eleven, Abe was too young to fight, and stayed to work our farm in Virginia along with the help of our sisters and mother. He was big for his age and looked thirteen, so the Home Guard wondered why he hadn't joined up. They would taunt him about being a coward, for hiding behind women, but them men wouldn't listen when our mama tried to stop them.

"Then one evening, the Yankees rode in, trampling our fields, ripping apart rail fences for firewood. They plundered our livestock and torched our barn. When one soldier tried to have his way with our eldest sister, Abe tackled him. My brother was strong enough to take the wind out of the man, but Abe took a beating. In revenge, the Yankees burned our cabin, so Abe had to hide my mother and three sisters in a cave. A pretty shallow one, but it was near a spring and provided a view of the road leading into the valley. But Abe never forgave himself for not saving our cabin and barn. At the end of the war, my older brother and I came home, leaving Daddy and another brother buried at Shiloh."

My aunts hadn't told me these details about my father's family. Watching the enemy burn down my home would seed anger into my soul. Fear and shame had pummeled my uncle when he was young, and twisted him into a bully. Not that I felt sorry for him. Like most of us, Uncle Abe's anger and fears caused him to clutch the reins to everything and everyone around him so he could control their lives. Running my fingers along the edge of my apron, my conscience reminded me how I had tried to manipulate Charlie's feelings for my gain, and look what my deception had harvested.

"After I wed your mama, we packed up for the Cumberland Mountains. Seeing how many of the local lads had died on the battlefield, your mama's sisters begged to come along. When we arrived on the ridge, we learned how most of the menfolk in Scott County fought for the Union, and didn't take kindly to our family being for the Confederacy."

"Back in Virginia, Abe stayed with our older brother until they quarreled, then Abe lit off for Wears Cove, hoping your Uncle John would invite him to live here. When an unmarried cousin died, Abe bought his farm and wed Sissy's ma. After the sufferings he endured from the war, it's a pity he lost two wives."

Hadn't Aunt Alta preached how we should learn patience from our sufferings? The less time I spent with my uncle, the better. Even my pity for Sissy wouldn't nudge me to knock on his door, instead she could visit us and find respite from her father.

"Jacob told me when you moved from Virginia, how Mama carried the beater for her loom through Cumberland Gap." I shifted my gaze to the windowlight, and counted four bubbles in the wavy glass.

Over the years, Aunt Alta had described my mother on that journey; barefoot, hunched over by the weight of the beater tied to her back, she had trudged between giant chestnut trees and waded streams as Jacob grew in her belly. While holding up her skirt with one hand, her other hand clutching at a sapling, she had threaded her way through the opening in the rocks, finally gazing into the promised land of Tennessee.

"She did. I had vowed that after raising our cabin, I'd build her a new loom and great wheel. And somehow, I'd give her a flock of sheep. Your mama had packed her carders in a poke tied to her waist. Come evening when we sat by the campfire, she'd take them out, just to inhale the scent of wool. I'd watch the weariness ease from her face, and a hint of gladness would raise the corners of her mouth." Pa rested his elbows on the table, his head nestled in his shaking hands.

"But you didn't build her either of them. Or give her even one ewe." My shoulder muscles knotted as I clenched my teeth, pushing down my fury. It would be easier to forgive this man if he recognized how he had hurt not only his children, but also my mama. Like her, I often buried my nose in a fluff of wool, dreaming of what the thread would turn into when I wove my latest design. Wool and weaving created more than coverlets, they flew me to a mountain peak where I found contentment, and my father had denied my mother that joy.

"I know." His voice quavered. "She birthed Jacob just after I laid the cabin's roof, and we started grubbing out trees so we could grow corn. Hard work clearing land, but your mama laid your brother on a quilt and swung an axe, determined to topple enough trees so sunlight could reach her garden. Two years after Jacob, Lizzie come along." He worked his lips, running his tongue over his bottom teeth. "Corn crop didn't bring much cash, so we had to spend our few dollars on salt and such. But your mama didn't whine. She'd pull a bit of wool off her cards and stuck it in the cabin wall near where she cooked."

I might look like my father, but my mother had given me her spirit. To lose the song of my loom as my feet pressed the pedals, to no longer feel wool twisting into yarn, while listening to the whir of the spindle, that pain would suck the marrow from my bones.

"Did my birth kill her?" My aunts would never answer my question.

"I think staring at her silent beater, longing to make something pretty, stole her spirit," he whispered. "I should have built that loom. I should have built a wheel for her spindle, but all I could think about was getting ahead. After her birth pains ended, and you had arrived, the bleeding wouldn't stop. She gave in to her sorrow." His eyes filled with tears. "She didn't fight to live."

Seeing him weep, I should have felt sorry for my father, but I couldn't. He should have understood how denying my mother the pleasure of weaving had loosened her grip on living. And yet, shouldn't she have wanted to live for her children? Why couldn't she find joy in us?

"I seen too much of death. Killed too many men, left others groaning on the battlefield. Your mama's screams, her blood flooding the bed." He looked away. "My selfishness killed her. If only I could start over..." His tears glistened on his beard.

"So you ran off." I tried not to spit out the words. Hadn't I seen Lizzie go mad with grief after George passed? Didn't I know what it was like to watch my Aunt Alta suck in her last breath and feel a piece of my heart tumbling away? But what sort of father left his motherless children?

His fingers rubbed back and forth along his horn spoon. "Death swallowed me. I walked west, to the prairies, looked for silver and gold in the Rockies, and hunted buffalo, trying to make peace with life. But I never could settle down, kept wandering; always thinking about Tennessee. Ain't no monster trees like these out west, nothing like our chestnuts. So, last year, I wrote Abe, and he offered to help me build this cabin."

"Why do you want me here? Why couldn't we have stayed in Rugby with Lizzie and Jacob?" The questions roared out of me. I wanted to shake him, but with each word from my mouth, his hands trembled more.

"I can't live on that ridge where your mama died, or in the cabin I built for her, smelling her roses, hearing the clickety-clack of a loom." My father lifted his head; his eyes pleading for mercy. "I want to know my children before I pass on. I want to make things right between us."

But did I want to make things right? The sorrow in Jacob's eyes when other boys went hunting with their daddies slid into my mind, as did the hurt in Lizzie's face when at frolics, other girls danced with their fathers. I had hated seeing their misery. My father couldn't make things right with me until I heard him say he was sorry. I picked up our bowls, wishing I had stayed home, but then Lizzie was right, each day at Rugby would have reminded me how Charlie wasn't coming back.

My emotions were as scattered as the crumbs I brushed off the table and into my hand. Standing on the porch, I flung the crumbs towards the mountain where James lived. Tomorrow, I would walk up and meet my girl cousins and their looms. If I could pick up a shuttle, throw it across a warp, hear the rise and fall of the heddles, and watch a pattern form, then perhaps my heart might find peace, and I could forget about Charlie.

• • • • •

In the middle of the night a thunderstorm rumbled across the mountains, and my father started hollering. Lightning lit the cabin as I raced down the ladder, and the next clap of thunder rattled the windowpanes. Sitting up in bed, he jabbed at me as if holding a gun with a bayonet, and I stepped back, smelling the sweat rising from him.

"Keep away. Or I'll slice your gut." Pa's white hair tumbled about his face, yet his eyes glared at me. His hands shook, but the growl in his voice sent shivers over me. He put me in mind of a coon caught in Jacob's trap that had snapped at us before my brother whacked him with the butt of his gun.

"Pa, it's me, Viney, your daughter. There's no battle. You're dreaming. It's just a thunderstorm." I leaned over to soothe him, but he flailed his arms, slapping my cheek.

"Get away! You won't take my brother." He punched me in the shoulder.

I fell backwards, and clutched the bedpost. My shoulder blazed, and I blinked back tears. Pa stood up, swaying from side to side, with his nightshirt tangled about his ankles. He took a few steps, and crumpled to the floor.

"Pa!" I lifted his head. He moaned. "Pa, it was all a dream. A bad dream. Let me help you back to bed." I hoisted him onto his mattress, wondering at how little he weighed. Pa clutched my hand.

"It did happen, at Shiloh. We thought we had won the battle, but after the Yankees shot our general, we floundered. More Union troops erupted from nowhere and sent us racing through the gun smoke. That's when a Yankee shot my brother in the head. Josh shrieked, and fell next to me, writhing."

My father covered his face with his hands. "I turned around and ran towards the blue coat. With my bayonet, I gutted the man who shot Josh, and can still hear his screams."

"It was war, Pa. You loved your brother and had just lost him. I'd do the same if someone killed Lizzie." Biting my lower lip, I wrapped my arms around my father.

He smelled rancid, and his backbone was as knobby as a mountain ridge. While I pondered how war ripped apart men, Pa wept until my nightdress grew damp. Like my mother, my father had lost the courage that keeps a body hoping tomorrow will bring something good. He shuddered and pulled away.

"But what if that soldier was from this cove? Most folks here sided with the Union." Pa swiped a hand over his tears. "I'm sorry, daughter. Thunder puts me in mind of the cannons booming. A single gunshot don't bother me, but several at once, and the memories take over my mind."

"Let's hope we'll be spared many storms." I stood up. "Reckon we need to go back to sleep." I tucked the coverlet around Pa, climbed up to my pallet, and lay down.

Seeing as the War Between the States was so long ago, I'd never pondered how ridge men talked about serving under General Grant. Come Independence Day, those men had donned their blue coats and shot off their rifles to celebrate the preservation of the Union. What had those men thought about my father fighting on the other side?

Staring out the small window, at the moon floating between ragged clouds, I stayed awake until I could hear Pa's snoring. Queer, how I had become like a mother listening to her child; it appeared that old folks and youn' uns needed the same tending. But if I didn't wed, who would take care of me when my fingers could no longer button my dress?

CHAPTER FIVE

Leaning against an outside wall of Saint Francis Catholic Church, Charlie watched Charlotte and Mr. Burnett stroll along the bank of the Boardman River. Dressed in a white lawn frock with a full skirt, Charlotte looked like a peony blossom. She carried a blue and white quilt while Mr. Burnett in his dark suit toted a wicker hamper. When Charlotte pointed at a large maple tree, they ambled to its shade, spread out the quilt, and unpacked their picnic. Soon, Charlotte's laughter mingled with Mr. Burnett's low voice as they ate their fried chicken and buttered biscuits.

The breeze carried the fragrance of chocolate cake to the churchyard, and Charlie's stomach growled. Why couldn't they have chosen some other location, instead of close to where his best friend, Seamus was attending Mass? Through the open windows, rumbled the voices of the worshipers repeating words in Latin. Charlie sat down on a granite step, waiting for the priest to bless the parishioners and bid them good-by. Not wanting to watch Charlotte sit shoulder-to-shoulder with Mr. Burnett, Charlie had skipped services at the Episcopal Church and walked to town. In his black robe, the priest opened the church door and positioned himself. Charlie stood.

"Were you wanting to speak with me?" the priest asked.

"No, Father, I'm waiting for someone." No wonder Seamus worshiped here, the priest spoke with an Irish accent similar to Seamus's. "And there he is."

Seamus grinned and embraced Charlie. "Fancy seeing you here. I thought a certain golden-haired lass claimed your Sundays." Seamus's blue eyes sparkled, and his black curls framed his wind-burned face. Dressed in a blue chambray shirt and black braces held up his woolen trousers. Although it was early June, Seamus wore a dark, red woolen stocking cap.

"Not any longer. In fact, she's eating a picnic with her new beau beneath that maple tree." Charlie gripped Seamus's shoulder. "We need a quiet place to talk."

"Come with me. To the harbor, it is." Seamus led the way through the streets, and down to the wharf. Waves lapped against single-mast sloops, tall schooners, and at the next pier over, smoke drifted from a steamer loading on firewood and barrels of salted fish. Gulls prowled the dock, looking for scraps.

"So did you buy your boat?" Charlie asked as Seamus hopped into a single mast vessel. The odor of fish lingered in the wooden planking and even in the hemp ropes.

"Aye, 'tis half paid for. Cutting firewood, working on Beaver Island docks, and fishing earned me the Selkie. Just delivered a load of whitefish for my uncle. Push off."

Seamus held the tiller and a breeze filled the white sail. The twenty-foot blue sloop slipped into Grand Traverse Bay. Small waves slapped the sides of the vessel as it leaned to port. They sailed along the wooded shoreline dotted with fruit farms. When they reached a small cove, he slackened the sail, and tossed the anchor overboard.

"Mr. Townsend's farm is almost at the end of the peninsula," Charlie said. "We can see the Old Mission Lighthouse from one of our hills."

"And now you won't be settling on his farm with his daughter?" Have you tried to woo her away from this new gent?" Seamus dug out a basket from a cubby, folded back the red-checked napkin, and handed Charlie a wedge of soda bread. "And there's cheese." With his knife, Seamus cut a chunk.

"I considered fighting for Charlotte, but when a man with more money arrives, she clings to his arm. Now, he escorts her to church and every social event. And besides, I've noticed her father lecturing Charlotte in his study. A couple of times I've overheard the words 'land' and 'secure future'."

"Ah, 'tis heartbreaking." Seamus dipped a mug into the bay and offered it to Charlie. "If her da is encouraging her to marry another, 'twill be hard for the young lady to deny his wishes."

"Charlotte hinted she wanted to marry me, and then she betrayed me." Charlie chugged the mug of water, and a bit dribbled off his chin. Sunlight shimmered on the highlights streaking his auburn hair.

"But perhaps, you are feeling what a certain lassie in Rugby must have felt when she read your letter. We know Miss Viney has a temper and will repay those who cross her." Seamus cocked his head and winked.

"You think I made her so angry that she wants to thrash a bear?" Charlie handed the mug back to Seamus.

"Yes, after she wept a long while." Leaning back against the prow of the boat, Seamus propped his boots up on a wooden crate.

"So what do you suggest?" Charlie trailed his fingers through the water, watching how the light bent his digits.

"Last summer, when the little miss from Tennessee angered you, what did she do to attract your eye?" Seamus downed a mug of water and bit into a chunk of cheese. "To regain your affections."

"She sewed that ridiculous dress that revealed too much of her flesh." Charlie slumped back against the side of the boat. "And caught the eye of every gentlemen in the crowd." Yet, with her hair in long curls, and her waist nipped in, Viney had rivalled any of the English girls. She had been even prettier than her sister. Charlie wished Viney sat beside him in her delicious gown, waiting for him to kiss her.

"And in a roundabout way, her plan worked. Within a month or so, you were engaged." Seamus stretched his arms over his head. "Though giving Viney your barometer might not mean as much as a locket or a ring."

"Yes, and then I moved north and met Charlotte." Charlie dried his hands on his pants. "I suppose I was a fool to run away, but Rugby wouldn't have been the same without you and George." He shouldn't have listened to Charlotte's prattle. Nor accepted her flattery that clouded his mind, making him forget his love for Viney.

"So now, you must perform the same deed. Turn Viney's heart back to you." Seamus handed Charlie another bite of cheese. "Too bad you didn't learn to play the fiddle. You could return to Rugby and ply the lady with lovely tunes. Or reels to set her feet to dancing."

"Well, I didn't learn, and Mr. Townsend operates like the old-fashioned hiring fair. I won't be paid until the end of summer when my apprenticeship is completed, so until then, I can't buy a train ticket. My father stated how I should find land in Michigan. If I write that I am returning to Rugby, he will cut off my inheritance. He will do all he can to convince me to remain here and not wed Viney." Charlie tossed a handful of water into the air, and the sunlight turned it into shimmering droplets.

"Aye, but listen to your heart. Dream of ways you can pursue your lady from afar, and as soon as you are able, head south." Seamus pulled up the anchor. "I'll sail close to your farm and drop you off. You might have to wade a bit."

Holding his boots, Charlie stood on the strand and waved farewell to Seamus. As the waves swept back, they sucked the sand from beneath his toes, throwing him off balance. He scrambled backwards, and landed next to a cluster of wild rosebushes blooming along the edge of the dune. Pink blossoms smothered the branches swaying in the breeze.

Dressed in a blue-checked homespun, Viney would have laughed at him, and bent to inhale the flowers' fragrance. Her long braid dangling across one shoulder; her bare feet digging into the sand, she would have fed herself on their sweetness and beauty. Charlie ripped the petals off the roses and dropped them in his hat. He would stuff an envelope with the dried flowers and send them to his beloved.

CHAPTER SIX

Leaves filtered the sunlight as I climbed the steep trail leading to the cabin where my cousins lived. I hoped to catch a glimpse of James and maybe find a moment when we could chat. A small creek tumbled next to the path; chestnuts and beech trees towered above me, and up high, a wood-pewee repeated his name. A bear had left his prints in the mud near a little pool, and I listened for any rustling in the brush that would reveal his presence. Rosy blossoms smothered rhododendron bushes while in sunnier patches, daisies bloomed. Bumblebees zipped across the path, and one bumped into me. Being such a gentle insect, I could almost hear him say, "Excuse me".

Near the top of the mountain, I stepped into a clearing and spied ridge after ridge of the Great Smokies as they flowed away from Uncle John's log cabin. Their hazy, blue peaks poured strength into my spirit, and untangled the knots in my shoulders. A red-tailed hawk screamed as he lifted off a tall hemlock, and a piece of me flew with him. Surely, the glory of the Smokies would wipe away the pain of losing Charlie. Even now, I yearned to slide my fingers through his and share this wondrous sight. But like the hawk, I needed to fling those longings aside and soar.

"Oh, Lord," I whispered. "Did you send down a scrap of heaven when you shaped these mountains?" Somehow, I knew God relished creating just as much as I did, and what joy He must have felt when He proclaimed this place as good. Somewhere behind the split-rail fence enclosing a pasture, a cowbell tinkled. Leaving the shade of an oak tree, a redbone hound barked, ambled over, and sniffed me. I scratched his chin, making his tail wag. On the other side of the tree stood a barn, corncrib, and springhouse.

The cabin's screen door banged, and a tall woman stared at me. "You must be our cousin, Lavinia, from far off." Two large wool wheels stood on the front porch with a basket of carded fleece between them. A riot of hollyhocks, cabbage roses, phlox, and other posies that I didn't recognize bloomed about the cabin. Honeybees buzzed above the fragrant cloud of yellow, red, and blue blossoms.

"I go by Viney." I offered her my hand. "Pleased to meet you."

"I'm Margaret Jane Walker." Her black hair was pinned into a tight bun, and she wore a linsey dress dyed butternut brown. Little buttons carved from a cow's horn marched up to a narrow collar, and met a stiff chin and brown eyes. "Polly, Marti, Nan, Louisa, Caroline, Hettie, come meet your cousin, Viney," she called. "Our pa's in the orchard with our brothers, thinning apples. Our ma died a year ago, God rest her soul."

"I'm the oldest gal," Margaret said as her sisters burst from the cabin and scattered around me. Most of my cousins were tall and big-boned; they ranged from about my age to eight-years-old. None of them smiled, but having recently seen their mother die, I reckoned their hearts still pinched them.

"It's a pleasure to meet you." I shook their hands, except for Polly who reached out and hugged me. "I heard from my pa how you are good weavers."

"Polly and Marti can weave a tight selvage," Margaret said, "The least ones can spin and card right well. They can even spin a fine linen thread."

"May I see your looms? I love to weave." I spotted a couple of looms inside the cabin, and my hands itched to throw a shuttle. I needed to hear the sweep of the heddles as the harnesses rose and fell as my feet tread on the pedals. The music of a loom is as glorious as a fiddle tune, and the dance of the heddles yields patterns like Whig Rose or Double Chariot Wheel.

Margaret pulled open the screen door. "Come on in."

With her sisters trailing behind me, I walked inside the one room. Newspapers covered the log walls, where their clothing hung on pegs along with all manner of saws, sieves, and baskets. Kerosene lanterns and other tools, plus a quilting frame dangled from the loft ceiling. Five beds bordered the room, and up in the loft rested more pallets. Three barn looms stood in a corner lighted by one window. On one loom, was a brown and white coverlet in the *Double Bow Knot* pattern; on another, linen covered the front beam, and someone was weaving dark linsey-woolsey on the last loom.

"Beautiful." I ran my hands over their weaving. "Y'all have that touch. Not too tight, but good firm cloth. I've never woven linsey-woolsey, is it hard to keep an even weave?"

"Our mama taught us; most folks sewed their clothes from it during the War Between the States. But after the war, they switched to store-bought cloth, but that's not as lasting," Margaret said. "We prefer to weave what we wear."

The least one, Hettie pulled on my apron. Her brown braids hung half-way down her back, and dark eyes gazed up at me from her oval face. "Sometimes I help Nan spin so she can finish fast, and go see her beau, Solomon David."

"Hettie! You shush your tongue." Nan's cheeks reddened. Although she pinned her black hair in a bun, a few shorter curls danced about her face as she ducked her head. Unlike Margaret, Nan had basted white linen cuffs and a collar onto her homespun dress dyed a light shade of indigo.

"As pretty as you gals are, I reckon your pa has a hard time keeping the boys away from your porch." From the way Nan's eyes sparkled and Marti's lips curved, I could tell they were the fun-loving sort of girls who would want to dance and spark with their boyfriends. Polly appeared the most tenderhearted; some fellows prefer that sort of girl who will make a gentle home.

"Pa don't have to, Margaret scares them off before they can climb up here." Marti frowned at her older sister. "Daddy says, Margaret should marry before the rest of us can wed." Marti had pinned a tiny bouquet of pinks to the collar of her dress, and brown braids crowned her head. Her eyes were as blue as the sky above the mountains. She straightened her shoulders and picked up a shuttle.

"Hell will freeze over before I take a man," Margaret scanned her sisters. "Like Saint Paul wrote, "'It's better to remain single'." Margaret turned to me. "We need to get back to work."

What had happened to Margaret to make her so bitter? Had someone like Charlie rejected her? Yet, I understood how much needed to be accomplished during the summer daylight. "I could card for a while, if'n you'd like that. Or I can spin."

Polly, Marti, and Nan began to weave, while the littlest girls and I followed Margaret to the porch. Caroline's bare feet slapped the porch floor as she walked back and forth, turning the great wheel with one hand, holding the fleece in the other hand, as the spindle twisted it into thread.

"Do you have a sweetheart?" Caroline asked. Two light brown braids swung on either side of a round face, and her green eyes met mine. A linen pinafore covered her tan dress, but she'd soon need a fuller bodice. No matter what Margaret preached, the local lads would want to court this covey of sweet women. But, Margaret was right about how loving a man could bring heartache.

"No, I don't." I picked up some wool and began to card it. Maybe by the end of the summer, James might become my special friend, but first my heart needed to heal. And I had to find out if'n Margaret ruled her brothers or just her sisters. It seemed odd how none of the girls would rebel against her. I'd never try and control Lizzie's future, and she would seek happiness for me. I wondered what Lizzie would say about Margaret's attitude?

"I'm glad to hear you have the wisdom to remain single." Margaret stepped forward, winding a fine thread onto the great wheel's whirring spindle. "I don't need these girls lollygagging around, listening to you talk about your fellar. There's too much work for them to waste time on such foolishness."

Her narrow fingers could have flown along a fiddle's neck, noting out a reel. This cousin needed the lift of a dance tune to drive her feet and fill her with joy. But Margaret's fear of the White Caps denied her the pleasure of swinging with a boy. Did James follow her notions? For a second, I recalled the warmth of his strong fingers on my waist as he helped me into the wagon, and the inquisitive look in his eyes. My ears filtered the birdsong, listening for the male voices working in the orchard, but the whirl of the spinning wheels muffled most other sounds.

"What about your brothers?" I looked at Caroline. "Do they plan to remain single?"

"At the moment, yes." Margaret wound the newly-spun thread onto yarn winder. "But being men, I'm sure they'll need to find wives to satisfy them and keep them from evil desires."

Caroline's cheeks blushed, and her hand jerked the great wheel, tangling her thread. I ducked my head, remembering the sweetness of Charlie's lips on mine. Not only men needed to be satisfied.

"Is Rugby like Sevierville?" Caroline asked. "What are English folk like?

I've never met any foreigners."

"Rugby is different in that most of the houses were built to look the same with gables and board and batten siding, like some of the barns in this cove. The English speak with a queer accent. They love their Queen Victoria, and put up a Christmas tree like she does. Some of the fetched-on settlers truly want to become farmers, but others are just frittering away a year because their parents paid for their apprenticeship. The visitors come to breathe the clean air and swim in the rivers, or play tennis, a type of game."

While my cousins appreciated their cold spring water and pure mountain air, they would never understand why grown men would spend time hitting a ball back and forth over a net. The first time I had spied such goings-on, I had tripped upon the gravel path and twisted my ankle. What possessed folks to whack a ball for fun? They would find more lasting satisfaction in a stack of split wood or a garden free of weeds. At the end of their ball game, the Englishmen had accomplished nothing.

"What do you like best about Rugby?" Caroline asked.

"The library, a fine building filled with over seven thousand books. Anyone can read them and not pay a fee." Last winter, I had tucked my skirts around me as I curled up in a library chair, reading each afternoon. Newspapers had arrived from New York City and London, and books about nature that had taught me about trees and birds in other lands. The library was a magnificent gift to the ridge.

We talked on, and I explained how Mr. Hughes preached that in Rugby, women and men were considered equals and supposedly there would be no rich and poor folk. And one day, he hoped to see former slaves hoeing corn next to the Englishmen. Of course, the wealthy visitors didn't think that way and treated the maids and other staff as beneath them. When the shadows slid across the porch, I stood up. "I best be heading home. Come visit Pa and me, sometime."

"We step out on Sunday, and for Wednesday's prayer meeting," Margaret said. "Thank you for helping, and come up anytime."

Polly walked with me and opened the screen door. "How's Uncle Jesse? Maybe some Sunday, I could visit and chat with him for a bit before heading home. Poor soul, it troubles me to see his shaking hands. He stood straighter last year and had more get-up-and-go."

"He'd be tickled to see you. This time of the year, not too many folks have time to stop by." I hugged Polly. "I'll climb up again, soon. It was wonderful to talk with you and to weave, again."

I headed toward the path just as Uncle John and his four sons walked from their apple orchard. James stood six inches taller than his brothers. His muscular hams expanded his britches as he walked, and even the sweat on his neck added to his ruggedness. His eyes widened when he recognized me, and he smiled.

"I heard about you from James," Uncle John said, and shook my hand. His long white beard hid most of his mouth, and reached to the middle of his chest. "Meet William, John Henry, and my youngest, Giles Daniel."

My cousins spoke howdy, and James stepped forward. "If'n you want, I can walk you down the mountain. I spied a female bear with a cub, yesterday. Might be best if you had some company. I could tote my gun."

"That would be kind of you, but we won't need a gun." I wasn't scared of the bear, seeing as we had plenty of them around Rugby. But with my innards smarting over losing Charlie, I relished James' attention and the idea of being alone with him. It tickled me how Margaret might not approve of James' offer.

As the trail twisted down the slope, around boulders and trees, James pointed out the place where he had shot a turkey, and the deer trail leading to his favorite fishing spot. Compared to our silent wagon ride, walking in the woods sparked his conversation, and I savored the sound of his soft voice. I liked how his shoulders filled out his linen shirt and how the fading sunlight highlighted his cheekbones. James walked with a smooth gait and long strides. What would it be like to dance with him, or to walk home from meeting with my elbow hooked on his arm? Once, he took off his straw hat, and wiped his forehead, and I looked into his hazel eyes. While a few of his quick comments reminded me of Charlie, mostly James was like my brother, Jacob, calm and steady as a pump bolt. At the end of the walk, he leaned against a tall, sugar maple, and snapped off a short branch.

"I hope you will come back, soon. I'm sure my sisters would appreciate your help." With his thumb, James chucked me under the chin. "If'n you'd like to stay later, I could ride you down the mountain on Red, my mule."

I hadn't expected his touch to set my insides tingling, and make my heart race. I steadied my voice. “Thank you. I’d be thankful for a ride, then I could help more.” I focused on his collar button, not trusting my eyes to meet his. For a girl who thought she still loved Charlie, why did being with James make me giddy?

After we waved farewell, I nearly skipped to Pa’s cabin. Uncle Abe or any White Cap couldn’t complain about me working with my girl cousins, so I planned to walk up the mountain as often as I dared to leave Pa alone. But from inside my brain a small voice asked, why didn’t such a handsome man like James already have a sweetheart?

Chapter Seven

Dearest Viney,

How I miss visiting with you on your porch, watching the sun set and listening to the mourning-doves. How I want to talk to you about William. He and his mother needed a ride to Rugby, so I invited them to come with me.

William loved the settlement so much, that he offered to teach at the new school and asked me to assist him.

Because his family is from society, his mother was not pleased with his choice, but soon returned to Cincinnati.

He is instructing me on how to shoot his pistol!

Take care with James, Viney, as it is only one month since you lost Charlie.

Don't let your desires addle your senses...

I folded Lizzie's letter into a tiny square, and tucked it into my apron pocket. I was thankful the settlement was offering my friends' children book learning, but the notion of Lizzie teaching puzzled me. She never could remember the date for when the Revolutionary War began, or how to diagram a sentence, or what twelve times eleven was, so how could she assist the schoolmaster? She had considered school a place to collect boyfriends.

Lizzie had charmed the local boys, giving them little pecks on the cheeks or squeezing their hands as she sashayed by them. At the corn-shucking or cider-making bees, she danced with every boy, until settling on Lucas as her beau who would do anything she asked of him. Poor Lucas hadn't lasted long when the Englishmen arrived wearing satin waistcoats, with gold coins in their pockets. Lizzie's flirtations had captured George's attention, but after a time, their feelings had grown deeper. Like a flooded river overflowing its banks, love had changed its course until they cared about each other's happiness and planned to wed.

For the first time in a year, Lizzie sounded excited about helping the students, and about Mr. William. With his pistol, she had even hit the bull's-eye on the target. What had come over my sister who loved lace and frippery? Could she be in love with this man? Or was she arming herself against something?

The last sentence of her letter set me to chopping at a clump of quack grass. Charlie had written me several letters, so Lizzie had asked, if she should save them until when she came to the cove in a couple of months or send them on?

Burn them! I wanted to shout, but curiosity clamped my lips. Why was Charlie writing me when he was the one who had ended our engagement? I didn't want Lizzie to forward the letters, because, when James rode to Sevierville, he picked up our mail. My sister's swirling penmanship looked feminine, but my handsome cousin would recognize that Charlie's script had been penned by a man. That double-minded Englishman was not going to interfere with my friendship with James.

I longed to flop down on Lizzie's bed and talk about James. I'd describe the highlights in his hair, the way the color of his eyes could deepen from golden brown to the shimmering green of a meadow, or how the sound of his boots on the steps to the Walker porch quickened my heartbeat. Lizzie would rub my back, while murmuring little comments, asking questions. But if she sniffed any sign of fickleness in James, she'd land on him like a duck on a June bug and warn me to send him packing. When I had needed advice about how to capture Charlie's affections, I had gone to Lizzie who had devised a cunning plan. Of course, being my sister, she had played a trick on me, altering the dress we had sewed so the bodice had revealed more than I thought was proper, but she had lured Charlie back to me. Bending over, I yanked out the long taproot of a yellow dock plant, and shook off the dirt.

But returning to Rugby for a sisterly visit wasn't possible, what with the shakes taking over our father's hands. During the past few weeks, he hunched further over his cane as he hobbled to the table. Some mornings, I had to feed him his mush because he kept dropping his spoon, and at supper I had to cut his meat into tiny pieces. He couldn't button his shirts, but thank goodness, he could hitch up his drawers and didn't need help in the outhouse. How much longer before I would have to assist him in the privy? What if some night he fell? Would I have to run for Uncle Abe, whom I had avoided seeing except on Sundays?

Over in the corn, my father leaned on his hoe, studying a large beetle. Although he didn't accomplish much in the garden, and kept me from doing all that needed to be done, he wanted to feel like he was helping me. So I walked him out and propped him up with his hoe.

"Viney, look at this here beetle. Have you ever seen such a large one?" He pointed his hoe blade at the bug. "Big as my toe. But not as hairy. Come here, daughter."

It made me squirm when my father called me daughter. I wanted to snatch back that word and keep it from his lips, because I couldn't forgive him. To let him call me daughter meant affection flowed between us, when duty and wanting to be near James kept me here. My aunts had loved me like a daughter, but that didn't make up for not having a mama and daddy. I walked over and stared at the shiny black shield coating the critter.

"Nope, never seen the likes. Hope he doesn't like corn or beans. Or squash. Best kill him." I crushed the bug with my hoe, and a spark of victory tingled in my belly. Having lost several squash plants to those gray pear-shaped beetles, now when I spied them, I'd squish them between my fingers.

"Viney! Viney!" Sissy hollered, running down the path with her sunbonnet flopping against her back. "You gotta come. It's Mama's time." Panting and red faced, she leaned over with her hands on her knees, sucking in air.

"Oh, Laws. Isn't there a granny woman in the cove?" I wasn't prepared to deliver a baby. "Or some married woman who could help?" Made my head swirl to ponder birthing an infant; my aunt deserved someone more experienced than me.

"Mark ran for the granny woman, but she's in Townsend helping another." Sissy pulled on my hand. "You gotta come. Mama's asking for you."

"Where's your pa? Or Sayward's mama, she'd know more than I do." I tucked my hoe in a corner of the porch, as my father's hand rested on my arm.

"Sayward's family lives in Cades Cove, and she needs help, now," my father said. "I'll sit here on the porch, waiting to hear the good news."

We ran toward my aunt's screams. The older boys had fled, but the five-year-old brother sat crying on the front porch steps with an arm around Hannah. Sissy pushed me through the doorway.

"Go on in. I whacked an ax into the floor, but her pain's still rising."

The scent of sour sweat, and the heat from the hearth blasted me. From her bed, Aunt Sayward turned and gasped. "Thank God, you came. This one's gonna be here soon." Her long braid twisted across the pillow, and sweat slicked her pale face. She writhed beneath the sheets, gasping. "Oh, Viney, I never hurt so bad."

"What should I do?" I washed my hands and opened the one window for fresh air. How could the mountains look so tranquil while life wrestled within this cabin? My mind sorted through any bits of information that I'd heard about catching babies as I swung a kettle over the coals.

Aunt Sayward panted. "There's clean rags in that basket, and sweet oil. Fetch a knife and thread from my sewing." She shrieked and clutched my arm. "Viney, help me!"

"You have to tell me what to do." The only experience I had with birthing was helping an old ewe bring forth twin lambs, a far different situation than being entrusted with a human life. Please, God, don't let my aunt die, I prayed. Guide my hands, please give me courage.

Aunt Sayward hitched up her legs. "Push, a mite on my belly. Had to do that to my ma when she delivered her last child." She pinched her lips together and groaned.

Closing my eyes, I pressed down on my aunt's stomach, and she screamed. I trembled, scared that I would kill her. I wished some other woman would come stepping through that door and relieve me of this trial. No unwed girl should have to do this. My aunt's screeching made my legs wobble.

"Pull, pull him out. Please, Viney." Aunt Sayward crushed my fingers. "Oh, Lord, save me."

I knew with sheep, you shouldn't pull the lamb until the final contractions, but what about with human babies? I inhaled, reached under the sheets, and instead of feeling a baby's head, I touched his rear end. Oh

Laws, if Sayward were a ewe, I would know how to reach inside the womb and turn the baby. But I'd never heard any tales of a granny doing that to a woman.

"He's breech." I couldn't do this, but I couldn't leave my aunt. "There must be another woman nearby who can help." Blood was creeping farther across the sheets, and reminded me of my father's description of my mother's death.

"No time for that," she whimpered. "Get him out." Aunt Sayward's face contorted as her womb contracted.

With one hand I held the baby's bottom and with the other, I pushed on Aunt Sayward's stomach. Her screams poured through the cabin, bouncing against the walls and swallowing us. Fear boiled inside me as I tugged on the child, hating the blood slicking my hand. Tears streamed down her cheeks as my aunt heaved, and the baby slid out.

I tied thread in two places on the cord, and cut him loose. Clearing away the mucus from his nose, I lifted his body and slapped his bottom. He gasped. I spanked him again, and he howled, waving his little fists. Helping the ewe had brought wonder, but this child filled the cabin with the mystery of creation. I wept, wondering if my Aunt Alta had felt this floating feeling when she had held me in the sunlight and love swept over her.

"It's a boy, thank God it's a boy," Aunt Sayward kept repeating. "Abe don't want no more girls. This one will never have to fear the White Caps."

For a breath, I questioned if my pa would have stayed home if'n I'd been a boy? Had he seen me as a burden to feed and clothe, and to marry off as soon as I was grown? I was glad this babe wasn't a girl because then Uncle Abe couldn't squish her spirit with his meanness, yet I hoped this lad would grow to be a gentle soul who would cherish his wife. Still, Aunt Sayward would birth a few girls before her womb closed, so she'd have to guard them from those wicked vigilantes.

After wiping the baby with sweet oil, I wrapped him in the clean flannel and gave him to Aunt Sayward. She set his wee mouth to her breast, and he began to suckle. Closing her eyes, she sighed. I remembered Aunt Alta quoting the Bible, about how a mother forgets her travail when she holds her baby, that children bring joy in the morning. I guessed a babe could bring happiness at any time of the day. A few minutes later, the afterbirth followed, and the tangle in my belly unraveled from knowing this birth was complete.

Once the little boy had filled his belly, I washed Aunt Sayward and slipped a clean chemise over her head. She scooted to one side of the bed, and I managed to remove the sheets.

"Where do you keep your bed linens?" I looked about for a large basket or trunk.

"Them's all I have. With eight other children still to wed, my mama couldn't spare me none. Just spread the coverlet over me. Sissy can set them to soaking and scrub them tomorrow. Please, bring in the youn' uns so they can meet their brother."

I could understand my aunt's folks not having bedcoverings to spare, but what kind of miser was my uncle to not give his bride a set of sheets? And why hadn't Margaret opened up her full trunks and helped out her father's brother? I vowed that I'd finish Aunt Sayward's baskets, so I could barter them at Rugby's Commissary for sheets. From the doorway, I called, "Y'all can come in now."

Hannah and Jessie ran to the bed and stared. Concern filled Sissy's eyes, so I slipped an arm around her waist, and she leaned against me.

"I was so scared. I thought she was gonna die," she whispered and wiped her eyes with her apron. "Mama Nancy screamed like that when she was birthing Hannah."

"Your new mama is strong and young. This was her first baby, and my Aunt Alta always said, the first one is the hardest." How tragic that death haunted Sissy, reminding her of the narrow gap between today and eternity. Yet, women defied their fear of death and kept birthing children to love. If'n I had wed Charlie, a little one might have been growing inside me.

"Want to hold your brother?" Aunt Sayward said. "Our newest blessing from heaven."

Sissy's face softened as she cradled him in the crook of her elbow, rocking him a bit. "Babies are the sweetest things. Can't wait until I have me a baby." Leaning over, she kissed her wee brother. "He even smells different, fresh, like spring air."

"Soon as you're sixteen, your pa said you can marry," Aunt Sayward said. "I've seen Jeremiah watching you at the singings. He's been building a cabin on a corner of his daddy's land and even has a milk cow. It won't be long before he's asking Abe for your hand and you'll be keeping house."

Blushing, Sissy cooed at the infant and showed him to her younger siblings. But I resisted the urge to shudder. Before Sissy married, this girl needed more flesh on her bones to fill out her curves, and more vittles to put shine in her hair. Hopefully, this Jeremiah fellow would agree to a long courtship.

"Your time will come, Sissy," I said. "But you might want to leave the cove for a bit, maybe return with me to Rugby, work there awhile, and see how others live." I wanted to tell her to enjoy her girlhood, but with Uncle Abe ruling her life, Sissy would surely wed to escape this cabin.

"I reckon I don't need to visit your Rugby. I'm ready to be a wife." Sissy shrugged, but a curious look had shone in her eyes at the mention of coming to the settlement. "Thank you for helping. I can take care of Mama, now. I best be cooking something up for Daddy and the boys."

"You've been a blessing," Aunt Sayward said to me as she sank back against her pillow, "but I know your daddy needs you."

"I'll stop by tomorrow." I touched her hand, thankful to leave before Uncle Abe returned. I didn't need to risk him fussing at me about James walking me home, unchaperoned. Knowing my uncle, he might do more than scold me.

Chapter Eight

Cherry juice dripped down Charlie's arms, gnats swarmed around his face, and yellow jackets hovered near his fingers. Picking sour cherries was as nasty as picking peaches. Instead of itchy peach fuzz sifting down his shirt and over his chest, Charlie had to endure the sticky juice that made bits of bark stick to his forearms. He climbed up a couple of rungs on the ladder and reached into the top branches of the tree. The ladder wobbled and Charlie clutched at a limb as one leg of the ladder settled into the soft dirt. He let out his breath and waited for a few seconds before pulling off handfuls of cherries and dropping them into his metal bucket.

Every other day, he had walked to town and visited the post office, yet Viney still hadn't answered his letter filled with rose petals. Had she taken ill? Had some accident befallen her? Or had his rash words damaged their relationship beyond repair? Or perhaps, some new settler was wooing her.

For the past two nights, before falling asleep, Charlie had envisioned a blond-haired man cupping Viney's chin in one hand as he kissed her and ran his fingers up and down her ribs. Charlie had thrown his pillow across the room, cursing himself for trusting Charlotte. His lust for land, and his longing to hold a girl in his arms and kiss soft skin had blurred his thinking. If he had married Viney, he would no longer thrash about, twisting the sheets.

Leaves rustled in the other trees as pickers moved their ladders, or climbed down in order to dump their cherries into large baskets that Mr. Townsend loaded onto his wagon. His team of horses stamped their feet, and their tails swished as they tried to scatter the flies biting their legs. The whistle of a steamboat rippled from across the bay as the ship traveled towards Traverse City.

"Are you almost finished with that tree?" Mr. Townsend called up to Charlie. "You need to pick it clean."

"Yes, sir," Charlie shouted. This was the fifth time today Mr. Townsend had reminded Charlie to pick faster and cleaner. If the man didn't like his work, then why did he demand that Charlie finish his apprenticeship? Why not agree to release him from his promise and allow him to leave? Charlie threw clusters of cherries into his bucket and descended the ladder. Maybe tonight, he would find a letter from Viney, instead of another missive from his father asking when Charlie would acquire a farm.

• • • • •

Charlie grabbed the ivory envelope from off the small table in the corner of the kitchen. The postmark declared Rugby, but the penmanship was not Viney's. With his penknife, he slit the envelope, and pulled out the letter. His heart stopped. Something must have happened to Viney and he wasn't there to help her, to tell her how he loved her. He would never forgive himself for leaving her.

Dear Charlie,

I have not opened any of the letters you sent.

Our father abruptly returned and Viney accompanied him back to Sevier County.

I asked her if I should forward on your letters, but she told me to burn them. As you can see, she is still angry with you. I decided to save your letters, because I believe that one day, she will want to read them.

May God bless you in your new position. Lizzie

Fool! Of course, Viney would rebuff his attempts to reconcile. Was there a more hardheaded woman in all of Tennessee? Yet, Viney's fierce stubbornness fueled her independence, and ignited her creativity. And now she was somewhere beyond Rugby, perhaps being held by a blond-haired man. Charlie had to find her. If she wouldn't read his letters, perhaps she would listen to him.

Chapter Nine

The next afternoon, I peeked in on Aunt Sayward, who rested with her little one tucked beside her. Pink had returned to her cheeks and the exhaustion of the past months had left her eyes. She thanked me again and hinted how I needed to find a man and start a family. Perhaps, this summer would bring about a courtship with James, but a sliver dug into my heart because I still missed Charlie. Sissy insisted how she could manage the household work without my help, so I lit out for my cousins' cabin.

Tiny yellow birds flitted from tree to tree, and fluffy pink blossoms glowed on some of the rhododendrons bordering the path. For a moment, I listened to the stream rushing over boulders; as soothing a sound as God ever created. I sank to my knees and drank, as speckled trout flashed into the shadows. When I reached my cousins' cabin, their redbone hound wagged his tail in recognition. Looking around, I didn't spy James, but he must be working nearby.

"Howdy, Viney." Polly grinned. "Come to help break flax?" She shoved down the heavy wooden four-by-four attached to a bench and pounded a cluster of dried stalks. Each whack separated the stems into finer sections, and raised an earthy scent. Her full bosom jiggled inside her bodice, and sweat rolled down her round cheeks. She kept pausing to wipe her face with the corner of her linen apron.

Dressed in a butternut brown wool dress, Marti bent over a low table and pulled the thin pieces of stalks through a comb with tall wooden teeth until the fibers were as fine as my hair. Today, she had tucked a daisy in her bun, and the scent of lavender floated from her.

"I've never worked with flax." I fingered the long, ash-blond strands. "Never grown it either. It looks like it takes more work to prepare it for spinning than carding wool."

"It does," Polly said. "But I like being able to stand, instead of sitting and carding."

"We plant it in the early spring. I just love the tiny blue flowers," Marti said. "After the plants turn brown, we rot the stalks until they begin to separate, next we dry them, and then whack them." She snuck a look at the garden where Margaret picked green beans with the younger girls. "Sometimes I pretend I'm thrashing the stubbornness out of the Boss—that's what we call Margaret. I sure wish some fellow would catch her eye and marry her, so Daddy would give his blessing to me and Johnny."

"See that little gourd hanging from my small wheel?" Polly pointed. "It's filled with water. Sit yourself down, dip your fingers in the water, then draw several strands of flax from the distaff, and spin it. The water helps keep the fibers soft so they can twist."

I sat on a stool, wet the fingers of my left hand, pulled off the flax, and began to treadle. A few thick places formed as the strands twisted, but slowly, the thread grew more uniform. That special peace I found in spinning settled over me as the wheel whirred and the bobbin filled. Spinning flax was almost as magical as turning straw into gold, and I liked the notion of taking a plant and transforming it into fabric. For a spell, the rhythm of the work quieted our lips until a red-tailed hawk shrieked as he dove toward his prey. He flapped his wings and rose, holding a critter in his beak. My foot paused on the treadle.

"Sissy warned me about a group called the White Caps. What do you know about them?" I scanned the grim set of my cousins' mouths and the way their eyes narrowed. "Have they bothered you?"

"Well, folks first welcomed the White Caps, thinking how the vigilante's threats would keep everyone's daughters pure. With so many women left unwed because of the war, wives feared that their husbands would seek out those single women's company." Polly said. "When the devils started beating women, and burning barns, folks' minds changed. But it was too late, the White Caps control Sevier County. Now, we bolt our doors and keep our guns loaded."

"Why doesn't someone fight back?" I asked, and started spinning. "Don't fathers defend their daughters?

"Too many of the beasts. A few of the men have attacked the vigilantes, but most have given up, just accepting things the way they are. Somedays, I think about moving to Knoxville or Gatlinburg, so as to get away from the White Caps and their meanness. Even if I wed, I don't want to live in fear until my hair turns gray, worrying them men will hurt my family." Polly resumed spinning. Bright red spots lit up her cheeks, and anger had stiffened her back. She thrust out her chin. "I'm praying that more fellows will find the courage to fight those varmints."

Marti jerked her head toward a couple of rifles sitting by the door. "Pa told the boys to shoot if the White Caps come. I asked him to teach me how to use a gun, but Pa doesn't want his womenfolk harming men. But James said how someday, he might teach me."

Margaret marched onto the porch with a basket of green beans on her arm. She stared down her long nose, eyes narrowed, lips pressed into a firm line. All she needed to complete the transformation was to stick out her tongue and rattle her behind like a diamondback snake.

"There's no need for the White Caps to meddle here. Everybody knows that we're God-fearing women. We mind our Pa. No drinking, no dancing, and no courting. That's the temptation that leads most folks into sinning and riles those vigilantes. And we only sing hymns."

Polly and Marti exchanged looks. Appeared that those two yearned for more than singing from *The Sacred Harp*. Hadn't Margaret ever noticed how after a hymn sing, young folk often left in pairs and vanished behind hemlock branches? Singing School was the time to catch a boyfriend with a wedding following. The old gossips usually counted the months when the babies arrived to the newlyweds. At least Charlie and I hadn't given them something to whisper about, but I almost wished that we had.

The low sun was flickering through the trees when Marti and I hunted for eggs in the barn. The hens had hidden them in the loft, in the corner of the cow's stall, and even behind the upright hollow log filled with corn.

"Do you like dancing?" Marti's blue eyes flashed. "Johnny asked me to go with him on Saturday night to a gathering in the holler up from your Pa's cabin. There'll be dancing and food. You could meet other folk from the cove. It'll be a dandy time."

"What about Margaret?" I flapped my apron at a hen when she pecked me for taking an egg out from beneath her. "She won't let you go."

"If'n you asked me to spend the night with you, then Margaret won't know that I've gone out with Johnny. Even Daddy says, I'm old enough to court, but Margaret keeps arguing with him that none of us should marry before we're eighteen. Johnny could fetch me from your place. Please say, yes, so I can slip away from the Boss."

"Surely, you can spend the night with me." It tickled me to pull a trick on Margaret who needed to swing a partner and enjoy a frolic. My father slept soundly, so it shouldn't be hard for Marti to creep up to the loft and tell me about the evening's pleasures. I'd missed having such talks with Lizzie, and sitting on my porch steps with Charlie.

"Does James ever take a sweetheart to the dances?" I placed an egg in Marti's basket.

"No, ma'am. Margaret would fuss something fierce at him. James likes keeping the peace with the Boss, makes his life easier." Marti placed a hand on my shoulder. "Are you wanting to spark with my brother? That would make for a merry summer."

"What's wrong with Margaret?" I avoided answering Marti's question and slithered around a mound of hay, spying two eggs in a dark corner. "Did some man break her heart?"

"No, even when Margaret went to school, she paid no never mind to the boys and ignored their teasing. Didn't even smile at the few fellows who tried to catch her eye, but pulled the brim of her sunbonnet further over her face. She's different, mighty independent, and doesn't want to obey a husband. Besides, she thinks that being the firstborn, she should inherit the farm."

"Queer notions for a woman with brothers, but my Aunt Alta left me her place." I figured living near Rugby had given my aunt the idea that a woman could manage land as well as a man.

"As the eldest son, if'n James were to wed, Daddy would deed him the farm, expecting James to care for his sisters." Marti picked up another egg. "Margaret wants him to marry a gal who comes with several acres so he'd move out, but most girls have a stack of brothers. Margaret will do everything she can to stop James from bringing home a bride and taking away her chance to own this place. Ever since Mama died, Daddy's been like a hollow tree and hasn't stood up to Margaret."

"What about your other brothers? What if one of them married before

James?"

"William and John Henry are studying to be teachers and hope to find schools in Cades Cove and over by Cosby. James is the one Margaret is fretting about because he loves this farm. And you're the first girl he ever walked home." Marti tossed ground corn to the chickens, and the rooster clucked loudly. The hens raced over to him and scratched at the grain.

I stared at my cousin. "But I would think any of the local girls would consider James a good catch. None of them have fancied him?" Charlie's father had not approved of him courting me, but that hadn't stopped him from asking for my hand. I swatted away the little voice reminding me of Charlie's letter. Might Margaret feel differently about me because I owned a farm back in Rugby?

"Because he's handsome, kind, hardworking, mannerly..." Marti winked at me.

"Yes. All those and much more." How could Marti so easily understand my feelings? Yet without Lizzie to talk to, it was comforting to share with her. Still, I wasn't going to tell her how I fell asleep comparing James to Charlie, and tallying up their good points. One night my heart yearned to hear Charlie's voice as he praised my latest weaving design or described how a cumulous cloud turned into a black thunderhead. The next night, I smelled the boxwood scenting James shirt, felt his hands on my waist, and I longed for him to pull me into his arms. Perhaps I had become as fickle as Charlie, or as folks said, I was seeing the dark of the moon in my heart.

"What you're not pondering is that until we sisters wed, James and his new wife will live with us. Not a girl in this cove wants to share a cabin with Margaret. But you could stand up to her bossiness, and I reckon James is thinking the same thing."

"I don't know. Besides, James has never acted as if he wants to court me." My cheeks reddened when I remembered him chucking my chin. If what Marti said was true, James was not a flirt who would tease a girl.

Marti laughed. "So if your daddy don't mind, can I stay with you, and if you like to dance, maybe Johnny can bring another horse so you could ride along with us."

"I love dancing." The blush traveled down my neck, but my insides pinched together as I remembered Charlie whirling me at a house raising.

His gait was as smooth as a pacer, and his fingers had smoldered on my shoulder. A shadow fell across Marti and me, and James led his mule into the barn. His shirt clung to his chest, and the top three buttons were open, exposing fine reddish blond hair.

"I thought you had left." His fingers moved up and down the mule's lead rope while his eyes wandered from my bare feet to the daisy tucked into my braid. "It's almost milking time."

Laws, we had chattered longer than I had thought. Uncle Abe wouldn't approve of me sauntering in during the hour when I should be serving supper to my father. I needed to pay more attention to the slant of the sun so I would skedaddle on time.

"You could ride down the mountain with me on Red," James said. "We'll have you home faster than a coon climbs a tree."

Marti nudged me with her toe. "Go on. I'll fetch you one of the chicken pies left over from our dinner. Your daddy would like it."

After James tied Marti's basket to the saddle horn, he hopped onto the mule's back and pulled me up. "Hold on," he said and guided Red toward the path where small cream-colored butterflies danced in the shafts of sunlight.

Wrapping my arms around his waist, I pressed my cheek against James' back. His linen shirt smelled of clover hay, and his sisters had patched the knees of his woolen pants. Feeling his muscles shift sent a fire rippling through me, and I licked my lips. With Charlie gone almost a year, I'd missed this closeness with a man, and wondered how it would feel to press my lips against James' mouth. Red splashed through a puddle where a spring trickled out of the rocks. James hummed the melody to one of my favorite hymns. When he began to sing the words, I joined him.

Peace flowed into my pinched spirit, and I wished James would pull on the reins and linger beneath the arms of a chestnut tree, so I could soak in the sweetness of this moment. But instead, the mule plodded onward. When we finished, I started *The Young Convert*, and James picked up the bass line. We completed the last verse where the trail met the road through the cove, and James reined in Red.

"You've a fine voice." He stared across the valley, as if he wanted to say more.

"Thank you." Realizing my arms were still wrapped around him, I removed them and sat up straight, hoping my uncle hadn't seen us.

James dismounted, placed his hands on my waist, and swung me off Red.

"I overheard you and Marti talking."

James' hands still circled me, and his thumbs pressed against my ribs as I stood on my tiptoes. I swallowed, trying to stifle the heat swirling through my belly.

"Hmm, yes. She's going to spend Saturday night with me." I straightened my skirt, avoiding his playful eyes.

"If'n you like riding Red, I could bring Marti to your cabin, and take you to that dance."

My heart jumped, and I lifted my face. "Are you or Red asking me to the dance?

He grinned. "I guess I am. Reckon I should add 'please'."

"Well, then, thank you. I'd like to ride Red to the dance, with you."

James laughed. "You looked mighty fine in that blue calico you wore to meeting on Sunday." He jumped on his mule, waved, and rode back up the mountain.

Holding Marti's basket, I hastened toward Pa's cabin. James' spicy scent and his strong arms haunted my thoughts, and I hoped neither Uncle Abe nor Margaret would discover our plans for Saturday night.

Chapter Ten

Even though I had lived in the cove for several weeks, I still fretted over what to call my father. Now and then while washing his clothes or making his bed, I would roll the word "daddy" in my mouth, but it tasted sour, so I still called him "Pa". His eyes had flickered the first time I spoke that word, as if he recognized how in a strange manner, sharing life had twisted us into a two-strand cord. And yet, I couldn't draw upon sincere affection to give him a hug or a kiss on the cheek, like my cousins gave their daddy.

One afternoon, I hiked a ways up Cove Mountain, and reached a lookout where I could gaze across Wear's Cove. With the sky opened up above me, I sat on a boulder, hugging my knees. I inhaled the scent of the winterberry plants crushed by my feet. How had I arrived at this moment when my heart struggled to let go of Charlie? Was I being foolish to think that by asking me to the dance, my cousin wanted to court me? And if'n James was thinking of making me his wife, was I ready to claim that joy knowing I would have to live with Margaret? Even though the Smoky Mountains were mighty and beautiful, I missed my sister and the freedom that Rugby offered to everyone living in the settlement. Each question pulled the tangle inside me into a tighter knot until even the beauty of the mountains couldn't fill me with peace.

Walking home, my feet turned onto a different path, and I stumbled upon a small clearing tucked inside a grove of hemlocks. Because of the ring of stones and the remains of a fire, the place didn't appear to be a natural bald. Nor did it look like a campsite for hunters or the work of moonshiners, seeing as no stream flowed nearby. Someone had been writing in the dirt, but had erased all but the letter Y. Or perhaps the lines were part of a map and not the ending of a word. Shivers prickled my skin, and I fled, hoping not to meet the men who had built the meeting site.

At twilight on Saturday evening, James and Marti trotted in on Red. Pa looked up from his chair on the porch and waved at them. Marti wore a red calico dress and had tied a red ribbon in her hair. James had on his best straw hat, and his black boots shone in the stirrups. Blast it all, Marti and I had decided that the fellows would wait in a nearby grove of hemlocks, and after Pa was snoring, she and I would slip off. James must have nixed that idea.

"Sit down, sit down," Pa called out. "What a blessing to see you two young folk. Viney, fetch some chairs."

"Howdy, Uncle Jesse. Didn't Viney warn you that I was spending the night with you?" Marti kissed Pa's cheek as I carried two rush-bottomed chairs to the porch.

James shook Pa's hand and set his straw hat on the porch railing. "We can chat for a few minutes, but the girls have plans, sir."

"I bet y'all are heading over to the dance at the Campbells'," Pa said. "Heard Abe ranting about how the devil was creeping into the cove, tempting the young folk to play fiddles and hold girls' hands. Poor Abe, the war stole his youth and sense of merriment."

"How did you guess?" I asked. Seemed Pa was more observant than I had thought. When my uncle had visited, I had looked at his angry face, grabbed my hoe, and run off to the garden.

"No lad slicks his hair down, and puts on his Sunday-go-to-meeting clothes to visit an old man. The pink in Marti's cheeks told me she's going to see her beau. And all day, daughter, you've been humming fiddle tunes."

Both Marti and James blushed, and I enjoyed seeing his neck redden. James looked handsome in his blue checked shirt and deep indigo trousers with black braces. I couldn't wait to slip my arms around his waist, and feel his muscles shift as we rode off. From the glint in his eyes, the same thoughts flourished inside him.

"May I go? You won't tell Uncle Abe?" I asked. "We'll be home late, but will rise in time for church." I patted Pa's hand.

"I won't tell Abe, and you can go if'n you'll dance the Virginia Reel for me. Your mama and I loved that dance and asked for it at every frolic. It's a pity you never met your Grandma Walker; her toes always were drumming out a beat. She'd clog while washing dishes or hanging up clothes; as soon as

I could walk, she had me beating time with my feet. Your Grandpa Walker played the fiddle and his brother, my uncle Adam, picked banjo." Pa half-closed his eyes, smiling. "Until the war, music filled our home most Saturday nights."

"I'll ask the caller for the Virginia Reel." I tucked away in my heart these new tidbits about my mama and grandma. My aunts had never said much about my Walker kin. Like I had stuck my big toe through a hole in the foot of a stocking, I had often wished to know more about my family. Now, Pa was darning the gap, filling it in with his memories.

"You and James help these old bones to bed. Then you can put on your Sunday dress." Pa's arms quivered as he tried to push himself from the chair, so James leaned over and gripped his waist.

"I've got you, sir." James lifted Pa from his chair.

"Never thought there'd come a day when I couldn't dance." Pa clutched James' arm and shuffled into the cabin. James guided Pa onto his cot where he plopped down with a moan.

While James took off Pa's boots, I unbuttoned Pa's shirt, and eased off his overalls. Pa had gained a little weight, but his ribs still showed. What had he looked like when he was my age and could swing my mama? By the time I slipped on his nightshirt, Pa collapsed back against the pillow, and I covered him with a coverlet.

"Thank you, daughter," Pa said. "Y'all best be going." Tenderness blossomed on his face as he gulped air. "You have a fine time."

"Night, Pa." I squeezed his shoulder while my innards struggled with feelings of pity and sorrow over the past. It was hard to stay mad at an old man, knowing how the time was short before he would leave us, but I longed for him to apologize. Outside the cabin, the sound of hoof beats sounded John Daniels' arrival, and he started talking to Marti.

I hurried up to the loft and buttoned up the blue calico dotted with red flowers. My heart thrummed as I tied blue ribbons in my hair, laced up my boots, and dashed to the porch. Gazing down at me, James' eyes glowed, and a little shiver rippled through me as he took my hand.

"Viney, meet Johnny Daniels," James said. "We went to school together. My best hunting and fishing buddy."

Johnny was a few inches shorter than James, with wheat blonde hair and mischievous brown eyes that focused on James holding my hand.

"Pleased to meet you. Folks in the cove have been talking about you." Johnny smiled, and slipped an arm around Marti.

"Good to meet you. Hopefully the talk is charitable?" I smiled at the way Marti fitted herself into the curve of Johnny's waist and rested her head against his chest. Margaret would be spewing warnings if she spied such a posture.

Johnny laughed. "Folks say that you're a mite headstrong, and a better weaver than Margaret. I heard you've even sold coverlets to the Yankees."

"Well, yes, I did, but Margaret and her sisters are fine weavers, too." I prayed that the gossip wouldn't turn my cousin against me. "I know that if Margaret lived in Rugby, she'd be busy weaving and selling her work to the visitors."

"Come on." Marti tugged Johnny's sleeve. "There's no need to talk about Margaret. We best be going or we'll miss the first big set."

James helped me onto Red, jumped up, and circled his arms around me. As much as I loved dancing, I wanted to beg James to make Red walk, to prolong the ride. Closing my eyes, I leaned back, and his shoulder muscles brushed my cheeks. Like flint striking steel, sparks flew inside me when my head rested beneath his chin.

"We fit together perfectly, don't we?" James' breath tickled my neck as his lips almost touched my skin.

"Oh, yes." A fire shot through my bones, and I knew by the evening's end that we would be kissing, even if I had to take the first step.

We rode into a narrow valley that slid between the mountain ridges. Trees rose above us, and a spring bubbled between cracks in the rocks, creating a small waterfall. As the hills hugged us, fiddle music crept closer, and my skin tingled. Like a bee smelling nectar, I dug my heels into the mule.

"The lady wants to dance, Red. Hurry up." James pressed his knees against his mule, making him trot.

As we rounded a bend, I spied a trio of musicians beneath a huge oak tree, playing fiddles, a banjo, and one man kept time with a set of bones. Children skipped and chased each other around a trestle table spread with platters of food. One fiddler stood in the center of the circle of dancing couples, calling while he played.

"Chase the rabbit, chase that squirrel,

Come back home, and give her a twirl."

James leapt down, and tied his mule to a tree branch while I slid to the ground. He grabbed my hand, and we ran after Marti and Johnny.

"We can make another foursome," Marti called to us. "Hurry."

Johnny pulled us into the circle. "Marti and I will be the active couple, that way James can learn the moves."

The caller cried out, "Birdie in the Cage" so James and I linked hands with Johnny and circled around Marti who peeped and hopped, before Johnny took her place as the old crow.

"Right and left stars," the caller shouted, and James mimicked us as we stuck our hands in the middle and walked in a ring.

Johnny leaned over and said in my ear, "You must be pretty special to convince James to defy Margaret and dance."

I grinned at Johnny. Every step and dance figure, sent gladness deeper inside me, pushing away the bitterness of losing Charlie. Like the bow drawing notes from the fiddle strings, the dancing drove away my anger. When James' fingers touched my waist or he swung me, pleasure and desire flowed across his face.

"Active couples move on," the caller said.

Johnny and Marti swung away, and a different couple introduced themselves and joined us. When the new gentleman took my hands and looked into my eyes, I swallowed my breath. He had the same blue eyes as Charlie, peering out of a similar shaped face, and the man filled out a blue-striped shirt like Charlie had worn the last time I saw him. Blast it all, would that Englishman haunt me until another man wed me? I smiled at the new fellow as he twirled me around, and vowed to banish Charlie from this evening.

After several more calls, the fiddler handed his instrument to a friend, broke into the ring, and linked hands.

"Everyone into one big circle and step to the left, then back to the right," he called, while his feet slapped the ground. Others began to clog, and my feet found the beat...shuffle, step, rock step. The musicians raced into *Mississippi Sawyer*. "Grapevine twist," the caller shouted.

He dropped a gent's hand, creating a single file, and wound us into a tight ring. Bunched together in a knot, like a centipede, we rocked and swayed. The rhythm of the reel throbbed in our veins, and our feet drummed the earth. The scent of lye soap and starch mingled as our bodies touched, shoulder to shoulder, hip to hip. The caller doubled back, cracking the whip as the line of dancers flowed faster and faster in a wave rippling across the grass.

"Swing her home," the caller said, picked up his fiddle, and bowed *Kitchen Girl*.

Instead of a two hand turn, I placed my right hand on James' waist and my left on his shoulder. "Do the same, and put your right foot next to mine, and pivot."

Matching my moves, James leaned back and we spun, with his eyes locked on mine. We twirled until my head reeled, and I collapsed against him. Instead of stopping, he grabbed me by the waist, lifted my feet off the ground, and swung me one last time.

James steadied me as I stared up into his joy-filled face. We stood panting, drinking in the cool night air. From somewhere at the edge of a pasture, a whip-poor-will called as small groups of couples chatted.

"See what Margaret has been keeping you from?" I said. With Aunt Alta failing, I had missed most of the local frolics. Courting James would give me a good reason to attend the parties in this cove.

"Now that you live here, I don't plan on missing any more dances." James slid an arm around my shoulder, and I liked being drawn to his side, feeling wanted.

"Couple up for the Virginia Reel," the caller announced. "Last dance before we take a break."

James and I stepped into the appropriate lines, with a row of men facing another of women. Each time the lines walked forward, James would sweet talk me, making me blush. His words were a honeysuckle vine, twining over me, pulling me closer. When James and I sashayed down and back up the set, the cheering couples clapped along with the tune. We danced until a chip of a moon rose in the east, then the folks drifted toward the pans of cobblers sitting on the table.

"Want some blackberry cobbler? And a sip of spring water?" James asked.

I could tell from the shine in his eyes that what he wanted was to kiss me. "Water first, then cobbler, please." We needed to find a more secluded spot before James lost his self-control. Twirling a girl on the dance floor was acceptable, but kissing her in front of others was not proper, and we didn't need anyone tattling to Uncle Abe.

James kept stopping to introduce me to couples, single fellers, and a gaggle of girls. While the lads punched James in the shoulder, the girls eyed James' arm linked with mine. I swapped names with them, knowing that these were the same young women who didn't want to share a cabin with Margaret. Perhaps Marti was right, and I had the grit to stand up to her oldest sister, but did I want to do that?

"Margaret know you're here?" one black-haired boy asked. "I knew Johnny was bringing Marti, but never thought you'd show your face."

"Nope, and unless you tell, the Boss won't know," James said and curled his fingers through mine. "And let us know where the next dance will be."

James led me through the cluster of sheds to where a small building covered the spring and a thread of water flowed across rocks and away from the farm. I dipped a mug of icy water, while James bent over and splashed his face. Grabbing the hem of my apron, I wiped his chin. His hand took mine, and James kissed my fingertips. My innards quaked as my heart thrummed. Moving his lips across my palm, he paused.

"I've been wanting to ask about these scars. How you got them."

"My hands were burnt when I pulled Lizzie out of a burning building." I tried to pull away, but his lips kissed the scar. My breathing quickened as a whirlwind rushed through me.

"Marks of courage." James pressed my palm against his cheek. "A brave and beautiful woman." He leaned over, his mouth covered mine, and I wrapped my arms around his neck.

Kissing James was like diving into a rushing mountain stream; the current of our passion swept us through the rapids and a whirlpool of desire spun us around. Sliding his hands into the middle of my back, James pressed me against him and his lips crept down my throat. As my legs melted, I ran my hands across his cheeks.

"Oh, Laws, his first kiss," Marti said. "Bet it won't be the last one, either.

Johnny whistled. "Got her swooning. James, you're a fast mover. Careful, my friend, best to stay standing."

My cheeks burned as James released me. Straightening my skirts, I glanced at Marti who raised her eyebrows.

"Don't worry, we won't tell Margaret." Marti grinned. "Wouldn't she be riled at the sight of you, two? Maybe I should tattle so I could watch her explode."

"But then she'd know that you went dancing," I said, making Marti laugh.

"Looks like you're eager to find a quiet place where you can spark," James said. "Reckon you could teach us a few tricks."

"Doesn't look like you need any of our advice," Marti said. "Johnny's right about taking things slow. Best be eating some cobbler, and give us some solitude."

"Our turn, James. You'uns find another place." Johnny laughed and pulled Marti's into his arms. "The north side of the barn is still empty."

With his arm around my waist, James and I strolled to the tables, claimed a bowl of cobbler, and sat on a log, brushing shoulders. Our spoons clinked as we dug into the sugary blackberries, and the buttery biscuit smothered with yellow cream. James fed me bites, wiping a splash of berry juice off my cheek. Laughing, I dipped a spoonful of cream and berries, and slid it into his mouth. At last, I scraped the sides of the bowl.

"Should I fetch you some more?" I cocked my head, and from his look, I sensed what he longed for. "Or should we see if the spot by the barn is still empty?"

James curled his arm around my shoulder. "I'd like more of you, but not here. When can I see you, again? Alone. I can't kiss you when you're weaving with my sisters." Moonlight chiseled his face, and shimmered along his swept-back hair as he brushed his knuckles along my cheek.

After Charlie left me, I never dreamed another man would so soon fill me with such longing. I didn't want to return to the quiet of my father's cabin, but yearned to dance with James until the sun rose. "I'll walk up Monday afternoon."

"Promise? I'll meet you by the big boulder, before the creek turns away from the path." James kissed my forehead. "Judging from the position of the moon, we'd best find Marti and Johnny. We need to ride in before dawn."

"I think they snuck behind the woodpile." James was right about needing to leave before we kissed one too many times.

He stood, pulling me up. My dress swept around my ankles and over his boots. "Why don't you fetch those two, while I get our mounts?"

Whispering, giggles and the scent of lavender floated from behind the tall stack of firewood. When I peeked around it, Marti stood against the logs, arms around Johnny's neck. He kissed each of her eyes.

"For the bluest eyes in all of Tennessee." Then he kissed her nose. "For the perkiest nose."

I shook out my skirt, making the fabric swish across the grass, and I stomped my boots. Their heads turned toward me.

"Don't mind Viney. If she snitches, I'll tell Margaret what I saw." Marti dropped her arms. "But I reckon it's time to ride out."

"Yes, we need to poke our heads from the loft if'n Uncle Abe should stop by," I said.

We thanked the Campbell family and said farewell to the other dancers. I loved how moving our feet together had made us friends, and we promised to gather again in a month at the Williams' homestead. James lifted me onto Red, and Marti joined Johnny on his horse. I rested a cheek against James' chest, listening to his heartbeat, as steady as the fiddler's tapping foot. Along the trail, clouds of fireflies flickered on and off as one body, and a barred owl hooted, "Who cooks for you?" Red's hooves clomped on the bits of shale and pebbles. Suddenly, James jerked on the reins. Darkness swarmed around us.

"What's wrong?" Sitting up, I only heard the drone of cicadas and tree frogs.

James pressed a finger over my lips. From further up the trail, faint horse hooves clip-clopped. He jumped down and led his mule to where rocks jutted out, hiding the mule as far back as he could.

"Johnny, quick. Beneath this ledge. Get your horse behind these laurels. Viney, Marti, climb up, and hide. Stay still and don't let anyone see you." He boosted us up the slope. "Hurry."

Marti and I scrambled behind a jumble of boulders and crouched on our knees. We peered between slabs of rocks as the creaking of saddles and horses marched closer, along with the smell of tobacco and burning pine pitch.

In the quivering glow of torches, ghostly shapes emerged, flickering between overhanging branches and boulders. White hoods with slits for eyes covered the men's heads, and some wore long white robes flowing down to their boots. They carried rifles and shotguns, and the man in the lead held a long whip. My mouth went dry, and my head whirled as I forced down bile. Marti and I huddled, powerless over what would happen if the vigilantes discovered us.

"White Caps." Now, I understood why folks feared the silent wraiths slithering between the hills and toward the Campbells' farm. Although they wore white, I had never witnessed such a gathering of evilness. I thanked God for the darkness shielding us, and hoped the men wouldn't spy us or notice the lads. While James and Johnny would try to defend us, I doubted if Marti and I could climb fast enough to get away from these men.

Marti whispered, "Must be a hundred of them. The Campbells haven't got a chance."

"And we can't warn any of them." I began to shake and hoped our animals would remain silent. The White Caps had trained their horses to walk as quietly as panthers. The Campbells wouldn't hear them coming.

Marti grabbed my hands. "Pray. There ain't no other way out of that holler other than to run up the mountain."

As the last rider passed beneath us, one of our animals shifted his weight, and his hoof crunched on the pebbles. Marti pulled me down as a ghost halted his horse. My ears roared, and my gut churned. Even if I begged for mercy, this man would punish us for being out at night.

Anger flowed from the hooded man, as he raised his rifle, scanned our hiding place and examined the outcropping rocks on the other side of the trail. "Blasted Blue Bills," he said. "We'll get you, yet." Slipping his gun behind his saddle, he flicked the reins and rode on.

Marti clung to me as we waited until the tree frogs began chirping again, and James crept up to where we sat. Far off, gunshots split the silence, and flames rose above the line of trees.

"Let's hightail it out of here. Looks like they're burning something." James slipped an arm around my waist guiding me down the dark slope. Johnny held out his arms to Marti who jumped into them, and he swung her onto his horse. On top of Red, James leaned over, sheltering me, and kicked his heels against the mule. "Move, boy."

"Will they beat Mr. Campbell?" I asked. "For having a dance?"

"The White Caps will tie his wife and older daughters to trees and make him whip them. Any of the young folk still at the gathering will feel their lash as a warning." Fear deepened James's voice, and he glanced behind us.

"Why doesn't anyone stop those men? Can't the sheriff arrest them?" Go, go, go, I wanted to shout at Red, get us away from here.

"The White Caps control the sheriff and the courts, and just about everything else in this county. None of us know who belongs. Someone invited to the party must be a White Cap, and he tipped off their leader."

"There must be a way to stop such meanness" I clenched my fists. "And who are the 'blasted Blue Bills'?"

"Another vigilante group trying to stop the White Caps, but with a thousand White Caps in Sevier County, we'd need the Army to battle them." James kicked his heels against Red. "Come on, boy."

No matter how I tried to rid my mind of those white hoods and the flames, they circled back, stabbing me in the gut. Why did folks believe that violent ways would keep their daughters pure? Why hadn't people stopped the White Caps before the vigilantes gained so much power? The image of the hidden clearing and the letter *Y* slid into my mind. Had the White Caps created that place, and had I seen part of the word, such as Saturday?

Lavender and apricot sifted across the eastern ridge when James and I reached my father's cabin, and a morning dove cooed from a dogwood tree. Martha and Johnny lingered in the grove of hemlocks, saying their good-byes. As James lifted me off Red, his strong hands pulled me closer.

"When you climb up on Monday, I'll take you fishing, to my special, hidden spot." His fingers cupped my chin as his lips found mine.

I knew I should push him away, but the heat coursing through me erased any sense of caution. Besides, Pa couldn't see us. Since swinging me during the dancing, James had lost his reserved manners and tightened his embrace.

Suddenly, someone leapt from out of the shadows, and a leather whip stung my ankles. I screamed, fearing a White Cap had followed us. James twirled around and caught Uncle Abe's raised arm.

"I warned her. No kissing. No dancing. If the White Caps hear of this, their lash would be worse." Uncle Abe twisted free of James, and shook me by my shoulder.

I tried to kick Uncle Abe's shins, but his huge hands held me at arm's length and lifted my feet off the ground.

"You stop that or I'll turn you over my knee. And you." He pointed his horse whip at James. "You never fell for temptation until this vixen arrived. I know she's to blame for your downfall. Stay away from her or I'll punch you." Uncle Abe shook me again. "I should lock you up until you'll obey me."

The cabin door opened. "Abraham." Pa clutched the door frame. His white hair floated about his shoulders, and his nightshirt billowed around his thin legs. "If'n my daughter needs correcting, I will apply the rod."

"You can't even button your shirt," Uncle Abe said. "She needs her rear end blistered."

I choked back my tears, mortified that James witnessed my shame. I tried to wiggle free, but Uncle Abe dug his fingers into me.

"I am her father," Pa said. "Let her go. James, cut me a switch from that sassafras tree."

Uncle Abe dropped me onto the porch. I fell to my knees, and scooted towards my father. If I had been a dog, I'd have bit my uncle, but instead, I wobbled to my feet, my calves throbbing.

"Yes, sir." James pulled out his knife, sliced off a thin whip, and handed it to my father.

How could James aid in this? His eyes avoided mine, and from the way James inhaled, he was struggling to control his anger. Did fear of Uncle Abe, or respect for my father keep James from defending me?

"Thank you, son. Lavinia, come with me. Good night, Abe, James." Holding the switch, Pa prodded me, and I walked in front of him, as he hobbled inside. Red's hooves clip-clopped away while Uncle Abe's boots stomped off the porch and then halted.

"Hold onto the bedpost and scream as loud as you can." Pa whispered. He gripped the other bedpost and raised his arm. The switch whistled through the air, and snapped against the mattress.

"Please, please don't!" I hollered. "Pa please! Laws, it hurts." I screeched and wailed. Even though it tickled me how my father was playacting and saving me from my uncle's beating, I hated that Uncle Abe would think this was how a father should control his daughter. "Stop, Pa! I'll be good. Please!"

"You promise to obey me?" Pa's hand shook as he raised his arm, and instead of the bed, the switch stung my bruised calves.

I shrieked, as pain raced up my legs. "Pa! I promise. I do." I collapsed on the floor and wept. Not only for the fire burning along calves, but I released my sorrow for the folks at the Campbells' who had suffered even greater agony. If'n not for James, I'd leave this sorry cove, tonight.

Uncle Abe's boots tramped down the path. Pa threw the switch on the banked fire, and sank down on his bed. He muttered something and shook his head. I lifted my skirt and petticoat. Blisters striped my calves, and blood trickled from the cuts, but what hurt most was my pride. Not the kind that makes a body think that she is better than other folks, but the spark that feeds a person's dignity so I could look at another and not feel ashamed. But I refused to hang my head like Aunt Sayward and Sissy, and other women. My uncle might be my elder and kin, but I'd never allow him to hit me, again.

"How are your legs? The tremors came upon me during the last one." Pa stared at his shaking hands. "Laws, I hate this. How long before I can't hold a spoon? Ain't no way for a man to live, or to die. Can't protect my child." Anger flushed Pa's cheeks. His eyes glinted as he chewed on his lower lip.

"My calves will mend. I best wash them, and soothe them with salve." I reached for a basin and filled it with warm water from a kettle hanging by the fire. Pa's words tugged at me; no telling when death would come for him.

"Daughter, you and Marti be more careful about who knows your plans. Somehow Abe found out the truth about where y'all were headed. And never ride up to the cabin on James's mule. He should say his good-byes over in the hemlocks or yonder laurel thicket where no one can watch you. Your cousin is an honorable man and I trust him, but my ears will be listening, just in case you need me."

"Yes, Pa." I understood he was warning me to kiss James good-night in a private spot. Tears wet my cheeks, and I heard Lizzie's reminder to seek the good in our father. "Thank you, for defending me."

He nodded, but couldn't look me in the eye. Pa pressed one shaking hand against the other, as if willing his fingers to rest peacefully. His knees trembled, making his feet jiggle against the floorboards.

"Pa, we spied a long line of White Caps heading into the holler. James hid us. The vigilantes burned something at the Campbells' place."

"Oh, Laws. Thought I'd heard horses on the pike. That poor family, feeling the lash of their whips. At least Abe ain't a part of that devilment, seeing as he was here. I was a-feared that he had joined 'em." He dropped his head into his hands. "How did such evil come upon us?"

"Guess Uncle Abe's too afraid of them," I said. Like other husbands and fathers, he claimed more power by bullying his wife and daughters with the threat of the White Caps' discipline. Men like my uncle didn't need a group to crush anyone; they knew how to slice women's spirits with words. But after tonight, I understood why the people of the cove dwelt in terror.

CHAPTER ELEVEN

Bunting decorated the Traverse City courthouse and draped the edge of a small stage that someone had constructed at the bottom step. Charlie lounged in the shade of an oak tree, listening to the mayor elucidate upon the passion of the American patriots who had won the Revolutionary War. Ladies in straw bonnets decorated with silk flowers clapped their gloved hands, making their full skirts sway. Gentlemen in top hats, wearing white shirts with blue and red ribbons tied around their upper arms, cheered as they celebrated Independence Day. At the end of the speech, the Civil War veterans dressed in their blue uniforms shot off their guns.

Charlie snorted. How odd it was to hear the American version of the story compared to the English history that he had studied back at Eaton. The rebels had been ungrateful colonists who had disregarded what England had done for them, and during the Civil War, his grandfather had fought for the Confederacy. His grandfather's tales of the lush soils of Tennessee had sparked Charlie's interest in coming to Rugby. How was Viney spending the holiday?

Last July, he and Seamus had picked early peaches, and Viney had baked a cobbler. The three of them had sat on Mr. Hill's steps digging into honey sweet peaches smothered with whipped cream. Afterwards, Seamus had fiddled, while he and Viney had danced around the porch, until she had collapsed against his shoulder. Charlie broke a twig off a low branch; he would go mad thinking about her.

As the crowd drifted away, he strolled to the school house. The room had been cleared of benches and desks. On a table covered with a white linen cloth, a stack of twenty boxes glowed. Decorated with red or yellow calico, or with colored paper, the boxes sported lace, ribbons, and silk flowers. The blue box with navy silk ribbons belonged to Charlotte, but the others belonged to the gaggle of young women clustered around one edge of the room.

"Ladies and gentlemen! We will begin the bidding on this handsome container, filled with delicious offerings bound to satisfy even the hungriest man in the room. Who will give me a nickel?" The schoolmaster said.

A short girl in a purple calico dress, with her thick brown braids wrapped around the top of her head blushed, as the bids rose. At last, the schoolmaster closed the bid, a gentleman claimed the box, and the girl accepted his offered arm.

One by one, the boxes left the table. Charlie dug his hands into his pockets. He wouldn't waste his few coins on Charlotte's box like the other fools who would try to outbid Mr. Burnett. Each time the schoolmaster cried out a figure, Burnett nodded his head and topped it. When the clerk from the mercantile gave up, Charlotte smiled at her beau, and he picked up her box.

Charlie hated the sound of Charlotte's satin skirt swooshing across the wooden floor, reminding him of the many times they had danced until the band packed up their instruments. He hoped Mr. Burnett would have indigestion from eating the meat pies and tiny cakes that Charlotte had baked.

One remaining girl stood by the wall, a slim blonde dressed in a simple dark-blue calico dress, thick, black stockings and heavy black boots. She bit her lower lip as the schoolmaster cleared his throat.

"And who would like to bid on this charming box? I can smell dill pickles and rye bread, and something else wonderful."

An older gentleman who resembled the girl lifted his hand. "Two cents," he said in a strong German accent.

Charlie waited, but most of the people had left the room. "A dime," he called out.

"Sold!" the schoolmaster called.

Charlie paid the man, picked up the heavy box, and smiled at the girl. "Where would you like to sit? My name is Charlie and your name is?"

"Gretchen. By trees," Gretchen said with a German accent. She linked her arm with his and they walked outside.

Charlie hoped Charlotte would notice Gretchen as he escorted her to a maple tree. She spread a gray tablecloth edged with blue cross-stitched flowers, and pulled blue enamel plates and mugs from a basket, along with silverware. Between bites of summer sausage, buttered rye bread and yellow cheese, Charlie teased enough words out of Gretchen to understand how her family had emigrated from Germany six month ago, and her father owned eighty acres.

The confusion that had swam in his eyes when he first came to Rugby, lingered on Gretchen's face as she sought the right English words. Charlie pulled up a handful of grass and tossed it away. Viney had been the person who had explained mountain ways and who had shown him how to farm. She had scolded and teased, her green eyes glinting mischief, but her laughter had eased his homesickness. Confound it, why did Viney have to interrupt even a simple meal?

"You have special friend?" Gretchen asked, her gaze hopeful and admiring as she handed Charlie several molasses cookies.

"Yes," Charlie lied.

CHAPTER TWELVE

Sunlight sifted through the dense oaks and beech leaves, and the creek chattered around rocks, as I strode up the mountain path singing:

"Hardest work I ever done,
Working on the farm,
Easiest work I ever done,
Swing my true love's arm,
Swing and turn, Jubilee,
Live and learn, Jubilee."

Another of Lizzie's letters had arrived, and she had referred to William fourteen times as she wrote about him playing the piano while they sang together, rode horses along the ridge, and had target practice. Appeared my sister and this gentleman had grown more than fond of each other, but a chill had filled me when Lizzie spoke of hearing someone walking outside her bedroom window. I was glad William had given her his derringer, and she could hit the center of a target. Maybe I should ask Lizzie to bring me one, and James could give me shooting lessons. Such a pretty sight came to me of James with his arms circled around me, helping me hold the pistol. Lizzie had also mentioned that two more letters from Charlie had arrived; one envelope was extra fat and smelled like roses. What in tarnation was that Englishman thinking?

As I rounded a corner and approached the big boulder, a turkey exploded from the underbrush and muscular arms grabbed me from behind. I screamed. James laughed, slid his hands over my eyes, and pulled me close. Relief weakened my knees, and I leaned my head against his chest.

"You shouldn't scare me like that! I thought you were a White Cap." I listened to his heartbeat, feeling the rise and fall of his lungs, and the heat from his arms. James laughed, again.

"What's sweet and golden? Fuzzy and soft?" He kissed the back of my neck, and the fresh scent of hay drifted from his shirt.

"A baby chick?" My heart danced as his thumbs caressed my cheeks. Despite the calluses, his touch was as tender as goose down.

"Nope, guess again." His breath tickled my ear as he kissed it, and I shivered

"A duckling?" I wiggled, trying to pry away his fingers, but James tightened his grip, curving his chest over my back.

"I don't name any fowl sweet." James' chin brushed my face. "What is soft as butter and full of sugar?"

"I give." I gasped as his hands fell away, and James spun me around.

"Peaches." James opened his fishing creel where rosy skinned peaches glowed; their scent floated toward me. Salivating, I reached for one, and he caught my wrist, pulling me toward him for a quick kiss. "You'll have to earn one. How many kisses for one peach?" His eyes reflected the green of the overhanging leaves.

"Name your price. Peaches are my favorite fruit. Please, I haven't had one yet this summer." The desire in James' eyes stirred waves of heat that rippled through me.

He pressed my back against a chestnut tree, tipped my chin. Firm but gentle, his lips explored mine, as lightning bugs dazzled behind my closed eyelids, until James released me.

"I'll claim more when we reach the trout pool. Come on." His strong fingers linked with mine.

A wren trilled as we threaded our way around laurel bushes and toward the sound of rushing water. When we reached the fishing spot, we sat on a large flat rock where James had left his poles, and a little basket of grubs. He gave me a peach. Lifting it to my nose, I inhaled its luscious fragrance, and then bit. Juice dripped off my chin, and James licked it away.

The silky fruit slid down my throat. "Hmm," I murmured and took another bite. Eve might have fallen for the taste of an apple, but peaches would be my undoing.

"You are tastier than any peach." Gold specks shone in James' eyes as his gaze wandered over me, pausing at my bare ankles.

With my palms pressed against the warm rock, I leaned back, eyes half-closed, basking in James' presence. How I had missed feeling wanted and admired. The imprint of his lips on mine lingered, as did the sweetness of his breath scented by teaberry leaves. Every part of me was rising, ready to float away in James' kisses.

James leaned over and tickled my feet. "Watching you takes away the misery of picking peaches. On a hot day, the fuzz coating my neck itches and drives me mad, but I can't wait to walk in the orchards with you during blossom time. Come fall, we'll pick apples and go nutting in our big chestnut grove."

Needles prickled my skin; Charlie and I had often strolled arm in arm through Mr. Hill's orchard. I had noticed the grape arbor and rows of apples and peach trees by James' family's cabin, but had not considered him a fruit farmer. His arms drew me to him.

"Oh, Viney, you're the best thing to ever happen to me. All week, I couldn't stop thinking about you." His mouth covered mine.

Like petals falling from apple blossoms, my misgivings fluttered away. Unlike Charlie, James was a man from these hills and loved the mountains. His accent matched mine, and he crumbled cornbread into milk. Butterflies floated in my belly as his fingers ran up and down my ribs, fueling my yearning, but I pushed him away before we would regret this meeting.

"Aren't we supposed to be fishing?" I inhaled, trying to quench the fire leaping through my flesh. "Didn't you promise to bring home trout?"

"Reckon so, but remember our bargain, there's still one more peach," James said, trying to hide his disappointment, but failing. Brushing his fingertips across my cheek, I sensed his longing like my own refused to fade. "But as soon as we fill my creel..."

We baited our hooks, and tossed in the lines. The sunshine shimmered through the overhanging tree limbs and tossed shadows on the rock. Dangling my bare feet in the stream, the water chilled my toes as I watched swallowtail butterflies land on a lip of sand. I squinted, seeing their colors swirl in my vision; I'd have to weave a coverlet in their yellow, black, and blue pattern.

I marveled how far James cast his line, as his muscles lengthened and contracted. And the way his hair fanned out from beneath the brim of his straw hat made my innards groan; I wanted to set the hat aside and run my fingers through his hair. Even with Margaret hovering in the background, it was a wonder that the local girls didn't flock around such a handsome fellow. Suddenly, James gathered in his fishing line and flipped a brown trout onto the rock.

He emptied the creel, winked, and tossed me the last peach. "I'm sorry about how our uncle shamed you Saturday night. I didn't want to cut that switch, but had to appease Uncle Abe."

"I'd about grabbed it from your hands, but my pa had a scheme. Once we were in the cabin, he had us playact a beating." I glanced at James' wide eyes. "And Uncle Abe believed us."

James laughed. "Your daddy is quite the trickster. Reckon I shouldn't mess with him. But still, Uncle Abe had no call to treat you like one of his women."

I was thankful James didn't think of me as belonging to Uncle Abe, but did that mean he considered me my father's property? Seeing as how I'd managed my life for nineteen years and owned more land than Pa, I didn't need or want my father telling me what to do. But I might enjoy having James think of me as his lady

"I'm not afeard of Uncle Abe, or his whip. Given a chance, I'd snatch it from him and lick his hide." My uncle's threats weren't going to change me. If'n I wanted to court James, then Uncle Abe would have to accept it.

"You and Margaret." James flicked his line into the trout pool and gently tugged it.

"That's not fair! I don't boss everyone around like Margaret, trying to control them." I didn't like being compared to Margaret with her sour ways. We might both be strong minded, but I didn't hate men like she did. If I moved into the Walker cabin, I'd allow those younger sisters the freedom to court, and encourage them to visit to Rugby so they could hear Mr. Hughes' ideas.

"Uncle Abe and Margaret have more in common." I scowled. "And I'm more fun than her. She can't tell a reel from a waltz." I pretended to pout, waiting to see what James would do.

"You're right about that." James cast again. "But we should fear the White Caps. Folks are saying they made Ian Campbell whip his daughters until there'd be scars on their backs. Most of the dancers hid in laurel thickets or climbed up higher while the White Caps beat up the musicians and smashed their instruments."

"Folks need to do something to stop their devilment." I had to think of a way to convince everyone to fight these evil men. As if voicing their agreement, cicadas buzzed from their hiding places between the oak leaves.

Setting down his rod, James wrapped his arms around me and pulled me into a shallow dip in the flat rock. Three boulders ringed the spot. "We need to be extra careful and avoid letting the White Caps see us together. I rarely see anyone here." He nuzzled my cheek with his chin; his fingertips tracing the bones of my wrist.

My insides melted like butter oozing across a hot biscuit, as his lips moved down my throat and back to my mouth. I pressed my hands against his chest, wishing James would tell me that he loved me.

Yet, when he released me, a flash of Charlie's shoulders as he lifted a hoe in my corn patch slipped through my mind. I hated how my memory played tricks on me. I was done with that Englishman, here was my Smoky Mountain love. Catching my breath, I leaned against a boulder, and through half-closed eyes, relished the dreamy expression on James' face.

"Is my payment for the peaches complete?" I poked James' thigh with my toe.

"For today, those were the first ripe ones, plenty more to harvest." James chucked me under the chin. "We best be off, if'n I'm going to clean these fish for you."

We linked hands and walked up the mountain. To my surprise, we found a city woman sitting on the Walkers' front porch. A gray hat adorned with pink silk roses perched on her blonde hair, and a gold locket sparkled at the collar on her white shirtwaist tucked into a brown woolen skirt. Polly and Martha leaned against the porch posts, eyeing Margaret who rocked while the woman talked. James nudged me.

"I'm not walking into that hornet's nest. I'll go clean the fish and leave you a mess by the back door. Hope your daddy enjoys them." He sauntered off to the springhouse.

I climbed the porch steps, and Polly fetched me a cup of sassafras tea and introduced me to Miss Dickinson. Next to a loom, little Hettie played with her doll. By the porch railing, a bumblebee rumbled inside a red hollyhock, and over by the barn, a calf mooed.

"Eventually, we hope to build a settlement school at the mouth of the cove," Miss Dickinson said. "I heard from a local woman that you and your sisters were some of the best weavers in the area. We would love to sell your weavings to our supporters up north. They are eager to decorate their homes with your crafts."

Sipping the spicy tea, I listened to the lady explain how flatlanders asked that their coverlets have matched seams, and they favored patterns woven with brown or indigo thread contrasting with natural wool. When the woman finished, Polly didn't wait for Margaret to reply, but spoke out.

"May I try on your hat, please, ma'am? I've never spied such a pretty one." Longing flickered across Polly's face.

"Polly," Margaret shook her head. "Don't pester Miss Dickinson. Such foolery is not for us."

The woman laughed and unpinned her hat. "If you were to sell your weavings off the mountain, you could visit Knoxville and buy one like it."

Polly modeled the hat, then Marti demanded to try it on, and even Hettie and Caroline begged for a turn. Margaret scowled.

"You're putting notions into their heads. Sunbonnets protect their skin better."

"Oh, they're just young women, wanting to wear something pretty and from a store." Miss Dickinson set down her teacup. "So, would you please sell me one of your coverlets?"

"I've none to spare." Margaret stopped rocking. "It takes a heap of weaving to cover this family and keep them clothed."

"Such a pity, couldn't you sell even one of them? You could also buy some pretty calico for your dresses, instead of having to weave your own cloth."

Miss Dickinson gave Margaret a pitiful look. Seemed this Yankee was as skilled an actress as me. I knew a certain chest held a dozen coverlets and a stack of quilts, and while the girls might be saving them for when they wed, Margaret could part with one. Polly's smile faded as she handed back the hat. Marti fiddled with her apron strings, hope simmering in her eyes. She probably pondered what Johnny would have thought if she wore such a bonnet.

"Maybe you could promise to sell the coverlet you're still weaving." I nodded at a loom with a cream and indigo Double Chariot Wheel stretched across the breast beam. "I'd be glad to help weave it, hasten things along. If'n I come every day, bet we could finish it yet this month, so you girls could have hats to wear to the next singing."

Margaret glared at me. She was too old-fashioned to scold me in front of company, and I planned to skedaddle before she could say much. I knew my cousins would take up the battle as soon as the screen door closed behind me. Miss Dickinson smiled.

"What a clever idea, Miss Viney. Please say yes, Miss Margaret. I would love to return to your beautiful cabin, so I might enjoy the splendid view and your amazing flower garden. I've never seen such tall hollyhocks or more fragrant pinks."

Marti and Polly stared at Margaret who studied her shoes. I reckon the Boss was wrestling with enjoying the praise for her garden, yet thinking such words stoked her pride, the worst of sins. Knowing to keep quiet, Hettie hugged her doll, and Caroline stilled her swinging legs from hitting the bottom rung of her chair. Beneath the porch, the hound scratched, his leg thumping the ground.

"By selling my weavings to the visitors, I bought my brother a harness for his mules," I said. "The cash money came in handy around the farm." I smoothed my skirt, acting innocent, resisting the urge to cut Miss Dickinson a grin.

"I reckon we can spare that one." Margaret stood up, and so did I.

"I can walk you down the mountain, Miss Dickinson," I said. "I need to be heading home, but I'll come back tomorrow to weave." I spied James at the back door, surveying us.

"That would be right kindly of you," Polly said, before Margaret could reply. "We'll watch for you, Cousin Viney."

Walking down the trail with my basket of fish, Miss Dickinson chattered about the opportunities the settlement school would provide for the mountain folks. I nodded my head, having heard such prattle from the men who had built Rugby. While I might have encouraged Margaret to sell her weavings, I had done it so my cousins could afford a few of the pretty things they desired. In their faces, I recognized the same frustration that had driven Lizzie off the farm and into being a maid at the inn. If'n Margaret didn't allow the girls a cunning hat or pair of shiny boots, someday, they'd walk off the mountain, and head to Knoxville and the mills.

"Where did you sell your coverlets, Miss Viney?" Miss Dickinson lifted her skirts as we rounded a bend where tree roots interrupted the trail.

"I sold most of my weavings to the folks from Cincinnati who came to visit Rugby."

"Ah, Rugby, Hughes's utopia. I had hoped to visit their fine hotel and view their lovely gardens."

"They're rebuilding the Tabard Inn so it will be even grander than the one that burned." Sometimes the smoke and heat from the fire still smothered me in my dreams, and I awoke gasping. I reckoned just like the war haunted Pa, the flames had kindled a fear that refused to let me go. When we reached the end of the trail, Miss Dickinson pulled on her riding gloves and untied the reins to her horse.

"Are there any other weavers in the cove you could tell me about? Or chair makers? I love those hickory chairs with woven, rush bottom seats."

"I don't know, but I'll ask around. My aunt makes pretty baskets, but her husband wouldn't like her selling them."

My uncle would rage if he found his wife earning money. The mountain men at Rugby had done the same until their daughters brought home cash money from working at the inn or other boardinghouses, then the fathers claimed how it had been their idea to allow their young folks work. Hypocrites, but in the end, my friends buttoned up new dresses and their fathers didn't worry about how to pay their land taxes.

"Maybe after the men see how much those Walker sisters can earn, other folks will want to participate." Miss Dickinson mounted her horse and trotted away.

If'n I could change Margaret's mind, my cousins could provide armloads of coverlets for Miss Dickinson. Maybe I should ask James to help me build a loom so I could set to weaving some of my own patterns. I strolled home, thinking about seeing James tomorrow, hoping we could kiss in the barn, remembering the feel of his fingers running down my ribs. As I stepped onto our cabin's porch, my bare feet hit something. I looked down, and sucked in my breath.

A hazel switch with a white scrap of cloth knotted at the end, rested like a snake on the top step. I picked it up and saw writing on the muslin. Untying the knot, I spied a drawing of a man wearing a white hood and read: "Mend your ways or we will."

Chapter Thirteen

Pa sat with his elbows on the table, winding that strip of muslin around his shaking fingers and then unrolling it, reading it again, and again. Tears shimmered in his eyes as he shifted his gaze from the muslin to the redbud tree outside our window, and back to the message. When I had shown him the switch, he had crumpled into his chair, and for the past hour, hadn't spoken. Once or twice, he'd open his mouth, and close it, shaking his head.

Stirring up some cornbread, I suspected the same questions circling in my mind pestered Pa. I poured the batter into a tin pan, placed it in the cast iron Dutch oven, and put on the oven's lid. Backing away from the fire, I noted the position of the sun. It needed to move to the other side of a cluster of tall oaks before the cornbread would be baked.

Pa moaned and rested his head on his hands. "Daughter, I'm afeard for you. The young women who dwell here, most of them know how to side-step around these devils. I should have warned you, given you better advice on how not to rile them."

"I reckon Uncle Abe tried to warn me." With one finger, I traced a knothole in the tabletop. "James said that we needed to be careful not to provoke them, but..." Someone must have seen us sparking at the river, or perhaps had spied us kissing at the dance, or had seen us walking along the trail where James liked to wrap one arm around my waist fitting me into the curve of his body. Why did our loving ignite such fury in these men?

Pa studied my face. "I remember those yearnings simmering, tormenting my mind; sometimes a fellow needs to be doused with a bucket of cold water. I should have spoken with James." Pa shook his head. "Abe's not used to women who refuse to obey him." His voice trembled. "He'll soon learn about this, seeing how fast news flies through the cove."

"I'd figured that since I'd only be here for a few months, the White Caps would ignore me." Being lost in my dreams about James, I had stopped ticking off the days until Lizzie would arrive and take care of Pa. A catbird mewed as I stared out the window at the black-eyed Susans blooming in a scrap of sun, realizing how July had arrived. In a few more weeks, Lizzie would come to the cove.

"No, daughter. Because you're an outsider, the White Caps aim to make an example of you, same as burning the Campbells' barn, a message to stop the dancing and frolicking. Because those men fought for the Union, they see you as the daughter of a Confederate rebel. They reckoned that I'm too feeble to resist them."

Pa didn't want any guns in the house, but Lizzie would be bringing her pistol. The thought comforted me. I picked up the linen strip with its walnut brown lettering, remembering the flames leaping above the treetops, and the parade of ghoulish white hoods shimmering in the torchlight. And the bullwhip of braided leather with its long handle that set my heart to quaking.

"I hate every one of those blasted White Caps. May the devil take them to hell." I picked up the willow switch and snapped it in half.

"No, don't hate them." Pa clutched the broken switch. "That won't end their evilness. Hating folks will heap more darkness inside you. Look at me, I hated the man I gutted, and even now, I can't escape from his screams. Sometimes I wonder if my shakes started on that night."

I knew Pa was right, but what *was* I going to do? The scent of baking cornbread mingled with wood smoke drifting from the fire. Such cozy fragrances, found most days in any of the log cabins dotting this valley. Yet, today was no longer like most days. It was if a cloud of locusts were buzzing around my head, and crawling along my neck. I needed to think of a way to end the White Caps' power.

"I'm sorry that I asked you to come here." Pa studied the knothole. "Them men see me as a sorry excuse for a father and blame me for not making you mind. Can't playact a beating for them." He brushed away tears. "Being a Confederate is my problem, and you shouldn't suffer for it. You must leave, before them villains act. Go back to Rugby."

For nineteen years, I had longed to hear my father say that he was sorry for abandoning me. While he hadn't spoken that particular apology, for the first time, my pa was showing remorse. His words flowed through me, pushing at the bitterness that had settled into my bones. Tears puddled in my eyes. I'd love to flee to Rugby, but how could I face my brother and sister who would want to know why I left Pa? And at some distant time, what would I think about my cowardice if I ran away? Seeing as the War Between the States had ended almost two decades ago, why did these men cling to it? Especially seeing as how their side had won.

"But who would take care of you? If you lived with Uncle Abe, mightn't the White Caps take their anger out on Sayward and Sissy? Maybe even burn your brother's barn?" My gut might roil at the mention of my uncle's name, but I wanted to prevent the White Caps from attacking my kin. What might they do to James? Before nightfall, he and his family would hear of this. Oh, Laws, what would Margaret do?

"Yes, there's that risk, and I wouldn't want to bring them harm. Your Uncle John hasn't much space what with all of his children still living at home. If I could ride James' mule up the mountain, I could live in their barn."

"No, you couldn't survive living like that. I best stay Pa, until Lizzie can come. She'll help me figure out how to protect you." Reaching out, I gripped his quivering hand. I'd write Lizzie tonight and warn her about this mess.

Tears dribbled through his fingers as Pa snuffled and wept. "I knowed you didn't want to come with me, but you did. You are a kind daughter."

"Thank you." From some deep valley in my mind, I recollected Aunt Alta telling me the Bible story of two brothers, one said that he'd come work for his pa, but didn't, while the other one said he wouldn't, but then did go help. My Aunt could have sorted through my snarled feelings and told me which boy I was most like.

Boots thundered up the porch steps. The screen door walloped against the wall. Uncle Abe towered over us, blocking the doorway. His dark eyes glittered, as his thick fingers clamped upon my chin. Sweat dripped down his forehead; red blotched his neck.

"You, whore! I shouldn't have allowed you on my land." Uncle Abe pulled me to my feet. Pain streaked down my neck; I couldn't swallow or speak.

"Abraham." Pa struggled to rise and gripped the table. "Release my daughter."

"Sit down." Uncle Abe threw me over his shoulder and with one hand, squeezed my ankles together. I pounded his chest with my fists until he grabbed my arms.

"I'll drop your drawers and tan your hide if'n you don't stop that."

Shame smothered me, winding me up like a spider wraps his prey in silk thread. I fell limp against him, hating him, sick to my stomach from the thick scent of his sweat. Someday, in some way, I would get back at him.

"Abraham, put her down..." Pa tottered toward us, reaching out for me.

"From now on, this vixen answers to me, and I plan to make her mind. Don't forget that those vigilantes might strike you, too."

The screen door banged behind us and Uncle Abe strode along the path to his farm. He opened the door to his corncrib, shoved me into it, and bolted it shut with a heavy board. My uncle glared at me as I stood gripping the slats. If'n he had been a wolf, slobber would have been dribbling from his lips.

"You belong in that cage. You should be ashamed of yourself, behaving like a wild cat in heat. Every gossip in the cove will be counting the days and watching your belly. The White Caps have spies everywhere, and saw you necking with James. I hope they see you sitting in here, and realize how I take their warning seriously. And if they come for you tonight, at least they can't hurt my brother. You deserve their whipping."

I loathed my uncle and those vile men. Swiping my sleeve across my eyes, I plopped down on the stack of corn waiting to be shelled. Mice had nibbled on some of them and had left little fragments of cobs. At the moment, my biggest fear was that a black widow or brown recluse spider might be hiding in a dark corner and bite me. But what if tonight the White Caps rode in, I couldn't protect myself or hide.

Little hands slid through the slats, and wide brown eyes looked up at me. "Why did my daddy put you in there?" Bobby, one of the twins asked. "You must be really naughty. Most times, Daddy spanks me in the woodshed." Bobby's blond hair was slicked down, and he wore a fresh set of clothes, all spiffed up and ready for Wednesday evening church.

O Laws. A passel of folk would soon be stepping down the road on their way to meeting, including my Walker cousins. I ran my fingers through my hair, trying to rid it of cobwebs and chaff. Bits of corncob peppered my skirt. My right sleeve was torn at the elbow and streaked with blood from where a nail had bit me. Seeing as the sun didn't set until after the service ended, everyone could still look at me on their homeward trip. I wished my body could shrink until like a mouse, I could squeeze through the slats.

"Didn't help much. You still look like AshPet." Bobby pointed at me with his clean little finger. "Want me to fetch some water?"

"Bobby." Sissy walked up to the crib. "Almost time to leave." She shooed him towards the cabin and pressed her face against the thin boards. "I'm sorry Cousin Viney. I'd let you go free, but Pa would take a belt to me." Sissy slipped me a piece of fried chicken. "It's all I could hide."

"Thank you." I hid the chicken in my apron pocket. Sissy ran and joined her family as Uncle Abe led them down the trail to the meetinghouse.

Bobby's reference to AshPet made me think of Aunt Alta who had told me the tale and another story about Mutzmag, a headstrong girl who outfoxed giants and villains. Mutzmag would have either tricked folks into thinking how she liked being locked inside a corncrib or she would have discovered a way to escape. Chewing on the chicken, I studied the slats for gaps or loose boards that I could pry off, but my uncle kept his buildings repaired.

Yet, over in a corner behind the pile of corn, a groundhog had dug a hole so he could sneak into the crib. The dirt was freshly moved, so he must have burrowed this afternoon, and my uncle hadn't noticed the critter's work. Judging from the size of the opening, he was a fat fellow, almost as big as my shoulders. But as the first of the churchgoers marched by, I plopped down on a sack half-full of corn, and hid the hole.

"She's a wicked one, the brat of a Confederate rebel," a man said to his daughters, and his wife nodded. "Girls who don't mind their daddies must be punished. This will learn her."

And so it went, as fathers pointed at me and warned their children. A few of their wives snuck me a mournful glance, but most stared at their dusty toes. One man stood for a few minutes, smirking, his eyes roaming over me until I wanted to curse at him. James and his family walked by without looking at me or saying a word, except for Polly who stepped off the path, and squeezed my hand. Did James shun me out of shame or to avoid the menacing eyes of the White Caps?

When the faint words of Old One Hundred drifted from the meetinghouse, I kicked at the groundhog hole with my heel, loosening clumps of dirt. When my heels began to ache, I clawed at the hole. But too soon, the families traipsed by on their homeward trips. Leaning against the sack, I sat hunched over, sniffling, wiping my eyes. Mutzmag herself couldn't have done better.

"See, done her good," one man said as he herded his flock down the trail. "She'll no longer act so high and mighty. She'll obey Abe, now."

But when Uncle Abe arrived, I put away my handkerchief. With his thumbs on his braces, he studied me, while Aunt Sayward and her brood looked on with concern.

"Are you gonna leave her there overnight?" Sayward asked. "Mite chilly. And the mist is rising, she'll get cold and damp." Sayward looked me in the eye and mouthed, "Say you're sorry."

For one breath, I considered sinking to my knees and begging to be released, vowing to obey him. But I wasn't going to add lying to my sins, and there was no way to know if he would believe me.

"She's just playacting. Too much pride on her face." Uncle Abe snorted. "Won't hurt her to ponder her willfulness. No husband is going to want such a wife until she accepts her lot. And I don't want to catch any of you sneaking out with a quilt," Uncle Abe said. "Come along."

I longed to spit at him, but didn't want to make things worse. Aunt Sayward gathered her youn'uns into the cabin and lantern light glowed from the windows. Uncle Abe checked on the livestock and stomped up the porch steps. At last, they blew their candles out.

Blackness filled the cove, interrupted only by clouds of fireflies. Bats' wings fluttered and whispered about the crib as they dove after insects. As nighthawks zipped overhead, they twanged their call, and a screech owl answered. Fog floated through the valley, threading between the trees and outbuildings.

Nighttime has never scared me, seeing as I love to stare at the stars and breathe in the coolness descending upon the mountains. But as the darkness surrounded me, I resumed scraping at the hole, praying the White Caps wouldn't come. My ears ached from listening for any faint sound of horses.

A crescent moon had risen when from the woods, two figures wearing white hoods walked through the mist toward me. Inching into the far corner, I cursed that my hole was still too small. My legs quaked, and my feet were stones. Terror squeezed my throat as one man lifted the heavy board that latched the door, as if to enter my prison. The other man peered through the slats; his white hood seemed to float in the mist. I crumpled to the ground and stuffed my fist in my mouth, knowing Uncle Abe would ignore my scream for mercy.

"Hee, hee, hee," The man staring at me pointed his finger, rocking back and forth on his heels, his high laughter sawing at my nerves. He slid his hands into the crib, reaching toward me. "Come on, give me a kissy. Like with your cousin. Hee, hee, hee. I seen it all."

Kathunk. The first fellow grunted and dropped the board, making sure it was secure. He cuffed his friend on the shoulder, and jerked his head toward the woods. They glided away; their white hoods flickering in the fog as it drifted along the valley. Trembling, I wept, listening for the faintest rustle of men's boots in case they returned. When the screeching of the locusts filled the night, I clawed at the dirt, gritting my teeth as my fingers bled.

A vesper sparrow called as the moon sank over the barn, and the black sky turned to gray. I slid through my hole and reaching into the crib, my hands packed the dirt back around the opening. Mr. Groundhog would find his doorway about the same, but terror overwhelmed my soul.

Chapter Fourteen

Charlie stared at the mirror while Charlotte lifted several locks of his hair and snipped them with her scissors. During the winter, he had relished her haircuts as her fingers brushed his neck. He would catch her wrist and pull her onto his lap. Charlotte would press her lips against his, and her kisses would overpower the numbness of leaving Rugby and the death of George. A fire would singe his nerve endings, and Charlotte's desire had conquered him. Had his father's demands to farm in the north pushed him away from Viney? Or had Viney's perpetual reminders of how she now owned land festered into a boil that had exploded in bitterness?

"Sit still if you don't want your hair to be lopsided." Charlotte's scissors pricked his scalp.

She hummed the tune Mr. Burnett had played on the piano last night; a tiny smile tugged at her mouth. Watching those two together made Charlie want to plunge into Lake Michigan and hold his breath until his head buzzed. What if Viney didn't reply because some fellow was courting her?

"Thank you," Charlie said after Charlotte removed the towel from around his neck.

"You're welcome. We want everyone looking their best for church tomorrow." Charlotte turned away, and replaced her scissors in her sewing basket.

"Yes." What did she mean by that? And did *we* mean Charlotte and Mr. Burnett? Charlie settled his hat on his head. In the slanted evening light, he hiked through orchards and pastures, aiming for the end of the peninsula. The voice of the waves as they slapped against the shore grew louder. Lake Michigan must be a female, contrary, capricious, and recalcitrant; Charlie listed adjectives that best described Charlotte.

Standing on the strand, the waves rolled pebbles away from shore. Charlie pulled the envelope from his pocket. His father had addressed the missive instead of his mother. With his penknife, Charlie slit the envelope, unfolded the letter, and scanned the lines.

Dear Son,

Your mother and I were shocked that you want to return to Rugby. Even if a match with Mr. Townsend's daughter is not in your future, we cannot bless your decision to leave the better farmland of Michigan. We will withhold any financial support if you choose to settle in Tennessee.

You will always be our son, but think wisely before you make your final decision.

Affectionately, your father

Charlie stepped backwards as a wave licked his boots. Perhaps he shouldn't have written about his plans until he had reached Rugby and married Viney. It would be harder for his parents to object to his decision if he presented them with a wife and a farm. Or maybe not. They had never approved of his relationship with Viney. After reading his descriptions, they had criticized Viney's low social station and her independence. Charlie stuffed the letter in his pocket and trudged onward. Life shouldn't be so complicated. Love shouldn't inflict such torment.

When Charlie rounded a dune, a riot of blossoms spread out like a quilt around the wooden lighthouse. In a dark wool dress and white apron, Mrs. Lane bent over a patch of pink, white and red Sweet William. With her dark hair tucked into a bun, the lighthouse keeper reminded Charlie of his mother, who stepped stately around their small manor house, giving instructions to the servants.

"Charlie! How good of you to visit," Mrs. Lane said. "How are things at the farm?"

"Fine. How's Mr. Lane?" Charlie pulled a stalk of grass from among the flower beds.

"Feeling poorly today, and from the look on your face, your mood matches his."

"I suppose so. With those mare's tail clouds, the sunset should be lovely this evening." Charlie gazed out at the pewter-colored waves rolling towards shore. Feathery clouds brushed the heavens, yet at the horizon, sky and waves melted into a satin shawl.

"Yes, sunsets always soothe my spirit."

"Yes." Lake Michigan's waves spoke of endless energy that could propel a ship or roll a storm into the bay.

"Word is that Miss Charlotte has a new beau. Might that be the reason you're here?"

"Partly." Charlie bit his lower lip. "There is someone I miss, who still lives in Rugby."

"And now because Miss Charlotte has tossed aside your affections, you regret leaving this young lady?"

"Yes." What a fool he was to think that Viney would never dance with some other good-looking fellow, or would never raise her lips towards another.

"And you've written her, but she doesn't reply?" Mrs. Lane cut several blue larkspurs.

Charlie sighed. "At least once a week, but not a word."

"So now you worry that she's met someone else?"

"Yes." Charlie rolled his hat between his fingers. How could he woo Viney back if she had fallen in love with another man?

"Hmm, keep writing. Don't give up. How many weeks until you can travel south?" Mrs. Lane set her basket on a bench and sat down.

"Six, and then I'm free." Although the calendar said a month and a half before Charlie could leave, his departure seemed as far away as Christmas. "But my parents aren't keen on me leaving Michigan."

"Ah, that's a pity. To have a father's blessing is important, but you're of age. Many a lad has chosen a wife contrary to his parents' will."

"Yes." Charlie leaned against the bench, gazing at the copper highlights shimmering between the waves as half of the sun slipped below the horizon. The clouds glowed orange and lavender.

"Time for me to light the lamps." Mrs. Lane stood. "Have a good evening, Charlie, and don't despair."

"And you, too." Charlie turned and walked through the gloaming, as trees shifted into shadows, and birds rustled in the leaves. If Viney were here, the evenings would be sweet once again.

At the end of the service, the Episcopal priest stood at the head of the church. His white robe rippled around his boots, and the high collar accentuated his graying beard. He nodded, and Charlotte and Mr. Burnett walked forward. Charlie clenched his fists; a bitter taste filled his mouth. So this was what Charlotte had meant by the pronoun, *we*.

"This morning, I have the pleasure of announcing the banns between Miss Charlotte Townsend and Mr. Henry Burnett." The priest drew their hands together. Pink flushed Charlotte's cheeks, but Mr. Burnett barely smiled.

What an old codger. Burnett was almost twice Charlotte's age, had soft hands, and streaks of gray in his hair. What did she see in him other than land and money? Why would Charlotte choose to share a bed with him? Charlie nibbled his thumbnail. How much of this betrothal was due to Mr. Townsend's influence? What if some well-to-do settler was wooing Viney with a marriage proposal?

"In one month, I shall unite them in holy matrimony. Today, they will join me at the door so you may congratulate them as you leave. And now for the blessing."

Instead of standing, Charlie slipped out of the pew and through the wide wooden doors. Somehow, someway, he had to depart from the farm before having to witness Charlotte's wedding. He had to return to Rugby and interrupt any man's plans to marry Viney.

CHAPTER FIFTEEN

Uncle Abe never talked about my escape. I reckoned that he didn't want folks to know how a slip of a girl had outfoxed him. I hoped the fog had erased the men's boot prints and that my uncle would never hear about the White Caps' midnight visit. When I had tiptoed into Pa's cabin, he had reached out and squeezed my hand before I climbed into the loft and collapsed on my pallet. I didn't tell Pa anything, so that Uncle Abe nor anyone else could weasel information out of him. But I wrote Lizzie about the switch and the terrible laughter floating from the white hood. For a few days, I stayed around the cabin, knitting, washing, and mending clothes.

Yet, it troubled me how James had not returned to release me from the crib. Or at least, he could have sat with his gun, guarding me until Uncle Abe set me free. Was his fear of the White Caps and our uncle greater than his affections for me? Charlie had raced into a burning building to save my sister and myself. Charlie, why had my thoughts circled back to him? Shaking such thoughts from my mind, I ambled up the mountain, to settle into the peace of weaving.

As I walked past the rushing stream, Lizzie's latest missive about *her* William plagued my mind. She had written three pages praising his good-looks, kindheartedness, and generosity. But she hadn't answered my questions about if her gentleman had proposed and when a wedding would take place. Instead, Lizzie had mentioned how Charlie had written me more letters and asked what to do with them? For a breath, I remembered the joy of feeling Charlie's fingers laced with mine, and not having to fear the White Caps when he folded me in his arms. If'n Rugby folks had noticed us sparking, they would have chuckled and teased us. After we were betrothed, Charlie and I might have kissed too much, but out of his respect for me, his hands had never wandered. Perhaps I should tell Lizzie to forward on his letters, but did I want to pick the scab off my wound? Gazing out at the

Smoky Mountains, I wished the spirit of Rugby could somehow descend upon the folks of the cove and destroy those vigilantes so James and I didn't have to sneak kisses in the barn.

At my cousins' cabin, I whacked the beater of one of the looms several times, thankful that they hadn't mentioned the corncrib or the message or the switch. I reckoned that Margaret believed James would now stop dallying with me, but I wouldn't allow her to win this battle.

Peace drifted about the porch as Polly spun, Margaret carded wool, and Marti plied yarn. By the set of Margaret's jaw, I knew she still fussed about me weaving this coverlet to sell to Miss Dickenson, but when my cousin realized how much cash money it would fetch, she'd change her mind. The crack of axes rang out from higher up where Marti's Johnny, James, and my Uncle John cut timber. I smiled, thinking of James with his legs apart and his boots sinking into the forest floor as his muscular shoulders swung an axe. I planned to weave until the shadows crept over us so James would have to give me a ride home on Red.

"Think you can finish that before the lady returns?" Polly picked up a fluff of carded wool and turned the great wheel, twisting the fibers into yarn.

"I reckon so. I'm caught up on the washing and mending. I'll hoe in the garden in the mornings, and weave in the afternoons." Whacking the beater also worked out my anger at the White Caps, and helped settle the river of thoughts about what might happen next to me.

"And in the evening, James can escort you home." Marti nudged me with her shoulder. She had wound her braid around her head like a crown and had pinned a few pinks to her apron. Ever since the dance, rose had often flushed her cheeks, and her eyes twinkled when Johnny was near.

Despite that frightful night and hideous laughter, thinking about James made fireflies swirl in my head. In a few hours, he would help me onto Red, slip his arms around my waist and draw me next to his chest. We would listen for sounds from up ahead on the trail or over in the undergrowth, so we could sit up proper-like before rounding a curve to avoid anyone catching us.

Margaret frowned. "Remember what Saint Paul said to women, 'avoid foolish talk and idle gossip'. You'll accomplish more if you pay mind to your work. Considering how agitated the White Caps are, everyone best behave, especially you, Cousin Viney."

Marti giggled, and Polly sighed. Hopefully, the three of us could chat in the barn before James arrived from his work in the orchard. Any day now, I believed that he'd ask Pa for permission to court me. James and I would need to build a loom so I could start weaving sheets and coverlets for my wedding chest.

The sound of the axes paused, a tree crashed, and a man screamed. Shouting rolled down the mountainside. We stilled, barely breathing. Marti dropped her carders and stood up.

"That was Johnny's voice." Her words quivered. "I'm sure of it." Lifting her skirts, she dashed up a game trail while Polly and I lit out after her.

Our feet slapped the path, aiming for the shouting and sounds of boots. I raced between the trees, praying. Lord have mercy, I spied James, shirtless, with blood streaking his arms. Marti screamed and dropped to her knees. Johnny lay twisted on the forest floor; his chest rose and fell as he gasped for air. A huge tree branch lay next to him. Blood flowed from his side where the limb had gouged his belly and crushed his ribs.

"No," Polly cried, and dashed to her sister. "Merciful heaven, save Johnny."

"Polly, Viney, hold Marti back," James ordered, kneeling beside his friend.

His father gently lifted Johnny's chest, and James wrapped it with strips of linen torn from his shirt. "Come on, Johnny, keep breathing. Don't leave us. We'll take care of you."

"Let me go," Marti screeched. "Oh, God don't take him. Not before we wed, please God."

Polly and I grabbed Marti by the shoulders as she sobbed, flailing her arms, trying to break free of our grasp. I scanned James for signs of mortal wounds, but only saw cuts and scratches. When he had finished with the bandaging, James nodded at us, and we released Marti who crumpled near Johnny's body.

"Don't leave me, please, don't leave me." Marti stroked Johnny's face and kissed his lips. "Fight, my love, so we can marry." She lifted one of his palms to her cheek. "Oh, God, please let him live."

Johnny's eyes opened for one breath, and Marti leaned over him. His fingertips pressed against her pale cheek. "My Marti." Blood trickled from the sides of his mouth. "I love you."

"Don't go. Stay with me." Tears dribbled off Marti's chin, and Polly wiped them away with her apron. "I want to share my life with you."

Gasping, Johnny shuddered and grimaced. His eyes closed, his body stiffened, and his arms fell limp. Marti pounded the earth with her fists, shrieking, "No, no," over and over. As she threw herself across his body, her hair tumbled from its pins, sweeping across Johnny's face.

James brushed away tears with the back of his hands, while Uncle John closed his eyes and prayed. Polly wrapped her arms around Marti, attempting to lift her off Johnny. Marti shoved her sister away. She arched and howled like a wounded animal. Her scream rose like a whirlwind, higher, stronger; it raced through the trees, echoed off the rocks, and vibrated in our hearts.

I sobbed, remembering how I had searched the flaming Tabard, and had found my sister in her trousseau trunk, waiting to be burned alive so she could be united in heaven with George. Staring at the scars on my hands, I thanked God that He had delivered Lizzie, Charlie and me from the conflagration. Squatting down on the other side of Marti, I slid an arm around her. She blubbered on my shoulder, moaning, gasping, as I rocked her just as I had consoled Lizzie.

"Please, let James carry Johnny to the cabin. We need to take his body down the mountain."

Uncle John bent over Marti, his long beard brushing her head as he placed a hand on her shoulder. "Marti, come away now. One day, you will go to him, but he ain't coming back to you. Polly, help your sister."

Polly swiped her apron across her face as James scooped up Johnny's body and trudged down the trail. Uncle John shouldered the axes and plodded after him. Polly and I linked arms around Marti's waist and half dragged her as she keened. Pain contorted her face, erasing the pink from her cheeks and the light from her eyes. When James laid Johnny on the porch floor, Marti sank down, curled herself around his body, and whimpered.

"Martha," Margaret said, "stop that." She reached to pull her sister up, but I grabbed Margaret's hand and shook my head. Margaret glared at me; her neck muscles stiffened.

"Stay out of this." Margaret shook her shoulders, trying to free herself from my grip.

"Leave her be." I gripped her hand. "Marti needs to grieve, in her own way." And if'n I might end up sharing a cabin with the Boss, then she had to learn how I wouldn't allow such unkindness.

"Have you no compassion?" I asked. For all Margaret's quoting of Scripture and preaching, seemed she had missed the verse where Jesus wept over his friend, Lazarus.

"Oh, how I loved him." Marti lifted her head and gazed up at me. "After the harvest, Johnny planned to ask Daddy for my hand. He promised we'd wed by Christmas and fill our cabin with babies. There'll never be another man like Johnny."

Releasing Margaret's hand, I leaned against the cabin wall, hearing Lizzie's voice saying the same words about George. There had been nothing I could do to stop Lizzie's sobs as I begged her to keep on living. Polly, Hettie, and Nan huddled by Marti, weeping with her. If only Lizzie were here, holding me, and drying my tears. I needed my sister.

Margaret pressed her lips together. "Polly, Viney, take Marti inside. James, find a fresh shirt and wash before you hitch the mule to the wagon. Better take Johnny's body to his folks. Giles and Caroline, let's go round up the cows. Time to milk."

Heartless witch, I wanted to shout. Thinking about chores when your family needs to grieve. But for Margaret, work was both her manner of escaping from conflicts and a way to control her sisters. I pitied my older cousin. One day, her sisters would break free and leave Margaret, locked in a corncrib of her own making.

Polly and I guided Marti into the cabin, and eased her onto a bed. Polly sat beside Marti, bathing her sister's face, whispering kind words as the others picked up baskets and buckets. I raced out the other door, surveying the yard, as the cows mooed from the pasture.

Uncle John sat in the grape arbor, head bowed; his lips moving. James stood by the springhouse, washing the blood off his arms and from the scratches etched in his shoulders. I dashed over to him.

"What happened?" I wanted to place my hands against his chest and feel him breathing, to have him wrap his arms around me. "You're not hurt?" Knowing Margaret might see us, I hid my rebellious hands behind my back and focused on his eyes where golden brown ringed his pupils.

"The tree fell the wrong way, and the limb snapped off, crushing Johnny. I tried to yank him out of its path, but I wasn't fast enough." James' face was ashen, and a bruise had turned his cheek purple. "His screams echoed off the hills, and still ring in my head. I should have saved him, but I didn't." He slipped a clean shirt over his head, tucked it in his trousers, and pulled up his braces, but tears glittered in the corners of his eyes.

"It was an accident. You aren't at fault." Cowbells sounded closer. "Margaret's coming. Let me help you harness the mule." I trailed James to the barn. Because his hands still shook, I buckled the leather straps, but he led Red to the wagon.

"Ride with me, please, 'till we reach the turnoff. Hauling a body is a fearsome thing. Johnny was my closest friend. I looked forward to having him as a brother. Marti's never going to forget him, and I won't neither."

Marti's wailing floated from the cabin's windows as James lifted Johnny's body into the wagon and covered it with a sheet. Even though Margaret watched, James helped me onto the wagon seat, and we started down the mountain. He clenched and unclenched his jaw, and I wanted to take his free hand, but he had slid away from me. At the turnoff, he pulled on the reins, stopping beneath a mighty chestnut. High above us, a wood pewee called his name, and sunlight drifted through the canopy of leaves. How could life roll onward so peacefully, without a hint of Johnny's death? James stared at the reins in his hands.

"You know what folk will say, that God struck Johnny because he and Marti went dancing and kissed too many times and too long. That they should have waited... until after their wedding. The White Caps will preach that Johnny and Marti deserved this judgment." His voice quavered.

"Do you think that way? That kissing is wrong?" I clutched the wagon seat. A chill rippled down my back as if a snowstorm had rolled over the mountains. "Do you believe God would kill people for showing their love?"

James looked up at Cove Mountain where an eagle circled the peak.

"I've listened to such talk all my days, that no woman should make free with her affections before she weds. Margaret is the godliest woman I know, and she says marriage is for the weak, who can't control their passions." A slight red color slid over James' neck. "If'n what folks preach ain't true, then why did Johnny die? And what might happen to us?" Fear simmered in his eyes. "Maybe them White Caps are right, and God sent them to chastise lewd women."

James rubbed his thumb up and down the reins, licking his lips as if he wanted to say more. I bit the inside of my cheek to still my tongue, and stared at the wavy grain in the wooden seat, forcing myself to consider my words. I had visited today to ask James about his feelings for me, and now, his questions erupted, dividing us. Yet, I didn't want to lose James like I had Charlie.

"I don't know why Johnny died, but I refuse to believe that it was because of kissing Marti, the woman he wanted to spend his life with. Terrible things sometimes happen in this world that we can't explain like my sister, Lizzie losing her fiancé a month before their wedding. The best thing folks can do is love and help each other, to show kindness." I placed my hand on his, but James balled his into a fist. "Do you want me to go with you to Johnny's family?"

"No." James shook his head. "His pa might be a White Cap, or maybe his older brother." He helped me down, and stepped back. "We best not be seen together for a spell. Let tempers cool down. I don't want to do anything to bring the White Caps looking for my sisters."

The wagon rattled down a narrow trail leading west, rounded the hillside, and vanished. I walked home, wishing I knew the answers to James' questions so I could convince him that his ideas were wrong. While it was noble how he was concerned about protecting his sisters, why didn't he worry about how the White Caps were watching me? No switch had been left for my cousins, so they shouldn't be in danger, but I was. Sitting on the front porch, Pa studied me.

"Something's troubling you." He patted the chair next to his. "What happened?"

While swaying back and forth in a rocking chair, I described the accident.

“Poor little Marti.” Pa rubbed his shaking fingers across his neck. “Such a sweet girl. Too young to face such loss.” Tears wet his cheeks.

I explained about James’ thoughts, and how he had separated from me. “I can’t believe that God would strike Johnny for loving Marti.”

“I don’t either,” Pa said. “We shouldn’t blame evil on the Almighty. We live in a world shadowed by a darkness that can cloud our minds when pain invades our hearts. James is speaking from a rawness brought on by desperate thoughts.”

Pa twisted a bit of his beard between his trembling fingers and gazed at the hazy blue ridges hugging the cove. Hollows sculpted his cheeks, and more lines wrinkled his forehead. The sadness in his eyes had deepened and foretold how his time on earth would soon end.

“But holding a pretty girl in your arms and kissing her *can* tempt a young man to beg for more. Don’t I know? Your aunts didn’t tell you how your mama was seven months wed when she birthed Jacob. We being newcomers to the ridge, no one paid much mind to what date we had wed. And when your aunts pointed out the early birth, I said how the long journey was the culprit, but I knew the truth. I should have heeded my mama’s warning to never be alone with a woman, even a good woman like your mama. Take care, daughter, with kissing.”

I sucked in my breath. Last summer, Lizzie had warned me about giving too many kisses to Charlie. And now after our time at the river, James was stepping back, pushing me away. Was I to blame for losing them? *Had* I been too free with my affections? Yet despite what James had said, his eyes had betrayed his longings for me. Pa’s gaze followed my footsteps as I opened the screen door.

“Reckon I best cook supper.” Kneeling on the hearth, I stirred up the fire and blew until the embers glowed, like the questions burning through me.

Chapter Sixteen

The funeral procession wound through the cove to Johnny's family burial plot. Six of his cousins dressed in black trousers and homespun-cotton shirts carried the coffin to the small knob. Because Johnny's folks blamed James for their son's death, my cousin had not been asked to help. Several versions of the tragedy swirled around the community, and Pa feared that sometime soon, the Daniel's clan would take revenge on our kin.

Johnny's mother wailed, and hung onto her husband's arm while their children and grandchildren trailed after them, holding bouquets of wildflowers. When Polly had taken food to the Daniels, she had spied Johnny's mother dipping the girls' dresses in a black dye pot, as she turned their cabin into a house of mourning. My cousin had offered to help, but Johnny's mother had shooed her away, saying how she couldn't abide the sight of any Walkers on her land.

The Colemans, Williams, and Walkers followed, first the men and then the women. Between Margaret and Polly, Marti trudged, her face as white as lard and her eyes red and puffy. The preacher gathered us into the little meadow on top of a small rise, where grassy mounds were marked by wooden crosses. Staring at the hole chiseled out of the hard and rocky earth, I recalled George's funeral, and how just before the men began to shovel in dirt, Lizzie had tried to fling herself on top of his coffin. Jacob and I had hung onto her until the hole was filled, and then she had sank upon the mound and keened. Why did God snatch away the lives of young men, and leave my father shaking in his rocker? I knew that Aunt Alta would scold me for thinking such, but I couldn't stop asking, why? Just this morning, Pa had shaken his head, saying he wished the tree had taken him to his final reward and not such a fine young fellow.

The preacher read from Job, the passages about repenting in ashes, then he told the crowd how Johnny now lived where all was gladness, never to be tempted again. I didn't listen to the rest of his sermon about how young folk would reap what they sowed in licentiousness. He didn't say much about men falling for temptations, but warned fathers to guard their daughters' virtues before any of them could turn into a Jezebel. A few folks said "amen" to that last comment, and one woman even glared at me. Poor Marti swayed, and I reached out to steady her. I prayed that she would find hope. After Johnny's kin shoveled dirt over the coffin, the elder brother stepped up to James, jabbing his finger at the grave.

"This is your fault. The Lord's punishing Johnny for sparking with your sister. You should have stopped them, instead of helping them go to that dance. I hope some night the White Caps come for your family."

Marti blanched and collapsed against her sisters. James' neck turned red, and he balled his fists inside his trouser pockets. Gold specks glimmered in his hazel eyes, as if he were a catamount, preparing to spring. My knees quivered, and Polly placed a hand on my shoulder. Beneath the brims of their sunbonnets, a few of the women's faces appeared shocked, but many others had hardened. Children hushed and gripped their mothers' hands.

"Mind your tongue, Brother Daniel." Margaret stood tall; her black dress buttoned up to her chin, the skirt touching her boots. "Did not Saint James warn us about our unruly tongues?" She looked around at the group. "That out of our mouths come blessings and curses, and these things ought not to be." Margaret nodded at her sisters and marched away.

I scanned the men as they filed out of the cemetery, some stooped with white hair poking out from under straw hats, another holding a young boy's hand, and then the fellows of courting age with slicked back hair. How many of those men were White Caps who might gather tonight and plot to act upon that curse? Did any Blue Bills stand among us, ready to defend my cousins? I walked along; my boots sliding on bits of shale.

"I reckon it's a far sight more merciful for the Lord to take Johnny home than to have the White Caps whip those Walker sisters, especially Johnny's gal, Martha," one older man said.

"That Margaret is a bossy shrew, and needs to follow her own advice," a middle-aged man in a slouch hat said. "No woman should scold menfolk. Her father needs to rein her in."

"Hard to fault Margaret for quoting Scripture, and she does her best at teaching her sisters to have a gentle spirit," Uncle Abe said. "The one who refuses to mend her ways is my brother's daughter."

I kicked a pebble with my boot, wanting to shush Uncle Abe. The other men nodded their heads, mumbling about how my Pa should use a belt on me in order to teach me my place. Shivers trickled down my spine. Back on my ridge, people clucked their tongues over my stubbornness and independence, but no one would whip me or any other woman. Even Lizzie hadn't paid no never mind to the gossips who complained about her flirting, and they hadn't threatened to beat her.

"Have you heard any more about them Blue Bills? Some folks are saying Doc Henderson over in Sevierville leads the band," one of the younger men said.

"For certain, they've got a clever leader, because the vigilantes haven't killed him, yet. And those Blue Bills have shot a few bullets into the White Caps," another man said. "They stopped a raid last week by blocking the only bridge that the clan needed to cross in order to do their business."

My heart thrummed. I slowed my steps and listened carefully, remembering how the rider had cursed the Blue Bills.

"Folks say how during daylight, White Caps and Blue Bills can pass each other on the street, saying 'howdy' even while knowing which side the other man is on. But come nightfall, the Blue Bills ride out, determined to clear Sevier County of the burning and beating."

Bless their hearts, I wanted to shout. We needed more men like these Blue Bills. Somehow, I had to meet this Dr. Henderson, so I could tell him about the switch on my porch. And I had an idea about how we could trick the White Caps.

A skirt swished against mine, and Sissy stepped beside me. "I've missed you," she said. "It's been a while since you came to the cabin." Her rough fingernails scratched my palm as she took my hand.

I bit my inner cheek, regretting my selfish desires to spend as much time as I could with James. "I'm sorry. I'd stop by now, but Pa is waiting to hear about the funeral. Can you come home with me?"

Sissy nodded at Uncle Abe. "No, Pa didn't even want me to pay my respects. He won't let me leave our place except when he takes us to Sunday preaching and Wednesday prayer meeting. Says he won't be having me become a temptress like Eve or like you." She let go of my hand, and looked at the dusty toes of her boots.

Over the past weeks, Sissy's body had claimed more curves that swelled her bodice and narrowed her waist. Her hips rounded the skirt of her dress and its hem brushed her calves instead of hiding them. If'n Uncle Abe wanted his daughter to remain modest, she'd be needing new frocks. Most-likely, Uncle Abe already fretted about the young men looking at Sissy, and keeping her at home was his way of protecting her. She would turn sixteen in a month and would accept the first feller who proposed.

"Can't see anything wrong with visiting your kin." I placed my hand on Sissy's shoulder.

Sissy dipped her head, and her sunbonnet covered her face, as she hid her chapped hands behind her mended apron. I had never seen her stand up straight and look into my eyes. Instead of a young woman ready to step into the future, she resembled an old basket of mine, with a few missing slats and a cracked handle. We linked elbows, and chatted as we tramped together until the path split.

I resolved to write Lizzie and ask her to fetch some blue calico for Sissy. When my sister arrived, we'd help our cousin sew a decent frock. I might even suggest that Lizzie bring a corset and muslin for new undergarments, such things would make Sissy feel like the woman, she had become.

"I'll try to stop by tomorrow." My heart pitied Sissy's bound life. She might as well be a slave, needing her master's permission to walk off the plantation. I hoped she would marry a man who was gentle and would respect her.

Uncle Abe strode up and gripped my wrist. "Don't you be teaching my gal any of your foolishness. You best keep to your cabin, caring for your pa. That's what he brought you here for." He herded his offspring toward his farm, but Aunt Sayward gave me a quick wave.

"Come see us." She silently mouthed the words. "I miss you."

When a few yards separated us, I spat at where my uncle's boots had dug into the dirt. Was Uncle Abe warning me because of his fear of the White Caps, or because he had joined them? I marched home while rage boiled inside my belly. Pa slept in his rocker with a gray kitten that Polly had given him. The little cat had curled up in the crook of Pa's arm and purred. I sank down in the other chair. Somehow, I had to find a ride to Sevierville because it was too far away to walk there and back in one day. I had to talk with Dr. Henderson before the White Caps attacked.

CHAPTER SEVENTEEN

"Blast it all!" Charlie swatted at a troublesome yellow jacket circling his head as he picked peaches. Beneath the leafy canopy, he rearranged his ladder so he could reach the peaches near the top of the tree. Peach fuzz ringed his neck, sifted down his shirt, and clung to his sweaty chest and back. His eyelids itched from fuzz, and Charlie licked it off his lips. Come evening, he would claim a dip in Lake Michigan, a ritual that would erase the misery of harvesting peaches. In a few more weeks, he could flee from this farm.

Lifting an earthenware jug, Charlie gulped cold water and splashed some over his face. If only he were sitting in Viney's cabin, eating her cornbread, but instead, he had to finish picking the peaches off this tree. Charlie slipped on the harness of the picking basket, and climbed the ladder. His hands gripped the sweet orbs and placed them in the basket, as the fragrance of peaches drifted about him. Over in the next row, Mr. Townsend worked on another tree.

Charlie couldn't quite reach the uppermost peaches. Stepping onto the top rung, he leaned forward. The ladder swayed and slid out from beneath his boots. He grabbed at a branch, but it broke. Charlie yelled as leaves and limbs slapped his face; peaches flew from his picking basket. Thrusting out an arm to protect his head, Charlie landed on his side with a rotten peach squashed against his face.

"Stupid peaches." A branch had stabbed a hole in Charlie's shirt, and another had ripped his trousers. Charlie dragged his sleeve across his face, wiping off the peach glop, and grunted as pain blazed up his arm. Mr. Townsend ran up to him.

"What happened?" The older man bent and helped Charlie take off the picking basket.

"What happened? I fell off the bloody ladder. And something is wrong with my wrist." Charlie cradled his aching arm with his right hand. "I need to see the doctor."

"I'll have Charlotte drive you, so I can keep picking." Mr. Townsend wiped his hands on his trousers, leaving streaks of peach fuzz.

Great, he had to share a buggy ride with the engaged Charlotte. Holding his elbow, Charlie trudged to the kitchen. All he needed was for Charlotte to take along her beau. Charlie nudged open the screen door with his shoulder, and Charlotte looked up from rolling out sugar cookies.

"My goodness, you're a mess. There's hot water in the reservoir."

"Your father said to drive me to the doctor." The pain raised the pitch of his voice. "I've hurt myself."

"I'm sorry." Charlotte dropped the cookie dough into bowl and covered it with a plate. "I'll go hitch up the buggy."

"Thank you." Charlie dipped hot water out of the reservoir and into a bucket. Resting his elbow on the small table in his room, he managed to wash the worst of the fuzz and peach flesh off his face and neck. Waves of pain shot through him, and he swallowed bile. The clip-clop of the horse drew him out of the house.

Each time the buggy wheels hit a pothole, Charlie gritted his teeth. Sitting in the backseat with his legs stretched out, he ticked off the mile markers, the Hansens' red barn, the Larsons' silo, the white clapboard Baptist Church. At last, the buggy rolled up to the doctor's home. While Charlotte tied up the team, Charlie walked into the one-story wing that housed the office and collapsed in a chair. Within minutes, the gray-haired doctor placed a hand on Charlie's shoulder.

"Let's have a look." Dr. Beaton escorted Charlie into a small room with whitewashed walls, two chairs and a table with a washbasin and other tools. "Let me help you with the shirt."

With a soft washcloth, Dr. Beaton bathed Charlie's upper body before examining his left arm. Charlie winced as the doctor ran his fingers around Charlie's wrist.

"You've sprained your wrist. I'll bandage it, and you should wear a sling for a week or so, mostly to protect it."

"So I shouldn't pick peaches with one hand?" Charlie clenched his teeth and grunted as Dr. Beaton wrapped his sprained wrist.

"I would advise you to avoid activities where you might bump or strike your wrist. Give it rest, and it will heal faster." Dr. Beaton arranged Charlie's arm in a sling. "Drink willow tea for the pain, or have a shot of whiskey if Townsend will allow it."

"He keeps a bottle hidden in the oat bin in the barn." Charlie snorted. "I'd have to add water if I poured out a dram. Townsend's a miser."

"I'll write you a prescription for it." Dr. Beaton winked. "Come back in a week."

• • • • •

Through half-open eyes, Charlie stretched out on his cot as the whiskey numbed the throbbing pain. He wished Viney sat next to him, so he could inhale her scent, a strange mixture of wool and lavender. Unlike Charlotte, Viney would bathe his face with cool water, give him sips of willow tea, and read to him. He was weary of *wishing* for Viney's presence. Hopefully Townsend wouldn't explode when Charlie asked for his pay and left for Tennessee.

Chapter Eighteen

Polly and Caroline unfolded the finished coverlet, and Miss Dickinson gasped. The white and indigo threads swirled, light and dark mingling, reminding me of the pattern of life in the cove. Most days were full of quiet moments, and then after sunset, the threat of the White Caps lurked in the shadows. The knife in my apron pocket knocked against my knee as my foot pumped the flax wheel. After James had slipped it into my hand, he had spent an hour showing his younger brother how to throw a knife, while from the porch, my eyes followed his moves. Back home, I had practiced each evening until I could hit the chestnut tree from thirty feet away.

"Perfect," Miss Dickinson said. "Because this is your first coverlet, I will pay for it now. Usually, we sell weavings on a commission basis, and pay the weavers after their work is purchased. But I'm sure someone will procure this one, instantly." She unsnapped the clasp on a small beaded handbag and pulled out an envelope. "This should buy all of you hats."

Margaret reached for it and stuffed it into her pocket. "I reckon there are other needs that should come first." Her butternut brown dress should have added highlights to her hair and set off her smooth skin, but the way she clamped her lips together gnarled her cheeks. I almost giggled thinking of what Lizzie would say about Margaret's sour face. Instead, I focused on the linen thread I was spinning, hoping one day it would cover James' shoulders.

"So you'll be wanting more coverlets?" I removed a full bobbin and replaced it with an empty one. "With fall not far off, folks will be needing more bedcoverings."

"Oh, yes, please," Miss Dickinson said. "Some northern women have asked if you would sell your quilts, plus baskets, brooms, and chairs. I will purchase whatever you can provide me."

"We don't have any of those to spare," Margaret said. "We can barely make enough for our use."

"Oh, I reckon I'll have that Chimney Sweep quilt finished soon," Polly said. "If'n we haven't another coverlet to give you, then I could sell my quilt. We might be needing extra cash money this winter, you never know."

Caroline and Marti glanced at each other, but their hands didn't stop carding wool, and my foot pumped the wheel even faster. The littlest girls looked up from a corner of the porch where they picked burrs and trash out of a brown fleece. Even the dog stared at Margaret.

"And if'n it's a cold winter, you might want those extra bed covers." Margaret shook her head and resumed spinning wool.

For a couple of mornings, I had visited Aunt Sayward and taught Sissy how to finish the two baskets. Somehow, I had to slip them to Miss Dickenson, and I hoped they'd fetch a good sum, or maybe she should barter them for extra bedsheets. My aunt and cousin needed a dose of taking pride in what their hands had crafted, and it might be good for my uncle to learn how others would pay for their creations.

Miss Dickinson tucked the coverlet under her arm. "Thank you, so much. I'll look forward to your quilt, and hopefully another coverlet when I return in a month."

"I'll walk you to your horse." I stood up, and stretched. "I'll be by again, tomorrow." I looked about, searching for a glimpse of James, but didn't see him. Most nights, I hugged my pillow, pretending it was my handsome cousin and his arms were wrapped around me. I even dreamed of standing in front of the preacher, repeating those sacred words that would allow us to be man and wife so he wouldn't feel ashamed of desiring me. But on other nights, the high laughter and the ghoulish shape of the White Caps invaded my dreams, and I'd awaken, whimpering.

Miss Dickinson and I waved good-by, and we walked to her big Morgan horse, resting beneath an oak tree. She squeezed the coverlet into a saddlebag and pulled on leather riding gloves.

"Would you like to ride with me? You would arrive home sooner." She offered me her hand.

I settled in behind her. We chattered on about the growing need for hand crafts, and her plans to build a settlement school. Seemed Miss Dickinson's church organization didn't want to draw folks out of the mountains, but wanted to bring jobs here. I told her about Aunt Sayward's baskets, and she offered to buy them. When we reached the cove, I scanned the position of the sun to determine the time, and noted that Uncle Abe was not in his fields, so he must be off fishing.

"Thank you for your assistance." Miss Dickinson drew on the reins and her horse stopped. "Hopefully next time, I'll have to hire a wagon to carry back all the crafts."

"My pleasure. Would you mind allowing me to ride on to Sevierville with you?" I reasoned that someone from the cove would be in town and could take me home.

"Certainly, after all you've done to help me, I'd love to repay your favor." Miss Dickinson clucked to the horse, and we rode off.

Her horse stepped more quickly than when Red hauled Pa and me in a loaded wagon. I reckoned Miss Dickinson was scared of the heights as she hugged close to the mountainside when we rounded the curves. After stopping to drink from a spring gushing out of the hillside, both Miss Dickinson and I ran out of questions, and we fell silent. I mused on how best to present my plan to the doctor.

If Dr. Henderson agreed to help me, and if the Blue Bills and I could rid the cove of the White Caps, then Pa would be safe and James wouldn't be afraid to court me. Yet, how would Margaret react when she spied James holding my hand or lifting me onto his horse? Even if the other sisters defied the Boss and wed, Margaret would never leave the farm. She would turn into dust while staying in that cabin. Living with her might parch my soul, but for James, I'd take that chance.

When we reached Sevierville, I said farewell to Miss Dickinson who rode off towards Cosby. I questioned a towhead boy lounging outside the church, and he told me the way to the doctor's house. I strolled down the road toward a two-story white clapboard house with a carriage shed behind it. A horse grazed in a small pasture fenced in with rails. A large vegetable garden flourished in the backyard. The scent of white and pink phlox blossoms spiced the air near the small front porch, and a honeysuckle vine curled along the railing.

A slip of a woman with blond hair and violet eyes answered my knock. Her green calico dress brushed the toes of her boots, and she had pinned her braid into a soft bun. Flour streaked her apron, and she had rolled up her sleeves. The scent of baking yeast bread drifted from the kitchen. For one breath, I was back in the Tabard kitchen, sneaking Charlie a warm dinner roll.

"May I help you?" she said, wiping her hands on her apron and smiling.

"Mrs. Henderson? May I see the doctor, please, ma'am?" I offered her my hand.

"Yes, I am the doctor's wife. Please come in." She escorted me to a small room with a couple of oak, bent-back chairs. "Please wait here. What ails you, honey?"

"Nothing, ma'am. I came to ask about my pa and his shakes. Perhaps the doctor can tell me of an herb that can stop them." I sat in one of the chairs and pushed back my sunbonnet. "Pa's palsy is growing worse."

"Poor soul. It pinches our hearts to see someone we love failing. Are you new to Sevierville? I haven't seen you about the village or at the general store."

"I'm Viney Walker, kin to half of Wear's Cove. My pa and I hark from Rugby, over in the Cumberland Mountains." Guilt trickled through me when she spoke about me loving my pa. What would this lady say if she knew my real reason for seeking out the doctor?

"Ah, yes, I've read about Rugby and Hughes's exciting experiment. If I were single, I'd consider moving there, but my family is here in the Smokies."

The door to the office opened, and a woman with a baby walked out. Wearing a white shirt, black suspenders, and woolen trousers, a tall man with a long nose looked down at me. Streaks of gray brushed his brown hair, and his blue eyes scrutinized me, giving me the jitters.

"Aaron, this is Viney Walker, from Rugby. She's come to discuss her pa's palsy." Mrs. Henderson nodded, and walked away.

"Pleased to meet you, Miss Walker. Like my wife, I admire Hughes's ideas and enjoy reading about his settlement." Dr. Henderson shook my hand and pointed toward the small room. "Please enter and sit down. And tell me more about what ails your father."

Rows of glass bottles filled with powders and liquids covered the wooden shelves lining his office, along with many thick, leather-bound books. The air smelled of camphor and valerian, with a hint of gunpowder. His doctoring bag sat on a table beside a line-up of special tools. Two Winchesters leaned against the wall, and a pistol rested on his cluttered desk. Dr. Henderson followed my eyes and chuckled.

"No, I don't shoot my patients—I prefer healing them." He leaned back in his chair. "Because of certain problems in our county, most men keep their guns at hand and loaded. And like them, I want to protect my family and my patients."

"Yes, sir. I know about the White Caps. While I would appreciate advice on how to help my Pa, I came to talk about those vigilantes. Some folks say that you command the Blue Bills."

"Folks love to speculate and gossip..." Dr. Henderson picked up a small, flat rock and rolled it in his palm. "What sparked your interest in the White Caps?" He studied me, as if to determine which side I believed in.

"They left me this, sir." I placed the muslin scrap with its writing on his desk. His eyes widened and met mine.

"Great heavens," he muttered. "Not another one."

"Where I come from, folks want their daughters to remain pure, but they wouldn't use beatings to keep them under control, sir. Their daddies appeal to their hearts, and tell their girls how much they love them, and that such wantonness would hurt their families. I aim to stop those devils from terrorizing folks." I leaned against the wooden back of my chair, pushing away thoughts of what I would do if this man refused to help me.

"I see. Would you feel comfortable telling me why you think the White Caps left you this?" He leaned forward and picked up the muslin as if it were a snake.

"Because my cousin took me dancing and kissed me, sir." I squared my shoulders. "He is an honorable man, sir. We did nothing more." My cheeks flushed as I remembered our time at the river, but I wasn't sharing those moments.

"I believe you, Miss Walker. Can you think of any other reasons?" Dr. Henderson's voice was calm, but showed his wariness. "Any other gossip that they might have heard?"

"Well, Uncle Abe says I'm willful, foolish, and should accept my womanly place. He doesn't like it that I'm helping the Walker sisters earn cash money, sir, and if'n I can have my way, his wife would sell her baskets. Plus, my father fought for the Confederacy." I crossed my arms against my chest. Hopefully, the doctor didn't hold the same opinions as my uncle.

"Hmm, the willful part sounds true, and because most of the White Caps served in the Union Army, they scorn Confederates." Dr. Henderson pitched the rock from hand to hand. "These days, it doesn't take much to ignite the White Caps' ire."

"And I spied two White Caps a couple of weeks ago by my uncle's place, sir." Fear shook my words as I explained about the night in the corncrib. I told him about stumbling onto their meeting place on Cove Mountain.

"Merciful heavens. They're moving quickly." Dr. Henderson set down his rock. "I hadn't heard about that particular site, and I wonder why they didn't do anything when you were caged. But sometimes the mere threat of violence gives them sufficient pleasure, especially when the threat changes a woman's behavior."

"Can the Blue Bills help me? Folks say they prevent raids, sir." I gripped the arms of the chair, feeling sweat trickle between my shoulder blades. Inside, a fly beat against a windowpane, and outside the cheesecloth screen, a mockingbird sang.

"That's right. When the Blue Bills learn about the White Caps' plans to discipline someone, they either try to block the route to the person's home, or ride in and halt the attack."

"After the dance, sir, we hid from the White Caps heading into the Campbells' holler. I was so angry. There was nothing we could do to stop them. One of the men cursed the Blue Bills. I wish y'all had come, sir."

Dr. Henderson ran his hand over his cheek. "I'm sorry you had to witness that ugliness. I wish the Blue Bills had known, but our normal informants failed. The leader has hired a spy to listen for any possible attack, and when he learns anything, he posts guards around the intended victim."

"I figured that the Blue Bills have spies, sir. But can you help me?" Even though I wiped sweat off my forehead, ice flowed through my veins. If this man refused to work with me, then what would I do to protect myself? To save my father from these devils' terror? I clutched the chair seat, willing my hands to stop shaking.

"Miss Walker, because of your plight, I will be honest with you. But nothing we say must leave this room." He sat up straight and measured me with his eyes. "Even though you grew up in the Cumberland Mountains, you are new in the area, and observe the situation from an outsider's perspective. And most of the cove would be suspicious of Hughes's utopia and his ideas that have influenced you."

"I understand, sir. At first, I felt the same way about Mr. Hughes's queer notions." I squirmed, remembering how I had fought against the Englishmen's presence.

"The folks here are weary of the vigilantes, but most are too terrified to act because there are over a thousand White Caps sworn to secrecy. Like their Scottish ancestors, the White Caps' first loyalty is to their clan. Every man who joins them must swear an oath of loyalty, forcing him to obey the leader whose word is supreme. If a member rebels and drops out, then he feels their whips and in some cases, they have killed men." He tapped the rock on his desk. "While this conflict is supposed to be over women's virtue, much of it erupts because of old grudges embraced by the next generation. Kentucky endures the Hatfield and McCoy feud, while our cove continues to fight the Civil War. A band of Confederates formed the Blue Bills, and there are only two hundred of them."

"I want to join them, sir." I lifted my chin. "I've a plan." I hoped it would work or I would have to take Pa and flee.

"Never. The Blue Bills protect women, and will not endanger them by having them join the battle. And frankly, Miss Walker, why would you offer to help? For all I know, the White Caps might have sent *you* as a spy."

I searched for an answer that would persuade Dr. Henderson to let me share my idea. "I hate seeing the terror in my aunt Sayward's eyes. My uncle is so afeard of the White Caps and thinks that I will mislead his daughter, so she isn't allowed to visit me, sir. Even those Walker sisters who can hog-tie a sheep keep loaded guns at their doors, and they live at the top of the mountain. I believe that Margaret's bitterness toward men comes from seeing how husbands' fears provoke them to rule over their wives. By not marrying, Margaret can live pretty much as she pleases, sir."

Dr. Henderson drummed his fingers against his waistcoat. "Have you stopped to think why the White Caps feel compelled to control the women?"

"No, sir." What was there to think about other than they were full of wickedness and enjoyed watching other people suffer?

"For four years these men were a tribe of warriors, fighting for ideals declaring that slavery was wrong. They returned home, reveling in the glory of winning the war and saving the Union. Yet, because of the economic woes crippling the South, they earn a pittance from their crops. They can't buy shoes for their children, or coffee or sugar. No longer do they feel like conquerors, but as failures without any control over their lives. What is the one thing they can rule? Their women and children. When one father complained how his daughter had kissed a boy, his friends encouraged him to beat her. Then another girl expressed notions about wanting more schooling, and the White Caps told her father to apply the rod, in order to drive out such foolishness. They offered to assist, and soon the rod turned into a whip.

They blamed the Confederates for causing the poverty eroding away the farm profits, and ganged up against those men. So even though it's 1882, and outside of the cove some ladies are working as shop clerks, our women live in fear. Elderly Confederates like your father are not forgiven, but harassed."

Maybe it had been a blessing that the war had driven away Pa. Lizzie and I hadn't grown up under the shadow of our father fighting for the other side, and we had been free to make our own choices. Because of the Englishmen settlers, I had grown accustomed to their ideas that allowed women new liberties. I sometimes looked down upon the local folks who disagreed with me about earning a living, although Aunt Alta had chided me about how I was becoming too prideful.

"Even if the war and being poor changed those men, that's no excuse for their devilment, sir. Someone should have stopped the clan years ago, before all this got out of hand."

"Yes, and to complicate the situation, most of the Blue Bills are Democrats and the White Caps are Republicans. So they battle each other over the new laws."

"Mercy, these men need to stop their feuding and treat other folks kindly." Men, so full of piss and vinegar that they couldn't see beyond their fists and their foolish politicking.

"I wish our preacher would speak against the feuding and teach kindness, because violence can't change the men's hearts. And while I don't know if the preacher belongs to the clan, he has never ridden with us."

"So you are their leader, sir?" From the look on his face, I had spoken the truth.

"I know their leader." Dr. Henderson gazed out the window, chewing on his lower lip, as nervous as a rabbit huddled in a briar thicket. "What do you want to tell him?"

"You'll listen to my plan, sir?" My palms began to sweat as I realized that the doctor might help me enact my idea.

Dr. Henderson nodded. "Go ahead." He rubbed one hand down his face as worry lines formed around his mouth. "Explain, but I make no promises."

"We know the White Caps are watching me, sir. If'n I did something that would prod them to raid my place, I would become the bait to draw them into an ambush with the Blue Bills waiting to attack." I took a deep breath.

"What if the White Caps learn that the Blue Bills have discovered the time when they will attack, and decide to arrive a day earlier? Or a day later? Like with the Campbells? And what if the White Caps are using you to draw the Blue Bills into an ambush? Why should I *trust* you, an outsider, with the lives of my men?"

I began to shake, remembering the ghostly white hoods and the man's laughter, recalling the crack of Uncle Abe's whip and the red scabs on my legs. The White Caps ripped a woman's dress open, and lashed her back, leaving scars no husband would want on a wife. They might even beat Pa. But Sissy's scared face and those of the younger Walker sisters swept across my mind. I didn't want my cousins or any other girl growing up in terror. Someone had to stop those men, and it might as well be me. If we failed, at least I could get shut of this place.

"I'm frightened, but willing, sir." I swallowed down the bile rising from my stomach. "And you'll just have to trust that I despise the White Caps and wouldn't help them. When you think about it, sir, the men in this cove live in as much fear as the women."

"I realized that fact shortly after I came to practice here. So what plan have you devised to spur on an attack?" Dr. Henderson thrust back his chair and paced the room.

"I thought next Tuesday, I'd ask my cousin to meet me at his favorite fishing spot for a little fun...to spark a bit." I gazed at the rug, feeling odd about discussing such private matters. "I assume you have spies that visit the vigilantes' rallies, and the spy could tell the White Caps, sir, about the meeting. I'd give him an eyeful to report." My neck reddened as the doctor's eyes narrowed.

"Yes. A courting couple seen kissing...or enjoying any other intimacies would set off their tempers. Once a woman receives a switch, any provocation results in a whipping. Have you spoken about this with your cousin? He might also feel the White Caps' wrath."

"No, sir. I reckoned that he might not want to get involved. But the Walker cabin is high up on top of the mountain, harder for them devils to reach, while my pa and I live in the cove."

"Yes, the distance might protect him, and John Walker is a respected elder in our community who fought for the Union. And the White Caps prefer hurting women."

"Yes, sir. " I picked at a small tear in my apron, not wanting to look Dr. Henderson in the eye, knowing that if anything went amiss, I would suffer. "So what do you think of my idea, sir?" I wasn't going to tell the good doctor that I still needed to figure out a way to convince James to meet with me.

"Very risky, but we've been searching for a way to trap as many White Caps as we can at one time. The ridges surrounding the cove would limit their escape routes, but even if the Blue Bills set ambushes for several nights, we might miss the attack."

"I understand that, sir." I stuffed my trembling hands beneath my apron. Had a similar fear filled my father's belly when at Chancellorsville, General Stonewall Jackson had shouted the orders to charge? "And you agree about not telling my cousin, sir?"

"Hmm, I don't approve, but perhaps the less information he knows, the less someone can wheedle out of him. So go ahead, plan your tryst. I'll ride out next week to check on your father, and bring any information I have unearthed."

"Thank you, sir. Is there something I can give my father, sir, to fight against his shakes? Some herb or medicine?" If'n anyone saw me leaving the doctor's home, I would have to prove my reason for visiting here.

Dr. Henderson moved various bottles and jars, poured a white powder onto a piece of paper and folded it. "Try this. Twice a day mix a teaspoon in his coffee. Feed him plenty of greens, and take him for walks, and appreciate the days you have left with him. You can pay me next time."

"Thank you, Doctor." I slipped the paper into my pocket. How odd that this man repeated what Lizzie had said, to be grateful for the time with my father.

"Unless I hear of an imminent raid being planned against you, I'll see you next week." Dr. Henderson shook my hand and opened the door to his office.

As I walked away, his words nipped at my mind. Somehow, I had overlooked the fact that the White Caps might already be plotting an attack. Maybe since James and I were not seeing each other, the devils thought they had squashed our courtship. Or perhaps they reckon the night in the corncrib had strangled my spirit. Skirting piles of horse droppings, I walked through the door of the mercantile, to see if anyone could offer me a ride back to the cove. The clerk handed me a thick letter from Lizzie and while reading it, I bumped into Uncle Abe.

"What in tarnation are you doing in town? Why aren't you at home, caring for your pa?" He snatched my shoulder. His thick jowls jiggled, and his dark eyes glittered.

"I came to talk to the doctor about Pa's shakes, something you could have done." I squirmed and pulled away from his hairy fingers. "The doctor gave me a powder for Pa."

"Don't you sass me! Look at me. Didn't your aunt teach you to address men as 'sir'? When are you going to do as you are told?"

I glared up at him, all he needed were tusks to make him a wild boar. I would say 'sir' to the doctor, and to other, older men who treated me with respect, but I would not offer such courtesies to my uncle. Nor would I allow his curses to slice away the blessings Aunt Alta had heaped on me. She would have scolded my uncle for hurting me, and would have reminded him how women were "the weaker vessel." Of course, Lizzie and I always laughed over that Bible verse because our aunties were the strongest people we knew.

"You worthless daughter of Eve." Uncle Abe shoved me toward his horse. "I'm taking you back to your pa." He swatted my rear end. "Get up there."

I climbed up, and his whip whizzed past my ear, as the horse trotted off. I clutched Uncle Abe's overall strap and he laughed.

"One of these days, missy, you're going to feel the White Caps' whip." He struck his horse again, and we cantered home.

I hated my uncle. Some night soon, the Blue Bills and I would teach him and those miserable White Caps a lesson.

CHAPTER NINETEEN

When we reached Uncle Abe's cabin, I jumped down and raced home. Leaning on two canes, Pa shuffled through the garden patch, fingering bean pods, gazing at the squash and corn. My father continued to shrink, and his pants hung on their suspenders. He tottered and swayed, but managed to right himself. I ran over and took his arm.

"You shouldn't be about unless someone walks with you." Guilt trickled through me. What if he had fallen while I was gone and had lain here in the sun, withering away? I could feel him trembling and the dark spots on his hands stood out as he clutched the canes. Bits of the cornbread he had eaten at noon clung to his beard.

"Oh, if I fall, I'll holler until someone hears me. The Good Lord will take care of me. James stopped by this afternoon and said that a preacher is coming through this Sunday. I want to be baptized, so I will need to walk into the river. I know my time is short, and I want to make things right with my Maker. Soon, the angels will escort me to your mama."

I didn't know what to say. My own death seemed like one of the far off high ridges, hazy and blue. Even if I started walking tonight, it would take weeks to reach those distant mountains, likewise I assumed many decades separated me from when I'd be called over the Jordan River.

But I reckoned pa felt something that only the aged could comprehend, some hidden knowledge that would enlighten me when my crippled hands could no longer spin.

Aunt Alta had quoted Bible verses, preached, and marched us to church, hoping to fill us with her faith. While I respected my aunt, I had figured attending church came with marriage and having babies. Sitting on a pew, I had stayed awake by daydreaming about weaving and then Charlie. Even now at meeting, if'n I wasn't forced to sit with Uncle Abe's clan, I'd settle in a spot where I could gaze on James' thick hair and wide shoulders. Pa's words jerked me back to the fact that while his body was crumbling, a deep peace filled his eyes.

"Pondering the glories of heaven helps silence the cannons of Chancellorsville." Pa gripped my wrist as we mounted the porch stairs. "Whenever those dark thoughts come to me, I close my eyes and see angels, hovering over me. A couple of times, one had the face of your mama."

Pa's words about angels and my mother frightened me, and yet, he spoke the truth. He hadn't had one of his bad nights for several weeks. Except when a thunderstorm had rattled the windowpanes he had panicked, and I'd found him huddling in a corner, his arms wrapped around his chest, humming "Amazing Grace". I had helped him to the table, and brewed peppermint tea. Until the storm had faded, I had listened to him talk about his childhood back in Virginia. A red bird had trilled its song as the sky had turned gray, and I had settled Pa back in his bed, for a few more hours of sleep.

"I went to Sevierville and spoke with Dr. Henderson, Pa. He gave me a powder that might help with your shakes. He said he'd ride over next week and see you." I guided Pa to his chair on the porch.

"That was right kind of you, daughter." Pa reached for my hand. "Thank you for being a blessing in my last days."

I squeezed his hand. What would Pa think of me if'n he knew the truth of why I had visited the doctor? Vowing to be kinder to him, I fried him a few slices from a chunk of smoked ham that Polly had given me when Margaret wasn't looking, and its rich scent flowed from the skillet. I also baked Pa's favorite, blackberry cobbler. While he ate two full bowls, I listened to him tell a fishing tale that I had heard at least ten times. Extra lines now wrinkled his neck and his cheekbones stuck out more than when I had arrived. I needed to tell Lizzie to bring Jacob and hasten to the cove before we lost our father.

After washing the dishes, I climbed to my loft and reread Lizzie's letter.

My dearest Viney,

It is hard to believe that you have been gone for almost six weeks. Weeks that have changed our lives in a sweet and glorious way. I can't wait to introduce you to William. Even though he helps his father run a hosiery factory, William hates the miserable working conditions endured by the laborers.

William believes in Mr. Hughes's ideas about unions.

Several more letters arrived from Charlie...

Up there in Michigan, Charlie's calloused fingers had dipped a pen in an inkwell and guided it across the linen paper, while the glow of a kerosene lamp had illuminated his auburn hair. Why did he write me more frequently after he broke off our engagement than during the winter when we were betrothed?

My fingers itched to open one of his envelopes and read what he had said, but seeing as how Lizzie would arrive soon, she might as well bring them. Even if Charlie had written how he had rediscovered his love for me and wanted to renew our courtship, was that what I wanted? Although James had never declared his affections, I was in love with him. I snatched up my brush and pulled it through my hair, hoping the long strokes would soothe my soul.

• • • • •

After the sun set, I arranged a pallet on the front porch, wanting to sleep where it was cooler. A breeze tossed the leaves, keeping the mosquitoes away. From up on the ridge, a bobcat wailed like a lost child, and a chill rippled over me. The corn shucks in my mattress rustled as I squirmed and wiggled. What was Lizzie doing? Playing the piano for Mr. William? Sitting on the porch, holding his hand? Or maybe they strolled arm in arm, pausing to kiss beneath the oaks near Lizzie's cabin site. I studied the stars, finding the Seven Sisters. I wished my sister lay beside me so we could talk about Charlie, Pa, James, and my conversation with the doctor. My misgivings about using James to trick the vigilantes, hopped inside me like fleas, whispering that I was conniving and selfish. If Lizzie knew about my plan involving James, she would call it foolishness and warn me about the risks.

"Blast it all." I knew my pride spurred me to fight against the White Caps, but ridding this valley of their terror was not selfish. Folks needed the freedom to make choices that might differ from the ways passed down from great-grandma to granddaughter. Whether in English society or in the mountains, narrow-minded ways constricted folks' lives. Hoping the chirping of crickets would quiet me, I closed my eyes. For some queer reason, I yearned to share the sounds of the night not with James, but with Charlie.

• • • • •

I drifted a bit, but jerked awake to the clip-clop of horses' hooves. I froze. Were the White Caps coming for me? Would the Blue Bills rescue me? Darting into the house, I slipped out of my nightdress, and pulled on one of Pa's shirts and overalls to protect my legs. Horses ridden by two men wearing white hoods and carrying torches passed our cabin, and thankfully, they didn't stop. Where were they headed? Even though fear snaked down my spine, I snatched a pillowcase, slit eye holes, and stuffed it in my pocket. At Uncle Abe's barn, I clucked to the horse and opened the gate, and he walked to me.

"Steady." Stepping on a lower rail, I mounted, and gripped his mane. "Not too fast now." As I slid the pillowcase over my head, his ears flicked back, and he danced about for a few seconds before realizing that the white mask wouldn't hurt him. I kicked my heels, and we rode down the trail. The White Caps had traveled too far in front of me to see them, but I followed the rustle of their horses brushing against bushes and tree limbs. At last, I spied the ghostly parade as they rounded a bend. I counted five more riders with torches who had joined them.

I nibbled my lower lip. Should I ride to Dr. Henderson and warn him, or maybe he already knew about the attack, and had prepared an ambush? If'n so, then I needed to keep an eye out for Blue Bills. Horse hooves sounded behind me, and two more white-hooded men on mules trotted closer.

"Better hurry along there, boy," one man said. "Or you're going to miss the fun we got planned for Trench's woman." The smell of sweat, whiskey, and tobacco passed me.

The other man cackled. "Good to have young blood in the brotherhood. Were you in the group that took our vow last week?"

"Yes, sir." I deepened my voice, hoping they wouldn't asked me more questions. I kept to the rear of the riders, watching the ghouls on horseback slip out of the woods, lengthening the troop heading into Trench's holler. When they paused near a homestead, I eased my horse a good distance off the trail. I led him to a sheltered spot behind a wide laurel thicket, where I peered through the leaves. The flickering torches filled the air with the smell of burning pitch, and the white hoods quivered in the heat waves.

"Shh," I said, stroking the horse's chin. "Easy now. Stay quiet." My ears searched for the sound of the Blue Bills' approaching horses, but only a screech owl screamed.

The gang jogged toward the cabin, and their torchlight shimmered in the windowpanes. Two men kicked in the door, and dragged out a young woman while two others hauled a dark-haired man. One socked him in the belly, and the other punched him in the jaw. He staggered backwards against a White Cap who grabbed his shoulders while the first man lashed the fellow's hands and stuffed a gag in his mouth.

"We'll learn you what happens to men who bed another feller's wife." The first man tied the battered man to a tree. "And teach a lesson to that slut." Cackling, the White Cap shook the man by his hair.

Oh, Laws. I recognized that same thin laugh from the hooded figure who had visited me. I wanted to gallop out of this holler, but knew if I did, one of the men would ride after me. Why hadn't the Blue Bills come?

"You watch good, so that we don't have to come back."

Near another tree, two White Caps pulled on the woman's hands, stretching her, pressing her face against the bark. They wrapped her arms around the trunk, and bound her hands. She cursed and attempted to kick them, until one man grabbed her ankles.

"Best tie them, too." He attached a rope to one ankle and pulled, separating her legs while another fellow ran the rope around the tree and back to her other ankle.

"I should cut out your tongue, you whore. You should have paid heed to our warning. When your husband returns, he'll thank us," their leader said. He grabbed the bodice of her dress and ripped it down to her waist.

I wanted to scream at them to let her go, to run into the gang, and flail them with my fists. How her heart must ache as the dress slumped along her shoulders, revealing her breasts. In the wavering torchlight, the men ogled and made lewd gestures.

The White Cap raised his whip, and like a panther's claws, the switch blistered her flesh. The woman screamed and writhed, begging for mercy as he struck her, again. Blood flowed from the welts and cuts crisscrossing her back and legs. Her lover struggled against his bonds, but they held him against the tree. What foolishness had made me come here? I hated myself for not having the power to stop this violence.

Waving their torches, the men cheered, and yelled for more. Why hadn't the Blue Bills rescued her? If my plans went amiss, would this happen to me? Lifting my hood, I leaned over and puked.

I wiped my mouth on my sleeve, the vigilantes passed around a couple of flasks. They joked and punched each other on the shoulders. Only the leaders wore long white robes with hoods, while the other White Caps had turned their coats inside out. Most of the men had left their shotguns on their horses, a detail I planned to tell the doctor. The main leader fired his rifle into the air, and the bitter smell of gunpowder swirled around him.

"Leave 'em," he shouted. "Trench's due back in the morning. Let him deal with them. She can be a warning to the other women of the cove." The man took a long swig. "And if she dies, well, at least, she won't sin no more."

"Got any more switches to leave?" another man asked and reached for the jug. "Any more fun planned?"

"No, but we're keeping an eye on the Walker gal. Her time will come, soon."

"Hee, hee, hee." The thin White Cap laughed. "Can't wait to hear her screams. Maybe we should stop by her place, now."

"Too late," the leader said. "Dawn's coming on. We best fly home." He mounted his horse, and the others climbed onto their horses.

Oh, Laws, no. I almost wet my drawers, from shaking so badly. What would these men do if they discovered me here? I should have stayed with Pa. Crouching behind my horse, I wept, yearning for the safety of Rugby, wishing that Pa was strong enough to travel, knowing I had to flee from this cove. The hooded men cantered down the trail, taking with them the torchlight. Only fireflies glowed, along with the growing moon.

It was queer, but as my anger flowed back through me, my body stopped trembling. Like lifting a hank of yarn from an indigo dye pot, and watching the wool change from light blue to a darker hue, something inside me grew stronger and deeper. I hated the evil that these cowards had done, and knew I wanted to be like my granny who had defended her family from the Yankees. And like pa, who had stormed through the Yankees at Shiloh. If'n they could find the courage to fight against wickedness, then somehow, I must do so, too.

"Come on." I pulled off the pillowcase and led my horse into the clearing. I slashed the ropes binding the woman, and eased her onto the ground. She appeared about Sissy's age. Next I freed the man, who swiped a fist toward me. I leapt back.

"I'm not a White Cap!" Because of wearing britches and a shirt, I hoped that he'd take me for a boy. Even if they didn't know it was me, I didn't need the bullies learning how a girl had helped these two.

"Who...are...you?" His black hair fell across his face, as he stared through swollen eyes. Blood smeared one cheek, and bruises darkened his jaw. From his battered lips more blood trickled down his neck. He looked to be about my age.

"A friend. We've got to help her." I untied him. He staggered to his feet and stumbled toward the girl.

I fetched a bucket of water from the porch, ripped a piece from the girl's dress, and washed her with the cloth. She whimpered and sobbed. The man fell to his knees.

"Katy." He patted her cheek, while I sponged away the blood. "Katy, them devils is gone," he whispered. "We've got to run. Before your man comes back."

"Her husband?" I removed her petticoat, tore it into bandages, and wrapped them around her back as she shrieked. I dribbled a little water between her lips, wishing I had something to relieve her pain.

"Yes, old man Trench." The fellow's jaw stiffened as he drew out the last two letters of the husband's name.

"Can't let...him find you..." the girl gasped. Whimpering, she clutched her lover's hand. "Oh, Laws, my back...hurts to breathe. Gonna die."

The fellow nodded toward a grove of hemlocks not far from the cabin. "My horse is over yonder. Could you fetch it, please?"

"First let me find a quilt to wrap her in." I ran to the cabin, and pulled a tattered quilt off a mattress on the floor. Only a table and two chairs furnished the one room. Either the husband was dirt poor or too miserly to provide his wife with basic creature comforts. Katy screamed as we wrapped her in the quilt.

Pewter moonlight burnished the clearing as I brought the fellow his horse, and the tree frogs trilled as if the cruelty of the White Caps had never interrupted the night. How could peace so soon return to this world where evil had invaded and changed Katy's life? Although my insides still quivered, a darkness had seeped into my bones. Perhaps, after seeing his brother shot, this same furor had driven Pa to stab a Yankee over and over. That anger had never left him and now it settled inside me.

The man and I lifted Katy to the front of the saddle, and she fainted as he draped her arms around the saddle horn. I stuffed her torn petticoat beneath her to soak up the blood. He climbed up and wrapped one arm around Katy.

"Go to Doc Henderson's," I said. The doctor would know how to protect them from further trouble, but what about the girl's lawful husband? While any decent person would help wounded folks, I knew that these two must stop committing adultery. But the doctor could deal with their problem better than I could.

The man studied me. "You've the voice of a girl. You be an angel?"

"Maybe." I backed away, as words from the Christmas story flitted through my head. "Fear not. Fear not," I said, and slapped his horse. They trotted away.

Uncle Abe's horse nudged me, blowing down my neck. His belly understood that a breakfast of oats wasn't far off.

"You're right." I jumped on him. "Gotta get home before first light and brush you down." We galloped past the couple and headed into the cove. No one had ever called me an angel before, and I rather liked it.

CHAPTER TWENTY

So as not to worry him, I never told Pa about that violent night, but in my next letter, I described it to Lizzie and waited for her response. If'n Pa learned what I had seen, I reckoned he'd send me back to Rugby faster than a duck could snap at a June bug. And then what would he do? Instead, we talked about his baptism, and I sewed him a new linen shirt from yard goods that Marti had woven for Johnny.

After the Wednesday night prayer meeting, the Walker clan threaded our way down a deer trail, ducking hemlock branches, and skirting around laurel bushes as we headed to the Greenbrier. From the riverbank, I watched as Uncle John and the preacher guided my father into the river and dipped him beneath the current. Polly stood by me, weeping, as the men lifted Pa and the water sluiced from his clothing. Uncle John wiped Pa's face with his handkerchief and kissed his cheek. A smile lifted Pa's lips as his eyes met mine, and I knew that he'd soon be going home to my mother.

• • • • •

Come Saturday morning, Pa clung to me as we strolled to the meetinghouse so as to join in the shaped-note singing. Those fluffy clouds that Charlie named cumulus floated above us, brushing the tops of the highest peaks of the Great Smokies, sending shadows across the mountains and over the cove. Charlie had called this weather, sunshine and shadow, because now and then one of those clouds would spill rain on a mountaintop and make the creeks rush around boulders. I missed seeing Charlie standing on the porch, reveling in the crack of thunder, and the lightning slicing the sky as rain cascaded off the porch roof. Even though he was a farmer, James didn't seem to pay much mind to the weather other than to say that the fish weren't biting. What made one man giddy about mare's tails clouds while another barely scanned the sky?

Inside the log building, Pa and I claimed a bench on the tenor side along with a dozen men and women, while young and old folks filled up the other benches arranged to form a hollow square. Most mothers with babies sat on the end seats so they could skedaddle out the door when a young child needed tending. Basses sat to our left, the sopranos in front of us, and altos on the right, where I should have been. But because Pa would need help turning the pages and finding the songs, I stuck close to him.

Like most folk, besides the Bible, the only other book pa owned was a copy of *The Sacred Harp*, now resting in my lap. My Walker cousins had settled into places with the altos and sopranos, while James and his father sang bass. Polly and Caroline smiled and nodded at me, but James refused to look my way. Instead, he turned and chatted with the fellow next to him. Blast it all. How dare he act as if I didn't sit eight feet away from him? If'n I didn't need him for trapping the White Caps, I'd about abandon my decision to plan a tryst.

One of the church elders prayed, and I bowed my head, squinting at the faces surrounding me. Behind those beards, which of the men were White Caps? Which were Blue Bills? All these folks resembled the people I knew back on my ridge. Despite what the doctor had explained, I hankered to understand why some men turned to feuding, while in another place, families limped along, hoeing corn and beans, shooting squirrels, and staying out of another man's business.

After the prayer, Margaret named the hymn, "Still Better", stepped to the middle of the square, and hummed the pitch for "sol". As she raised and lowered her hand, we called out the shapes before singing the verses instructing us to do our duty in life. Naturally, the boss cousin would choose words that warned about the toils and seriousness of living. Yet, with the White Caps preaching about what was fitting for women, didn't folks find it queer how Margaret was leading the first song?

Around the room other hands rose and fell with the flow of the tune, as if flocks of sparrows beat their wings. One by one, men and women, and even a girl of about ten years, stood in the center, leading us. At first, Pa's voice trembled, but soon pink flushed his cheeks and his eyes twinkled. During a lull, he called out for "Sweet Morning."

“That was your mama’s favorite,” Pa said. “She had the voice of a dove. We met at our settlement’s singing school, and whenever we could, we’d go to other towns and sing. She’d ride in front on my mule, with my arms around her, warbling fa, sol, la, the whole way.”

I enjoyed learning my parents had loved singing, and had made friends with others similar to them. With each memory that Pa shared, his words were a shuttle, weaving another section in the tapestry of my mother. It tickled me how Lizzie had inherited my mother’s sweet voice. Had our mama crooned her lullabies? Perhaps, Lizzie had heard our mother singing ballads, and the words had floated into her head. I cherished the image of Pa and Mama cuddled up on his mule, like James and I had traveled on Red. Pa nudged me, and I turned to page 412.

“I’ll lead it for you, Uncle Jesse,” Polly said, and walked to the center of the square. In a brown linsey-woolsey dress, with her black braid pinned like a crown on her head, Polly stood with authority, free from Margaret’s bossiness.

As we shouted out the shapes, tears glazed Pa’s cheek, and I reckoned he was thinking of Mama, playing her harp in heaven. Like so many other times, I wished that my mother hadn’t died, but could have given me her attention and love. With extra passion, I sang those beloved words:

“The happy day will soon appear,
And we’ll all shout together in that morning.
When Gabriel’s trumpet you shall hear,
And we’ll all shout together in that morning.
Sweet morning, Sweet morning,
And we’ll all shout together in that morning.”

After the hymn, Polly came over and gave Pa a hug. “Bless you, Uncle Jessie. That’s one of my favorites, too.”

Suddenly, James stood up and called for, “Wondrous Love,” My throat constricted as his long legs strode away from the bench. I wanted to feel his arms around me, once again, and cursed those dratted White Caps. Why didn’t James join the Blue Bills and defend me? His boots clomped on the wooden floor, and his shoulders seem to swell when he reached the leader’s position. James had combed his hair so it swooped back around his face, and even his fingernails were clean as he lifted his hand.

Facing, the tenors, he drew out the syllable, "la," waiting for everyone to note the pitch.

My mind went dizzy, as I smelled James' scent so close to me, a mixture of hay and leather. I gave up following the shapes and just sang, "la," until we launched into the words that Aunt Alta had taught me,

"What wondrous love is this, oh, my soul, oh my soul,
What wondrous love is this..."

Once, James glanced at his book, but otherwise, he watched me, his strong hand keeping time, his rich bass pouring out the harmony. Oh Laws, I longed to press his palm against my cheek and feel his lips against mine. Had James led this hymn because he reckoned our love could be wondrous, again?

As the last notes vibrated, folks held their breaths; their faces softened as the singers recognized that we had touched the gates of glory where so many of our loved-ones now resided. Marti wiped her eyes with her hanky, weeping over her Johnny. Uncle John unfurled himself from the bench, and gazed about the room.

"We welcome any visitors to our Greenbrier singing. Our womenfolk have brought a feast to share, so please join us for dinner on the grounds and eat heartily. Let us give thanks to the Lord for the work of their hands." He bowed his head, and we did, too.

Outside the meetinghouse, the women spread quilts on the grass while men laid boards across sawhorses. Folks also scattered the benches underneath the clusters of trees. I helped set out crocks of baked beans, stacks of cornbread, kettles of greens, platters of fried chicken, plus apple stack cakes, blackberry pies and cobblers. While James escorted my father to a bench, I heaped a plate with chicken, green beans, new potatoes, and chess pie. Pa's spoon trembled in his shaking fingers, and he dropped bits of food, but he could still hold and drink from a mug. Sitting with Polly, not far from Pa, I nibbled on a slice of salt-rising bread spread with spicy apple butter.

"With all this fine food, and that's all you're going to eat?" Polly nudged me. “You best try the chicken and dumplings, and the blackberry cobbler is heavenly.”

I shook my head. My stomach flip-flopped at the mention of blackberry cobbler, and the memories of sharing a bowl with James washed over me. I glanced over to where James lounged under a tree, talking with a few other fellows as he plowed through a second plate of food. Polly followed my gaze and smiled.

“I know James misses you,” she said. “Since Johnny’s death, I’ve found him staring out across the ridges, his hands idle. His expression matched our hound’s face when Pa goes fishing and leaves him home.”

“How do you know it’s me he’s missing? More-likely he’s grieving over Johnny.”

“I reckon it’s fear that’s keeping him away from you.” With her spoon, Polly scraped the last baked beans from her plate.

“Why doesn’t he talk to me? Say a few words when I’m at your cabin. I’m having a hard time believing that he still feels any affection for me.” I turned my eyes onto Polly. “He hasn’t even said howdy to me today. And we are family.”

“So are more than half of the folks at this singing,” Polly said. “While the Boss is busy with Aunt Sayward, I’ll drop James a hint. Want me to bring you a slice of pound cake?”

“Yes, please.” I finished my scrap of bread while my cousin ambled over to James and whispered in his ear. He rubbed the toe of his boot in the grass and nodded. Polly smiled, walked to the feast and cut three slices of pound cake, one she gave to James and then brought the others to our bench.

“Wait and see.” She handed me my slice. “Come on, take a bite. It might settle your belly and sweeten your countenance.”

After Pa and I finished eating, I stacked our dirty dishes in a bucket and carried it to the stream that wound around the meetinghouse. James’ shadow followed me. I tried to swallow my fear that James would refuse my proposal, yet thoughts of spending time with him made my cheeks flush.

“Allow me.” James dipped my bucket into the water. Sunlight shimmered on his hair, and I longed to run my fingers through it.

“I miss seeing you, alone,” I said, watching his shoulder muscles expand as he drew out the bucket. I wanted to feel those arms lifting me off the ground and twirling me around.

James set the pail at my feet, and our shoulders brushed as I leaned over to rinse the plates. He licked his lips, and I sensed the desire rising inside him, matching the quickening of my heartbeat. Yet, guilt invaded my mind, scolding me about how I planned to deceive my cousin in order to bring revenge.

"We could meet at your favorite fishing place on Tuesday." The dishes clinked as I stacked them back into the bucket. Cicadas buzzed, stirring up the humidity. A swallowtail butterfly fluttered to a frothy Queen Anne's lace blossom and sipped its nectar. James' chest rose and fell and with each breath, my fears grew. Even though James always wore a straw hat, his face was tanned, and blond streaks highlighted the hair close to his neck. Starch stiffened the collar and cuffs of his linen shirt. Because of the singing, he had shaved, and I yearned to run my hands over his cheeks.

"Mid-afternoon? Meet by the big boulders?" James thrust his hands into his pockets. Gold specks glittered in his hazel eyes, as he gazed at the current tumbling over the boulders.

"I'll be there, with a fishing pole." My eyes followed the swing of his legs as he strolled away, and I longed for the days when he would have chucked me under the chin. The hem of Sissy's skirt flickered near my feet. Concern shimmered in her blue eyes as she watched James enter a group of men.

"Take care, Cousin Viney. Who knows which of those fellows are White Caps." Sissy scanned the crowd. "James would be a fine catch. Maybe even worth the hardship of living with Margaret. But best have a wedding before you're alone with him, again."

"I'll be careful. And there's always a chance some man will change Margaret's mind about marriage." I stared at a red-tailed hawk, a white-winged speck circling over us.

"Mama says, pigs will fly before that happens, but I hope the other sisters find good husbands. I thought you might like to know, Mama's helping me make the baskets. Hard work to beat the ash log and pull off the splints." She showed me her fingers. "Even have nicked a few places with my knife when trimming the slats."

"I'm so proud of you. Do you enjoy the work?" I picked up my bucket.

Maybe seeing her hands form something would help Sissy look for a different future than seeking an early marriage as a means to independence.

Sissy smiled, easing away the wariness that usually flooded her face. "Yes, I do. After hearing how Miss Margaret and her sisters are selling coverlets, I'm hoping to follow their example and sell what I make to the fetched-on lady." Sissy stood straighter. "I hope to save up some cash money so as I can buy sheets and such for when I marry."

"What about your father? What does he say?" My uncle would explode if he knew what Sissy was planning, and he might blame me for her rebellion. Worse yet, what would the White Caps think?

"He's fine with me learning to make baskets. If'n I can't sell them, I'll need them when I set up housekeeping, for storing potatoes and turnips." Sissy gazed at the mountain peaks, lowering her voice. "I've been thinking about what you said, about waiting for a husband. I wouldn't want to be as old as you when I wed, but I want to find a man who would let me sell my baskets. I'm not settling for any man like my pa." Sissy lifted her chin. Not only had curves shaped her body, but she no longer hid her hands beneath her apron, and she looked me in the eye. "Besides, Polly showed me those verses in Proverbs about the woman who earned cash money for her family. If'n I work like her, my children will always have shoes."

"I hope you will find someone, perhaps one of the men who rides with the Blue Bills." Those men risked their lives for the changes that Sissy now coveted.

Sissy nodded. "I wish those White Caps would fade away, go shoot turkeys or something. It's high time, they and everyone else forget about which side of the war a man fought on. When I have some cash money, first thing I plan to buy is my own gun, then I can protect myself and my little sisters."

The light in Sissy's eyes fed my courage, and I wanted to tell her about my plan, but knew I shouldn't. When the White Caps attacked, I'd repeat Sissy's words, knowing I was facing those devils for her and her sisters. But another idea returned to me.

"When I leave, you could come with me to Rugby. You could work at the new inn, as a chambermaid or help in the kitchen. You could live in a place where women are encouraged to work and go to school. Some nights, we attend musical concerts and lectures. You could meet gentlemen who think women should be doing those things."

"Maybe someday." A glint filled Sissy's eyes. "It would pleasure me so, but I can't leave Mama with all those youn' uns. A couple of my friends heard me talk about Miss Dickinson, and they're thinking of selling their quilts. We need to stick together."

"Well, if you change your mind, just hop on a train and ride west." I spied Pa looking at me and he waved one hand. "Looks like my pa needs me. I'll try to visit soon." I squeezed Sissy's waist.

"It's been a blessing to sing, but I'm plumb worn out." Pa's shoulders drooped, and his back curled until his elbows touched his knees. "You best take me home, daughter."

Home. Strange how images of Aunt Alta's farm were sliding far away, like trying to recall a blurry memory from my childhood. Yet, thoughts of Rugby still haunted me. Even if I married James, would I ever truly feel a part of this community?

I raised Pa to his feet and gave him his cane, and we said good-by to folks. Polly urged me to come weave every day, next week. As we headed toward the path, a shadow fell across us and James approached us. His hat shaded his eyes so I couldn't measure the look on his face.

"I'll walk with you, sir." James slipped an arm around Pa. "Lean on me and let me know if you need to stop and rest."

A redbird sang its evening song as the waning sunlight sifted through the leaves, and we left behind the sparkling sound of the Greenbriar. Trailing behind them, I delighted over James' hair dancing around his collar. He could have picked my father up and carried him. But instead, he matched his steps to Pa's shuffles while they chatted about the good corn crop, how James had to prop up the apple limbs because they were so bent with fruit, and a new litter of ten piglets. From the tone of Pa's voice, I knew he relished such manly talk. When we reached the cabin, James undressed my father, and his tender ways showed how one day, James would make a fine daddy. After I washed Pa and buttoned his nightshirt, James eased him into bed.

"Sweet sleep, Uncle Jessie." James pulled the quilt over Pa.

"Thank you," I said, as we walked out onto the porch. "For being so kind." I wanted to press my chin against James' chest, and listen to his heartbeat as he rested his head on mine. Too many days had passed since he had touched me.

James leaned against the porch post, and with one finger, he tucked some loose hair behind my ear. My breath quickened, but I pressed my hands against my thighs.

"Kindness never cost a body anything. I've been watching your pa's sliding away from us. He's grown punier these past few weeks. Not much time left before he says good-by to this world." James put on his hat, and his boots clomped down the porch stairs. "'Til Tuesday."

"See you then." Sitting on the railing, I watched until James turned onto the upward path, and the drooping tree branches closed over his back. Hugging my knees, I rested my eyes on Cove Mountain, as the last rays of the sunset slid behind the hills, and clouds of fireflies blossomed. A whip-poor-will called from the edge of the woods, and another echoed over by Uncle Abe's home. I prayed that James would make good on his promise and nothing would go amiss.

Chapter Twenty-One

With his injured arm in a sling, Charlie stared at the gravy oozing from a mound of shepherd's pie, even the radishes and cucumber slices didn't look appetizing. He yearned for a chunk of Viney's cornbread, slathered in butter and dripping with honey, and a bowl of soup beans. Although he enjoyed watching the waves of Lake Michigan roll onto the shore, Charlie missed standing at Wilson's Lookout with Viney and gazing at the mountains dappled in red, gold, and brown fall colors.

"I thought you could weed around the young trees this afternoon," Mr. Townsend said. His slick-back hair revealed the man's high forehead and long nose. Sunburn flushed his neck and cheeks. "Next week, we'll start picking the early apples. So you should move the sheep from the orchard."

"The doctor said that I shouldn't work at any activity where I might bump my wrist. He suggested taking a week off so my sprain can heal faster." Charlie speared a forkful of mashed potatoes.

"A week's holiday, now? Richard should know how this is the busiest time of the year! I understand you can't pick peaches, but surely, weeding won't hurt your wrist."

"I suppose he'd be concerned that I might lean on my arm or fall on it." Charlie glanced at Charlotte but her face remained passive. No help would come from her. "So he prescribed a week's rest."

"Harrumph." Mr. Townsend bit a bread roll. "Use caution and weed those young trees. We'll see how it goes for you."

A dozen long rows of three-foot-high apple trees stood midst patches of thick orchard grass. Sweat dripped down Charlie's neck and forehead as he yanked out a clump. This was silly; he would be weeding in this apple orchard until midnight. With merely two weeks left in his apprenticeship, Mr. Townsend should release him from his commitment. A gust of wind off the bay blew Charlie's hat off. Leaning over, he snatched at it, and bumped his wrist against his shin. He gritted his teeth, and held his hurt arm with his good hand until the flash of pain subsided. Rising from his knees, Charlie stalked towards the house. He began to pull open the screen door and paused.

Charlotte sat on Mr. Burnett's lap, her hair a golden curtain as she arched her neck. Her fiancé's lips moved down her throat while his fingers ran across her ribs. Unbuttoning Mr. Burnett's shirt, Charlotte pressed her hands against his bare chest. Charlie stepped backwards, and strode to the barn.

Shouldn't Charlotte be busy making butter or canning peaches? What if her father spied them? Or what if Mr. Townsend had encouraged Charlotte to entice Mr. Burnett into a proposal of marriage so that he could merge their farms? A bitter taste flooded Charlie's mouth. He plopped down on a thin layer of straw that had drifted outside the sheep's stall. At one time, he had wanted to spark with Charlotte. Even now, he recalled the feel of her fine hair brushing his stubbly cheek. Good gravy, he had to untangle himself from this place and from Charlotte. He longed to return to the woman who could hoe a row of corn faster than him.

The rumble of Mr. Townsend's wagon loaded with peaches awoke Charlie. He stared up at the man's face, shadowed by his straw hat.

"What do you think you're doing?" Mr. Townsend's gray eyes narrowed.

"Resting, like the doctor said." Charlie inhaled, waiting for a gale of cursing.

"I told you to weed." Mr. Townsend's neck blazed as he pressed his lips into a thin line.

"I did, and hurt my wrist." Charlie rose and faced Mr. Townsend. Not one ounce of compassion flowed from the man's flinty stare. Perhaps Townsend should direct his anger at the fellow making free with his daughter. "If you had come earlier, you could have watched your daughter and Mr. Burnett pleasuring themselves."

"Speak no ill of my daughter. Besides, they are engaged, and the wedding is next month. Never forget that Burnett owns two-hundred acres while you have nothing." Mr. Townsend turned away and pulled crates off the wagon.

Money. Land. That was all this man cared about. When would Charlotte realize that she was the nectar used to attract the bee? When would her father comprehend that Burnett would outlive him and add the Townsend land to his farm?

"Perhaps it would be best if I leave early, if you are willing to break our contract." Charlie licked his lips.

Mr. Townsend grunted. "I'll have to prorate your pay for those two weeks."

"Fine. I'll start packing." Charlie tramped to the house and stomped up the steps.

Mr. Burnett toppled backwards as he shoved Charlotte off his lap. Her cheeks flaming, Charlotte shrieked and began to button her bodice.

"Your father's on his way." Charlie laughed, and slammed the door to his room. His father was thousands of miles away and hopefully at some future time, would understand why Charlie was done with northern women.

• • • • •

Fog off the bay drifted around the station. The train's whistle screamed, its brakes screeched, and steam roiled around the locomotive as it stopped in front of Charlie. Dressed in his blue suit, the conductor's calloused hand reached for Charlie's ticket.

"Bound for Tennessee?" The gray-haired man spoke with an Irish accent.

"Yes, sir. Going home."

CHAPTER TWENTY-TWO

On Monday morning, Dr. Henderson rode up while I was weeding the butterbean plants. He shook Pa's hand, sat down on the porch, and questioned my father about his palsy, before examining his eyes, ears and throat. Dr. Henderson nodded at me when I leaned my hoe against the porch railing and climbed the steps.

"How's my pa, sir?" Pulling off my sunbonnet, I wiped my face with my apron. "Sure is hot and sticky."

"Yes, hot enough to bake biscuits." Dr. Henderson tapped Pa's knees, listened to his heart, and ran his hands down Pa's arms. "We should go jump in the river, sir, a swim would cool us off."

"My swimming days are gone." Pa chuckled as the doctor held his shaking hand. "I'll let you young men jump in the swimming hole."

"Let me fetch you a drink, sir." I dipped a gourd of water from the bucket by the door, and wished that I could provide chips of ice like the maids at the Tabard dropped into guests' glasses.

"Thank you." Dr. Henderson took a long swig. "You are doing well for someone with palsy. Did the powders help?"

"A mite. Having my daughter caring for me helps the most." Pa reached out a shaking hand and took mine. "Good cooking. Clean clothes. Having Viney to talk to, gives a body strength. I look forward to getting out of bed and watching her work, hearing her sing."

"She's an angel in calico," Dr. Henderson said, and wiped his forehead with a handkerchief. Little frown lines wrinkled at the corners of his eyes as he stared at me. "A guardian angel."

My heartbeat pounded in my ears. I had known the couple would tell the doctor what had happened, but who else might have heard about the girl who rescued them? Would the White Caps find out that it had been me?

"Try to walk a bit every day; keep those legs moving. I'll leave some more powders." Dr. Henderson stood up, and with his handkerchief, mopped his forehead. "Viney, if you will come with me, I'll give them to you."

From his saddlebags, he pulled out a white paper envelope and turned so that Pa couldn't see us speaking. "How did you come to be at the raid? That was plumb foolish and dangerous."

I slipped the paper into my apron pocket, next to my knife. "I couldn't sleep, sir, and saw the men riding down the trail, so I decided to follow them, and ended up in the middle of the parade. I considered riding to your house, sir, but reckoned there wasn't time to gather the Blue Bills, so I hid. When they whipped her, I kept hoping that y'all would gallop in, sir."

"We were told the raid would be the next night. Usually, the White Caps do not strike on a Sunday night, but I suppose they figured that in the wee hours of Monday morning, the Sabbath had ended. Thank you for sending the couple to me." He tapped his fingers against his saddle.

"I know they were sinning, but I had to help them, sir." I shook off an ant that was trying to cross my foot.

"Katy's father treated her dirty, then dumped her on an older fellow in order to settle a gambling debt. The lout cuts timber up on the mountains for a week or two, returns to his cabin, and leaves her black and blue. Once he even tried to strangle her because he had heard rumors about her having a "step-husband." Naturally, Katy yearned for someone to love her, and her longings led her back to the young man who wanted to marry her."

"Isn't there some way to help them, sir?" I gave thanks that I hadn't grown up with a father like Katy's, and that my aunts had sheltered me from such meanness.

"Because she committed adultery, I've filled out the papers to have the marriage annulled, and Katy went to live with an aunt in Cosby. I sent young Daniel to Knoxville, to look for a job. They both need to start over in a larger town." Dr. Henderson glared down at me.

"But do you have any idea what could have happened to you? I've a mind to call off everything."

I wiggled my dirty toes, digging them into the soft earth. "I was reckless. And so scared, that I considered giving up on my plan, sir." I looked up. "All I wanted to do was grab Pa and run from here. But then, what if I hadn't been there to help Katy? Besides, that's the first time a man called me an angel."

"Angel, indeed." Dr. Henderson shook his head. "Don't do it again. Next time you might not be so lucky. And I'm afraid that it's too late to move your pa; the trip back to Rugby would kill him. The best we could do is bring him to uncle John's cabin. Now, did you arrange a meeting with your cousin?"

"Yes, sir. Tomorrow, at the fishing hole I described to you."

"Stay alert. If you see more than one man, restrain yourselves, understand?"

"Yes, sir." My cheeks reddened, even having one man watch us sparking would be awkward. "After tomorrow, how long...?" I focused on a crow walking by the side of the trail, pecking at something.

"I never find out until the last minute." Dr. Henderson mounted his horse and took hold of the reins. "I'll stop by or send word as soon as I learn anything. If need be, I'll come with a wagon for your pa and a horse for you, plus a few men to guard your escape."

"Yes, sir." Watching him ride farther into the cove, I prayed that when my night came, the Blue Bills would arrive on time.

• • • • •

Come Tuesday, I ambled up the path holding a fishing pole and a basket lined with moss, wondering if I could convince James to kiss me. Heat waves shimmered across the valley, and the sassafras leaves drooped like hound's ears while at the mountaintops, giant, dark clouds wrestled. Above the treetops, buzzards rose on the updrafts. Sweat rolled down my back, making my chemise and the bodice of my dress cling to me. I wound through the underbrush, watching for snakes. Patches of lichens encrusted the rocks sticking out of the damp earth, while ferns brushed my ankles, and from a red oak tree, a Carolina wren sang. Ducking beneath low pine branches, I spied James's straw hat behind a jumble of boulders. He perched on the flat, sunbaked rock, dangling his bare feet in the river. He looked up and smiled as I sat down next to him.

"Let me bait your hook." He took my fishing pole, slid a worm onto the hook, and handed it back. "We need to catch some fish first." His eyes lingered on my unbuttoned collar, while I stared at his rolled up sleeves; fine red-gold hair crossed his forearms.

"I hope they're biting." I cast my line, and the bobber drifted downstream until the line played out. I wedged the pole in a gap where the boulders met and cozied up to James.

I wanted to lean over and kiss him, but remembering my father's words, I waited until James reached for me. He slid an arm around my waist and ran one finger down my back and up, as if counting my ribs. Had Eve touched Adam in this way, seeking the spot where God had taken out a bone? His pole jiggled. James grabbed it, and pulled in a brown trout.

"For your daddy's supper." He cast his line. "Next one's for Margaret's frying pan."

Did he have to remind me who ran his kitchen and his life? Would he ever find the courage to stand up to his sister? When I pouted, James laughed.

"None of that." He eased me down on the moss, and twisted a bit of my hair around one finger. "I've missed you." His thumb traced my cheekbone and wandered to my lips. Longing shimmered in his eyes when my hands slid along his shoulders.

"And I've missed you. Don't see how this can be wicked." Especially if you're thinking of marrying me, I wanted to add as fire filled my veins, and my flesh tingled.

"We have to be careful," James said. "I know we shouldn't meet, but..." He kissed me hard as his fingers loosened my hair, and moved to the small of my back, pressing me closer to him. Even the sound of the stream couldn't cool what bubbled up inside us. As the kiss continued, our breathing quickened, and my mind spiraled into a smoky haze, reveling in the salty and sweet taste of James' lips.

James exhaled, and cupped my chin in his palm. "Every time I sat down at our table, I knew from the look on Margaret's face that she was praying that I'd forget about you. But she and I both failed."

His lips inched down my neck to the hollow of my collarbone. 'Twas mortal sweet to be wanted, and I ached for him to continue. Somewhere higher up, thunder rumbled, and lightning flashed through my body when

James' fingers undid the buttons on my bodice. If'n Mr. White Cap lurked on the bank, he was getting an eyeful, and I didn't care one whit as my own fingers unfastened James' shirt.

A horse neighed. James jerked up. From across the river, a man on horseback watched us, but he was far enough away that we couldn't see his face. He pulled his rifle from behind his saddle, as a second man rode into view. My fingers fumbled with my buttons.

"The wretches." James swore. "Quick. Get between the boulders." James shoved me behind him, and crouched down. I wrapped my arms around his waist, and tried to draw him in but there wasn't room. The only way out was to run for the path and expose ourselves. Why, oh, why had I brought us here?

"Having some fun?" the first man called. "I heard your doney-gal is a vixen. Maybe you should share her?"

"Sounds tempting." The second man urged his horse down the rocky bank. "Shallow enough to cross. I'd like a little time with a saucy woman."

"Ain't you the oldest Walker boy? The one that killed my cousin?" The first man pointed his gun. We ducked as buckshot struck the rocks, and grit splattered us. "Just a warning that we'd better not catch you two, together, ever again," the man shouted, before thumping his heels against his horse. "Come on, we've a job to do."

The other man grinned and turned his horse away from the river. "Reckon you'll be seeing us, soon."

When he laughed, chills raced through me, and I forced down the bile rising in my throat. Not him again. The image of his ghostly hood floated through my mind and my legs gave way. James took my hands and lifted me up.

"Hurry. Follow me." James' voice shook. "We'll hide in a laurel thicket I know, in case they should decide to cross over."

Tears blurred the game trail as I stumbled through the underbrush, and tree limbs slapped my face. My knees kept buckling, until James wrapped an arm around my shoulders. At last, he pointed to a small opening in a dense laurel thicket, and we slithered on our bellies into the tiny green cave. I brushed cobwebs from my face and listened for the sound of hoofbeats.

"When I'm sure they are gone, I'll take you home by a different trail."

James pulled me to his chest.

Weeping, I clung to him as he stroked my hair. I longed to explain my plan and what should have happen today, then he would understand my terror. Two men had seen us, and not the single spy sent by the doctor. Like the buzzards circling overhead, trouble had found us, and I was to blame for its arrival.

CHAPTER TWENTY-THREE

At dinner, the sight of those black-winged buzzards flapped in my mind, and my hands trembled as I cut Pa's ham into tiny pieces. I had already forgotten to set the table with forks and spoons, and slopped milk when I poured it into his mug. Pa's eyes followed me and he chewed his lower lip.

"Can you tell me what's plaguing you?" Pa touched my hand. "Did something happen this afternoon? You met with James? Did he...force himself upon you?"

"I saw James, but no, he's not that type." I stuck my fork in a mess of collard greens, and stirred them, watching the steam rise. Shame blazed my cheeks as I remembered the way my flesh had ached as James unbuttoned my bodice. My cousin might not be that kind of man, except when tempted by me. Oh, Laws, how could I have done such a thing? Even during her flirting days, Lizzie had never dragged her boyfriend into danger.

"I'm glad to see y'all courting, again. When my time comes to leave this world I'd be pleased if'n James was your husband. He'd do you right." Pa sipped his milk, and a little sloshed from the mug because I had filled it too full. "But something's troubling you."

Trouble, yes, I had ripped open a wasp's nest. I grabbed a cloth and wiped up the spilled milk. How much about today should I reveal?

Being a man, Pa wouldn't like that I had involved my cousin in a risky situation without James' permission, even if the events of the afternoon were supposed to hasten the demise of the White Caps. It wasn't fair not to warn my father about the perils racing towards us. He should have a say in what we should do to protect ourselves. Yet, even with my worries biting at me, I cherished the memory of James' lips on mine, and his soothing caresses when he held me as I wept. But I also knew James would be vexed if he learned what the Blue Bills and I had been plotting.

Swallowing a lump of greens, I tried to speak about the encounter. "Two

White Caps saw us, alone. We were very close together." From the red moving up my neck, Pa understood how we had been kissing.

"Oh, Laws." Pa slumped over his plate. "Young folk. Different time, same temptations. How much did they see?"

"Too much." My voice trembled. Why had I thought I could get away with my scheme? From the glint in Pa's eyes, he understood that more than kissing had taken place.

Pa shook his head. "No telling when them devils will come. You must leave."

"I can't abandon you." As Pa winced, I regretted speaking the word abandon. Sorrow crept over his face, and pinched my heart.

"Thank you. After what I done, I don't deserve your loyalty." He stared at the tabletop, tears glistening in the corners of his eyes. "But thank you."

Closing my eyes, I savored his apology. I had dreamt how this moment would wipe away the anger that the years had piled onto me, but instead, a weariness seeped through my veins. I longed to escape from the peril confronting us.

"Even if I tried to flee, you know that one of them would see. They'd catch me in Sevierville, and whip me there." I shuddered, hearing the sound of the lash on Katy's back.

Pa nodded. "You should tell Abe. He might know what we should do."

"After how he's treated me, never." Knowing my uncle, he might hand me over to the White Caps and encourage them to beat me.

"I could send Abe to tell James to marry you. Most likely, that would calm the clan." Pa stared out the window. "Even if there ain't no need for a wedding, James has sullied your name, and only by marrying you can he restore your honor. Wouldn't be the first such wedding in our family."

I dug a laurel leaf out of my apron pocket. I didn't want James to marry me because Pa ordered him to do so. James should propose because he loved me and wanted to spend his life with me. That was what had supposedly motivated fickle Charlie to ask me to marry him.

"There's no need for a wedding. I reckon many courting couples been seen kissing," I said. But if'n those White Caps hadn't interrupted James' fingers on my buttons, who knows what we might have done.

"There must be something I can do to protect you." Pa straightened up and tried to grip the sides of the table, but his hands slid away.

What would Pa say, if I told him my plan with the Blue Bills? Would he order me to stop? But after this afternoon, my confession might bring one of those crying times upon Pa. Like the tree that had slammed into Johnny, my night with the White Caps roared toward me.

"I don't think there is anything we can do." I began to clear the table.

Pa rose, tottered over to his cot and curled up. I tucked a coverlet over him, hoping he would find a measure of peace in sleep. His face was a thin seed pod, cracked and bleached by time. No matter how hard I tried to imagine him giving my mother a hand as he had guided her through the Cumberland Gap, all I saw now was the dust of a man.

Standing at the table, I washed the dishes, staring at a storm cloud and a sweep of rain smothering the top of Cove Mountain. For some queer reason, I longed to tell Charlie about this muddle, of what I had hoped to do for the women, here. I reckoned that he'd groan and warn how no good came from trying to trick folks, but he'd understand why I had started this journey.

• • • • •

The following afternoon, the sun slanted through the chestnut leaves as I sat on our porch, threading green beans for leather britches. With each stab of the needle, the scent of the beans grew, as did the green garland. Footsteps sounded on the path, and Cousin Caroline ran to the cabin; her sunbonnet bounced on her back, her eyes wide and frightened. For a moment, she stood panting with sweat beaded on her forehead, and then she began to cry.

"Cousin Viney, you've got to come. Polly's packed and planning to leave home. Margaret and Marti are about ready to hog-tie her. The others are sobbing, begging her to stay. Pa's off fishing with Giles and Willie; be gone the whole week. James sent me for you. Said you're the one who can wrestle with Margaret."

"Let me check on Pa." I peeked in the screen door. He was curled up sleeping. Compared to when I first arrived, Pa slept more hours each day. "Let's go." I pulled my sunbonnet off a nail.

Caroline grabbed my hand, and we lit off. Seeing as she was only ten, I hadn't talked as much with her. Her dark brown eyes were sunken into her pale face, and her thin arms stuck out from sleeves that could no longer be lengthened, and her skirt was shorter than Margaret would approve, plus her pinafore bore several patches.

"Looks as if you're growing as fast as a willow tree." I tugged one of Caroline's braids. "In no time, you'll be pinning up your hair, wearing aprons, and wanting to keep your bonnet on."

"You don't like wearing a sunbonnet." Caroline stepped over a big root snaking across the trail. A rabbit scurried away from us, and farther into the woods, a larger animal crashed through the undergrowth.

"If I wear mine, will you put on yours?" I pulled my bonnet around my face and tied a bow.

"Yes, ma'am." A tiny ruffle ran along the edge of her bonnet's brim, adding to the child's innocent look. Lizzie would have liked to add bows to Caroline's braids, lace edging along the bottom of her pinafore, and perhaps even a slim white collar to soften the somberness of the brown homespun. Lizzie understood how those small details would add cheer to a child's outfit. Our feet flew up the path until we reached the cabin, and Caroline dashed towards the barn.

"I fetched her, Jamie!" she called, her petticoats flying.

James emerged pushing a wheelbarrow of manure and spent straw. He jerked his head toward the cabin. Sweat and dirt streaked his face and ran down his bare chest. He put me in mind of a drawing in one of Rugby's library books that showed a Highland chieftain. I wanted to run into his arms, but instead, I walked towards the shouting.

Polly stood on the porch with a black carpetbag and wearing shoes. Tears glistened in her eyes, but she stiffened her jaw when I hailed, "Hello".

"I'm leaving, Cousin Viney. Even you can't stop me. The preacher agreed that the Lord was calling me to serve Him, and suggested that I study the Bible at Carson College."

"How far away is the school?" I climbed the steps, eyeing the weeping sisters.

With arms folded against her chest, Margaret glared at me. "No girl needs that sort of learning. Religious training is for menfolk. She's wasting her time and money."

"Carson's in Jefferson City," Polly said. "Far enough away that Margaret can't tell me what to do. I'm only spending money that I earned, thanks to you." She tied on her new gray hat with blue silk flowers. "And there won't be any White Caps bullying folks. I'm tired of their wickedness, of living in fear."

"She's just going to look for a husband," Margaret said. "After some fellow breaks your heart, you'll come whimpering back." She glared at me. "See what you started! Giving her notions. Before you came, she was content here. All this comes from selling her quilts. Too much pride."

"I'm nineteen and can make my own choices." Polly picked up the carpetbag. "Besides, you should be glad. Maybe He's calling me to serve Him in Africa or some other far parts. The preacher's always saying how we must obey the Lord."

"How do you plan to travel to Jefferson City?" I asked. "It's a far piece to walk, must be over forty miles. Might take you two or three days to walk there."

"You'd walk it, if'n you had a mind to go." Polly wiped her eyes. "Nothing stops you."

Everyone recognized that she spoke the truth. Perhaps I hadn't been the best example of meekness for my cousins, but I certainly wasn't going to hinder Polly from leaving. Yet, Polly had never traveled farther than Sevierville, and had returned the same day to her mountain home. Hettie and Caroline stared up at me, as if expecting me to work some miracle. I felt as if I were swinging on a grapevine between two trees, but couldn't latch my legs onto either one of them.

"What if you don't like living in a town? College classes aren't like studying at the Greenbrier School. Some of your fellow students will have graduated from high school, and you might not be as advanced in your learning."

"I love to read and study, so I aim to try, and find out for myself." Polly stroked the handle on her carpetbag. "I can't know what I'm missing if I never leave. Daddy even said that I'd make a fine preacher's wife."

Margaret snorted and shook her head. "Just plain foolishness."

But Uncle John was right, Polly had a heart as big as her mountain and could quote even more Scripture than Margaret. Her sweet voice often led the hymns as her hand kept perfect time. The Boss needed to realize that her sisters should follow their dreams, even if their path led off the mountain.

"You ain't missing anything, except noisy streets, shiftless men, and wild living," Margaret said. "You have all you be needing here, with your family."

"It's true that cities are noisy and filled with all sorts of folks." I swung my sunbonnet by one finger. "But meeting new people, hearing new ideas, makes life interesting." I ignored Margaret's scowl. "Did the preacher say how long you'd need to study?"

"Two years, but I'd spend the summers back here, helping out, and be home for Christmas." Polly dabbed her eyes with a hanky. "And every Sunday, I'll write. Hopefully, Cousin Viney, you'll write me."

Out by the barn, I spied James harnessing Red and hitching him to the wagon. Caroline also noticed him, and her eyes widened.

"Looky yonder." Caroline pointed as James led Red to the cabin. Anger snapped in his eyes and made him look even stronger and more handsome. I reckoned he'd had his craw full of Margaret's bossiness and stubborn ways. His brothers had gone after more learning so they could escape from Margaret, and perhaps James believed that Polly should have the same chance. I wanted to hug him and thank him for not being a stiff-necked man.

Margaret marched down the steps with all of us following. "What do you think you're doing?"

"I'm needing to sell these peaches, so I aim to take Polly as far as Sevierville. Hopefully, she'll find a teamster headed to Jefferson City." James lifted her carpetbag into the wagon, glancing at me. "Reckon I can take Viney home."

"Ain't fitting or safe for you and her to be seen together, and you know it," Margaret said. "You can't take chances with her, anymore."

"I'd appreciate a ride to town and can sit in the back," I said. "I need to see Dr. Henderson for more of his powders, for Pa."

"I could go with them," Louisa said. "I ain't never been to Sevierville. Please let me go along and keep them company." She stood up straighter, and gave James a pleading look.

"You lollygagged all morning, and got chores to finish." Margaret shook her head. "All of us need to be getting back to work."

"Louisa can chaperone, so Viney and I are not alone," James said. "You were younger than her when Pa took you. If'n you don't let her, she's bound to run off, too." James lifted Louisa onto the wagon and she settled on the seat as he gave a hand to Polly.

I jumped up and hopped into the back of the wagon, where the wooden sides hid me so there was less for a White Cap to see. Polly tucked her carpetbag next to me. James clucked to Red, and the mule trotted off, leaving Margaret in a swirl of dust. Leaning back against the wagon's side, I waved at my cousins. A dozen baskets of peaches scented the air, so I chose a ripe one and bit in.

"Thank you, sweet brother. When I'm on the mission field or helping in a church, I'll never forget your kindness." Polly leaned over and kissed James' cheek. He merely nodded and clucked to Red.

"Thank you. Tomorrow, I'll bake your favorite gingerbread." Louisa snuggled her head against James' shoulder, and I longed to do the same with him.

The rattle of the wagon's wheels snuffed out any bird songs, but the fragrance of new-mown hayfields filled me with a quiet peace. Staring up into the cloudless sky, I watched a red tailed hawk drifting in slow circles. Town life might disappoint Polly, but at least she would have a chance to discover whether she wanted to live off the mountain. Margaret needed to honor her sister's choice.

The word *honor* wiggled around inside me. Was I being honorable to James? I studied his hands holding the reins, thankful that his sisters sat on the bench with him, removing certain temptations. What if he knew that I needed to talk to Dr. Henderson about the two men who had spied on us at the river? What would James say if he knew how I had used him? Sitting up straight, I eyed the various trails running off the main road out of the cove. White Caps lived down those two-tracks. I shuddered, as though a spider crept up across my back.

Once we reached Sevierville, I hugged Polly good-by. "You write us when you reach the college. I know you'll love the book learning. And I hope you will meet some special gentleman." Stepping back, I smiled at the pink in her cheeks and the sparkle in her eyes. Time away from Margaret would strengthen my cousin.

"I'll come visit you at Christmas." Polly squeezed my shoulder. "You take care, Cousin Viney. Last Wednesday when walking home from meeting, I spied a man sitting beneath a cluster of hemlock trees, keeping an eye on your cabin. He didn't look charitable."

"Thank you for the warning." I said. Had the fellow been a White Cap spy or a Blue Bill? Polly's words churned in my belly, and a bitter taste flooded my mouth. Hopefully, the doctor would tell me something to ease my fears.

"I'll ask if anyone is heading to Jefferson City," James said. "You go on down to the doctor's and I'll meet you there." James escorted Polly and Louisa into the general store.

When I reached his home, Dr. Henderson was nailing boards over two smashed windows and pulled me inside. "It isn't safe for folks to see you coming here. The White Caps found out that you released Katy and helped Daniel escape, and they're more riled than I've ever seen." He wiped his brow with his handkerchief.

"Two men saw us at the river, and I assume the second man was not sent by you." I nibbled on my lower lip. Several crates lined the hall wall; one was filled with the doctor's son's toys, another with books. A stack of hat boxes sat next to them, along with a large round top trunk.

Dr. Henderson sank into a chair. Circles shadowed his eyes, and a few more lines creased his forehead. "My spy told me about the men. When they ran into him, they asked him how he had known to come to that particular spot on the river. He fed them a tale but they wouldn't believe it and roughed him up."

"Oh Laws, was he bad hurt?" Why hadn't I thought that this might happen because of my foolishness?

"A black eye and a split lip. He'd have fared worse except that he's a second cousin to one of the men who spotted you. Of course, now the White Caps suspect that he is on our side, so my man took his wife and baby over to Cades Cove where she has kin, I told him to stay there until things calm down."

Tremors ran down my spine as I walked around his office, resisting the voice telling me to fly away from here. I picked up his smooth rock from the river, but even rubbing my fingers over it couldn't soothe my mind. My willfulness had hurt a man who had to flee the cove, how many others would be injured because of me?

"My cousin, Polly noticed a fellow watching my cabin. Did you send him?" I set down his green and gray rock.

Dr. Henderson sighed and ran one hand along the back of his neck. "No, he was another White Cap, taking note of your comings and goings, when your uncle stops by, that sort of information. The clan tries to find out any patterns that might interrupt their attack."

I paused at a window, staring out at the pink and white phlox bobbing in the wind. A squirrel leapt from one tree branch and soared to another tree. The leaves on the limb quaked. I longed to ride off like Polly and return to Rugby, but I had no money for a train ticket or for lodging in Knoxville.

"Seeing as how enraged the White Caps are, I should help you to escape, but first I want to care for my family's safety." Dr. Henderson paced the room. "Yesterday, the clan threw rocks through our windows, and shot our dog. So, I'm sending my wife and son to her parents over in Gatlinburg."

"But what about Pa, sir? Could you take him with you?"

"Traveling even to Gatlinburg might kill him. He's failing, and hasn't much time left in this world."

"That is my concern, too, sir." I gripped the back of a chair. "So, what should I do? How can I protect Pa?"

"I will post a nightly guard near your cabin, not that one or two men can do much." He picked up his rock and tossed it back and forth. "But if they see or hear anything while you are sleeping, they could make a lot of noise, shoot off several guns, and perhaps give you time to escape and hide."

"When do you think the White Caps will attack? I'm so jumpy, sir. I can barely sleep." I inhaled, wishing I had stayed in Rugby, weaving, spinning, and minding my own business. But along with those thoughts rose, the image of Aunt Sayward's weary shoulders, and of Sissy dreaming of selling her baskets, and I heard Polly's yearning for peace in the cove.

"I don't know when, but probably within the next week. Maybe even tonight." He unbuttoned his high collar and wiped his neck.

"If'n the White Caps know you are the Blue Bills' leader, why don't they attack you?"

"They leave me alone because there is no other doctor around for thirty miles. If they killed me, who would set their broken legs or cure them of typhoid?"

Aunt Alta had often quoted a line from the Prophet Amos about letting "justice roll down like a river". I reckoned that was what I was trying to do, break through a dam of hatred and let a river of justice sweep through the valley. I hoped it wouldn't carry me away in the flood.

"You should stay close to home, and keep away from James." Dr. Henderson set down his stone.

"But I rode here in his wagon! Along with a couple of his sisters. I'll have to return with them." My head ached from the heat, from the strain in the doctor's voice, and from knowing that I might be endangering my cousins as we rode home. "Do you think the White Caps will harm us?"

The doctor frowned. "No, your uncle's service to the Union keeps those devils away from his daughters. But from today, use your head. Stay clear of John Walker's place. Go help Sayward. Do her laundry, weed her garden, and play with her children. Act in the manner of other women, and that might appease some of the vigilantes. The smaller the mob, the shorter the punishment."

Someone knocked on the front door, and Mrs. Henderson answered it. She walked into the office, carrying her baby, and from the set of her mouth, I knew she fretted.

"Mr. Coleman's wife's having a difficult labor."

Dr. Henderson jumped up and grabbed his satchel. "As soon as I ride off, you should leave." He ran from the room.

I pulled back the lace curtains and peeked out the window. From down the pike, James drove his wagon. "I see my cousin coming."

"Oh dear, it's not safe for Mr. Coleman to see you with your cousin." Mrs. Henderson moved to a corner of the room.

"So, ma'am you don't know what side Mr. Coleman is on?" I let go of the curtain and stepped back. At least, I knew James wasn't a White Cap.

"I am afraid not. Aaron feels it is safer for me to know nothing. Even when the doctor rides off at night, I'm never sure if it's for a medical reason, or to fight the White Caps." She stared at me. "I believe in my husband's work, especially after he cared for Katy. Thank you for helping that young couple." Her little boy squirmed, so she placed him on the floor, and he crawled towards me.

"Do other women feel like you do, ma'am?" I knelt down and reached out to the little feller, and he grabbed my hand.

"I know a handful of women have expressed the same outrage, but none of them know if their husbands might be White Caps. In fact, the clan's members refer to their group as the Graveyard Hosts, so if the law asks them if they are White Caps, they can answer, no."

James called to his mule and the wagon rattled to a stop. Mrs. Henderson placed her son on her hip, and we hurried outside. As we approached James, she handed me a piece of folded paper.

"Don't forget these. You can pay the doctor later. May the Lord protect you, Viney."

"Thank you, ma'am." My shaking hand stuffed the paper in my apron pocket. Thankful that she had given me the powders so I could truthfully account for the doctor visit. James helped me onto the wagon seat, and Louisa scooted over and sat in the middle. He handed me a letter from Lizzie, clucked to the mule, and the wagon rumbled off.

"Why did she say, 'may the Lord protect you?'" Louisa asked, "instead of 'God bless', or 'come back soon'?" Louisa gazed up at me with braids now sporting wide blue ribbons. From beneath the rim of my sunbonnet, I spied James's frown, as his fingers tightened on the reins.

"I reckon that's just the way she talks, probably because she sees folks with broken arms and such." I fingered her hair ribbon. "That color is perfect for your eyes."

"James picked it out." Louisa pulled pink ribbons from her pinafore pocket. "He bought me these to wear on Sundays. Cousin Viney, is the general store in Rugby so full of wonders?"

"Yes. The commissary sells ribbons and lace, boots, and other..." I blathered on, as Louisa pestered me with countless questions until James put one hand over her mouth.

"I need some quiet." He eyed me. "Give Cousin Viney some peace." James pulled his hat lower, and urged on the mule.

Peace. As long as I lived in this cove, I'd not find peace, but only fear.

CHAPTER TWENTY-FOUR

Glancing around the Sedgemore station, Charlie searched for one of Rugby's wagons, and recognized a team of Percheron horses that he had driven last summer. He hauled his carpetbag over to it, and extended his hand to the driver.

"I'm Charlie, formerly of Rugby. Do you have room for one more traveler?"

The youth's brown hair brushed his collar, and his innocent blue eyes gazed back. Charlie winced. One year ago, his face had worn a similar look of being enthralled with the mountains and optimism of Rugby. How many months would it take before blisters thickened this young man's palms and fatigue filled his eyes?

"Pleased to meet you, I'm Nathan. I need to load some freight that just arrived, and then you're welcome to ride along." Nathan wrestled a barrel from off the station deck and rolled it up a plank into the wagon bed.

Charlie shoved his carpetbag under the wagon seat. Around the station, a couple of men in muslin shirts and woolen trousers helped women into buggies. The ladies adjusted their bonnets, stowed parcels behind the seat, and smoothed their skirts. Charlie studied every woman's face, hoping that he wouldn't spy Viney with one of the men. At last, Charlie and Nathan jumped onto the wagon seat, and the horses trotted off.

"What brings you to the settlement?" Nathan tipped back his hat but kept his eyes on the road.

"I left last fall to try farming in another location, but I missed Rugby. This is a special place." Charlie gripped the wagon seat, as the wheels bumped over ruts, and rattled over a wooden bridge. "I helped build that bridge, along with six other fellows. We worked on this road so that it was completed before the settlement's grand opening."

"Yes, Rugby has a special feel about it, this air of expectation and great possibilities. Who did you intern with?" Nathan pulled on the right rein, and the team avoided a large puddle.

"On Mr. Hill's farm, but I also worked at the sawmill, and in the tomato fields." And he had helped out at Viney's homestead, hoeing corn, milking the cow, and cleaning stalls in the barn. Each activity had drawn them closer until he yearned to hear Viney whack the beater of her loom and sit with her on the porch, listening to Seamus play his fiddle.

"I'm swatting nails on the new Tabard; it should open soon, but without the grand ceremony." Nathan glanced at Charlie. "So you were at the opening, when that girl planted a snake in the flowerpots?"

"Yes, the trick scared the ladies and angered the gentlemen." Only a lass like Viney would have had the courage to pull such a prank. Charlie hoped that part of Viney hadn't changed.

The men traded stories while the wagon rumbled around curves, as the road rose and descended. Charlie rubbed his itchy palms against his trousers. One more mile, and they would arrive in Rugby.

"At any of the dances, have you met a Viney Walker? Or Lizzie Walker?" Charlie gazed at a red-tailed hawk gliding in an updraft.

"I came a little over a month ago, and don't recall a Viney, but Elizabeth Walker is helping the new school master. She's a beauty, and those two make a stunning couple when they dance."

"Lizzie? Do you know where she's living? Could you drop me off there?" Charlie's hands gripped the wagon seat. How had Lizzie turned into a schoolteacher?

"I'm headed for the commissary, so I'll tell you where to find her boardinghouse. Gee!" Nathan guided the team to the hitching post, and gave Charlie instructions.

"Thanks for the ride. Hope to see you, again." Clutching his carpetbag, Charlie jumped from the wagon. He avoided passing the house where George had died, and instead, strode up the dusty road towards the gray, board and batten house with maroon trim. In the past year, Rugby had returned from its post-epidemic ghost town to a place filled with wagons and teams. From various streets, swelled the sound of hammers pounding and men shouting orders. If Seamus could be here, seeing the changes and renewal, he might choose to return, also.

Charlie knocked on the beveled glass door and peered into the hallway. A kerosene lamp with a shade decorated with prisms hung from the ceiling and heavy wallpaper with a hunting scene on it covered the upper wall while walnut wainscoting protected the lower section. Boots tapped across the wooden floor, and a tall woman with dark red hair opened the door.

"Come in and make yourself welcome. How can I help you? I'm Mrs. Carroll, the owner." Mrs. Carroll wiped her wet hands on a stained apron covering a lavender dress dotted with springs of green leaves.

She sounded like Seamus. Charlie bit his lower lip. "I'm looking for a Miss Viney Walker or her sister Lizzie. I need a room for at least tonight and perhaps a bit longer." How many days would it take to convince Viney to marry him, and to arrange the wedding?

"Ah, Miss Lizzie will return soon, but her sister, Viney, well, Miss Lizzie should tell you the tale. Why don't I show you a room, and would you like a cup of tea?"

"Yes, please." Charlie followed Mrs. Carroll down the hall that smelled of beeswax and lemons. The whitewashed room held a single brass bed with an indigo and blue woven coverlet, a small oak table and chair, along with a nightstand with a bowl and pitcher. Cheesecloth covered the open window, allowing a breeze to filter through the muslin curtains.

"Simple, but clean, with a lovely view of the ridge. And there's tea and shortbread on the sideboard in the parlor." Mrs. Carroll dropped a skeleton key into Charlie's hand and hastened away.

He plopped down on the bed. Why wouldn't the good mistress tell him anything about Viney? Had she died from the summer flux? Or married someone else?

CHAPTER TWENTY-FIVE

"Read it again," Pa said. "Looks like Lizzie's found herself a new beau. Going to have a wedding or two this fall." He tried to wink, but only wrinkled his face in a way that accentuated his protruding cheekbones. From a nearby tree, a flock of crows flew upward, cawing as they expanded into a web of black against the sunset. I unfolded my sister's letter and spread it out on the table.

Dearest Viney,

My wonderful William asked me to marry him!

I know you and Pa will love him as much as I do.

He has encouraged me to cultivate new skills as a teacher and leader with the local women. As soon as the term ends, we will depart for Wear's Cove..."

I folded up the letter so that Pa wouldn't notice Lizzie's warning to not use James as a lure. She begged me to move Pa to Uncle Abe's cabin, and to arm myself. My sister still didn't realize how I distrusted our uncle.

"No." Pa shook his head. "From the worry in your eyes, I reckon you aren't telling me how bad things are with the White Caps. You tell Lizzie not to come, ain't safe."

"But Lizzie and William want your blessing, and you can't travel to her. Besides, there isn't time for a letter to reach her. She'll bring her pistol, and having weapons in the cabin could be helpful."

Pa's brown eyes grew misty and he sighed. "Lizzie's like your mama's mother. Your grandma was a crack shot. No Yankees messed with her or with her daughters. When her husband and sons were away fighting, she taught her girls how to shoot so that if marauders came scrounging around their farm, they'd send out a volley of bullets. General Lee could have used her as a sharpshooter."

"My grandma? I wish I could have met her." Why had my aunts never told me this tidbit? Perhaps because they already had lamented my wild ways and didn't want to encourage such boldness. But every time Pa told me something new about my family, he darned another hole in that tattered stocking. Sometimes though, I would pepper him with questions, but he would shake his head. Seemed something had to spark the stories before his words would flow.

"Before your grandma married, she dressed in her brother's clothes and rode over to a turkey shoot in the next town. She came in second place, but when she wiped the soot off her chin and flung away her hat, the men refused to give her the prize."

"Well, that wasn't fair, at all. What about my mama? Was she good with a gun?" I had always envisioned my mother singing, setting out rose cuttings, but not aiming a gun.

"Your mama was a good shot, but didn't take to hunting like your grandma who kept her family in meat during the war. But even with pistols and her beau, tell Lizzie that she shouldn't come. And it troubles me how you're staying; I can get by on my own."

In my last missive, I had written Lizzie about how Pa was fading, and had encouraged her to hasten to the cove. I had also added a note to Jacob and recommended that he come along, too. Yet, even now might be too late for their visit. Most mornings, it took over an hour to wash Pa, get him dressed and escort him to the privy, and back to the cabin. I would have given him a slops jar, but he refused it, saying, because of his shaking, he'd miss the pot. Between meals, he slept, only waking when Uncle Abe or some other visitor stopped by to chat.

"You can pen my blessing and send it in a letter, that way Lizzie will have my written words to keep with her when I'm gone. With a letter, she can read it over and over."

Pa's voice shook as did his arms, and his feet tapped the floor. I hated to see the palsy consuming him, turning him into a marionette like the ones I had seen at a Punch and Judy show during Rugby's Christmas celebration. What had my father been like when he chopped down trees for our cabin and plowed fields with his mule? I knew he regretted losing those years when his children could have known a healthy man. And what might I regret if I didn't fight for what I believed was a better way for this cove?

From outside the cabin, a whip-poor-will repeated his name while a moth batted against the glass globe on Pa's kerosene lamp. I couldn't brush it away without burning my fingers. Flutter, flutter, its wings tapped the glass until they singed. The moth fell to the table, and I crushed it. Scooping the moth into my palm, I threw it onto the hearth.

"I'll write Lizzie and warn her." While I would explain the danger shadowing us, I would not tell my sister to stay away. Every part of me needed her, so I could talk to her about James and draw strength from her. And she and Jacob should see Pa before he joined Mama in heaven. I helped Pa to bed before I slipped out to the porch.

Lizzie had also written how Charlie had sent me five more letters. Five! What in tarnation was he writing about? Now, my curiosity wanted to read that stack of letters. Lizzie hadn't burned any of his epistles and would bring them with her. If I was calculating correctly, Charlie had written over a dozen letters. For someone who said our engagement was over, he was acting real friendly. Reckoned I only had myself to blame for not being able to see what Charlie had said, but what would I do if he wanted to renew our engagement? What *did* James feel for me? Why wouldn't he say that he loved me?

Like most nights, I rocked while the moon traveled higher and bats swooped after bugs. While tending to my father during his last days, a tenderness had snuck into my hands. Sometimes they squeezed his shoulder or my fingers twined with his. When my hands did so, tears would spill from his eyes, and he always said, "Thank you, daughter." Appears that my anger had shifted, like when a river cuts a new course and leaves behind an oxbow lake. My anger had pooled in that leftover lake, settling towards the White Caps.

I stared at the ribbons of stars. What would happen to my father when the White Caps arrived? The doctor had assured me that the vigilantes wouldn't hurt an elderly man. But then, the doctor had also said that he had never seen the White Caps so furious. The scene at Katy's cabin erupted in my mind...the torchlight accentuating the angry faces, the jeers and taunts, the whistle of the whip, and Katy's screams. I trembled. May the Lord have mercy on my father and on me.

The chestnut tree's leaves rustled, but there was no wind. I stiffened, squinting into the darkness. Two large shapes sat beneath the tree, but without white hoods. They must be Blue Bills sent to guard us. I knew what I must do, and walked toward them.

When I was about twenty feet away, one man spoke. "Don't, miss. Can't have you seeing our faces, so you could recognize us." A horse shifted its weight, and I saw it hidden behind the lowest branches.

"We'll be here till dawn, so you go rest yourself," the other man said. "Just leave your latch string out so as if'n we need to alert you."

"I will. Thank you for guarding me and my pa. Can I ask a favor of you?" I swallowed. "About my pa."

"Sure, miss. What?" the first man said.

"If...when the White Caps arrive, would one of you please put my pa on your horse and ride up the mountain to my uncle John's, or some safe place. Please don't let them hurt him, He's just an old man."

"Sure thing, miss. And we'll pass your request on to the others to rescue him," the second fellow said. "And thank you, for your courage. I've four daughters, and I don't want them living this way no more. We're obliged to you."

"Thank you." I slipped inside the cabin, and collapsed onto my pallet. I remembered a Negro servant who had accompanied a gentleman to the Tabard Inn, and how the Negro had described when he and his parents had run away from a plantation in North Carolina, so that their son would grow up free. Quaker folks in Pennsylvania and Virginia had sheltered them, before sending them on to Michigan. The Negro kept talking about the Quaker folks' courage, and now, a man had called me courageous, when I felt only puny and scared.

Chapter Twenty-Six

Heeding the doctor's advice, I kept away from James and his sisters, and stepped over to help Aunt Sayward and Sissy. As soon as I arrived, and saw the endless pile of diapers and baby garments, shame swept over me for having neglected my aunt. Sissy and I scrubbed laundry until our hands were raw, and we draped everything on bushes and the porch rail. Uncle Abe had brought home baskets of peaches from my cousins. As Sissy and I peeled them, my cheeks flushed, remembering James feeding me a peach and kissing away the juice. We dipped the slices in sulphur water, laid them on boards, and covered them with cheesecloth. Baking in the late August sun, filling the air with their sweetness, the peaches dried in no time. On another afternoon, my aunt set me to gently stirring a pot of curds for cottage cheese while I scanned the hillsides and the trail for any movement.

"They never ride in during the day, Viney." Aunt Sayward rocked as she nursed her baby, who waved his little legs and touched her face. "Them White Caps are part of the night, like heat lightning. Maybe you and your pa should come live with us? So's Abe can protect you."

"Thank you, but when I suggested that to Pa, he refused to move." More likely, if'n the White Caps arrived here, my uncle would throw me to those dogs.

"Best thing would be for James to marry you." Sissy grinned at me. "That would settle down the White Caps. They might fuss at missing their chance to discipline a woman, but there'd not be any reason to whip you if'n you had a husband. James would do right by you, and you know you want him." She picked up the framework of a basket, and drew a splint from a bucket of water. "Don't worry about Margaret, you'd stop her bossiness."

"Sissy's right. Marrying Abe saved my hide." Aunt Sayward stopped rocking and shifted her baby to her other breast. "Reckon you don't know this, but I had a shotgun wedding."

"Pa didn't need to see a gun." Sissy threaded another splint through the web of a melon basket. Aunt Sayward pulled the quilt over her little man, and gazed up at Cove Mountain.

"When you look at your uncle, you see a man with thick hands, a frown, and a loud voice, like that giant in the tale of Mutzmag. But remember how in the story, the giant loved honey and would sneak some when the witch wasn't watching. Before we wed, I had recognized that beneath Abe's gruffness, was a man aching over the deaths of his wives. Think of how you hurt over losing your aunt, and Abe had also watched two babies die. Death can wrestle even a strong man to the ground and weaken his spirit."

"I was visiting kin in this cove, when I met Abe at the singing school, and just like you and James, a fire filled my bones with desire. Then he introduced me to his children, and I wanted to gather them in my arms and wipe the sorrow from their faces. I knew that Abe had been without a wife for several months, and had watched him struggle with his longings when he walked me home. One night, after the singing, I snuck away and met Abe at that there apple tree, and we spread a quilt beneath it. Many kisses and Abe's wandering hands lit what both of us wanted." Aunt Sayward smiled.

My cheeks blushed when I realized what my aunt was admitting. With Aunt Sayward being so much younger than my uncle, I hadn't credited them with such fleshly ways. Appeared how Aunt Sayward wasn't as meek as she acted, and for all his bellowing about purity, my uncle was a charlatan.

"I was wrong to tempt him, and once we dove into that pool of pleasure, we couldn't hold back the next night, and the next. That's why Abe was so rattled about you and James. He's seen what happens and knows how hard it is to stop." Aunt Sayward bit her lower lip. "We should have known that some passerby would see or hear us. By the end of the week, I found a switch on my aunt's porch, and a warning for me."

I remembered the feel of my feet stepping on the switch and how a single piece of linen had changed my life.

"Abe married me that day, a good thing, because he had already seeded me this boy." Aunt Sayward kissed the top of her son's head. "While I know we shouldn't have dallied, I'm thankful for a man who restored my honor and didn't leave me in the hands of the White Caps. If'n you want, Abe can talk to James and order him to wed you."

"Thank you for telling me about your past and for making that offer...Pa already suggested it. But there's no need...." My neck turned red, and I focused on the buzzard swooping over the pasture. My aunt's words about restoring her honor gnawed at my belly. If James felt any responsibility for protecting my reputation, he hadn't expressed it.

"Honey, even if you ain't in the family way, marrying James is the one way out of this mess." Aunt Sayward gripped my hand. "Sissy can fetch the preacher while Abe brings James to your cabin, and by sundown, you'll be wed. No more fearing them devils, and free to love whenever you please. We can even hold a shivaree to celebrate your marriage vows."

I stirred the small pillows of cheese curd, and they circled around the kettle in their sea of whey. Should I heed everyone's advice and force James to marry me? Despite our sparking, James had never said that he loved me. His sisters and I had been the ones who had assumed that our courtship would eventually end in a wedding. But if James took me to his family's cabin, Margaret and everyone else would hear the nightly rustle of our mattress, and I didn't relish that thought. Even the hay mound would offer little privacy. James wouldn't want to move in with my pa and live so far from his orchards. Was that the problem that stilled his tongue from saying the words? He didn't want to leave his farm?

"Again, thank you. I'll ponder the notion." A shotgun wedding might prevent the White Caps from attacking me, but it would not solve the problem of them disciplining other women. Aunt Sayward winked at Sissy, who grinned back; for them, marriage was the answer to everything.

Like unrolling a finished coverlet from my loom, images of Charlie declaring his love, of proposing to me, and his insistence on having a chaperone when he visited rippled through me. There had been kissing, but Charlie had always stopped before temptation dulled our senses. For some queer reason, maybe because of the letters he had written, I longed to feel Charlie's fingers laced through mine, one more time. If'n Charlie had stayed in Rugby, then his love wouldn't have crumbled. Closing my eyes, I shook away such thoughts.

From the kettle, I spooned a few curds and tasted them, testing that they were squeaky. I drained the cheese in a muslin-lined riddle sitting on a bucket to catch the whey. The little pillows glistened as I salted them. I didn't want my uncle to drag James to the cabin. My future husband needed to wed me because he loved me.

CHAPTER TWENTY-SEVEN

At the sound of Lizzie's voice and the rumbling response from a gentleman, Charlie set his teacup in its saucer. Hands behind his back, Charlie stood in the foyer, bracing himself for whatever Lizzie would tell him, yet praying that Viney was alive and hadn't wed.

"Hello, Lizzie," he said when she walked through the doorway. In a white shirtwaist and long brown skirt and her curls pinned up, Lizzie looked the part of a schoolteacher. The tall black haired gentleman beside her withdrew his elbow from hers. In a top hat and black frock coat, with matching wool trousers, he was no settler.

"Charlie!" Lizzie's eyes widened. She dropped her satchel and hugged him. "I'm so thankful that you returned. Please meet William Fraser, the new schoolmaster."

An hour later, Charlie rubbed a hand along his chin. He should have shaved before dressing for dinner, but he could only think about talking with Lizzie. His stack of letters rested on the round walnut table near the maroon settee. Settled next to him, Lizzie sipped her tea while William sat at a table near a window, correcting his students' essays.

"So that's what Viney has written to me about James. While she believes that he will ask her to marry him, she's perplexed because he hasn't declared his love. You and I know that the feeling of being in love, and committing to love someone are different. I fear that James is dallying with Viney."

Charlie pressed his palms against his knees. He should have come earlier and stifled the romance. This night, Viney might be marrying James. Charlie clenched his jaw. He could only blame himself.

"But there's more happening. Much more." Lizzie bit her lower lip. "First, you need to know about the White Caps." Lizzie traced the stripe in her silk skirt as she unfolded what Viney had written her. "The worst is her determination to follow through with this plan, and Dr. Henderson continues to support her. Just before she arrived in the cove, those devils beat a woman to death."

"Why is she doing this?" Charlie sank lower into the settee. What had fomented this gang of vigilantes? "If this cousin sincerely loves Viney, why isn't he protecting her? Or urging her to escape?"

"You know how my sister is; she should have been one of King Arthur's knights. And ever since Viney found the switch, I've asked the same question. Why won't James defend her? I'd guard the one I love." Lizzie glanced at William. "Viney hasn't explained her plan to him. I told her that she is deceiving James. I guess she didn't learn her lesson from when she used you to silence the gossips."

"Good gravy, that was to stop a couple of old ladies from badgering her about getting married. These men will kill her. Unless, do you think Viney might have wed him?" Charlie couldn't say the man's name because to do so would give him a shape and the rights of a husband.

"It's possible. She wrote that my aunt and our father were pestering her to make James marry her. Belonging to a husband should turn away the vigilantes." Lizzie ran her hands over her cheeks, wiping away a few tears. "I'm terrified for her. When it comes to seeing justice accomplished, Viney hasn't much common sense."

Charlie stood up. "I need to ride there, and stop this madness. Do you know when the next train leaves for Knoxville

"The school term finished today, and we plan to leave tomorrow morning. Wait and go with us." Lizzie gazed at William. "Viney told us to come, and we bought our tickets last week. This is why I don't think she'll marry before we arrive. She would want me at her wedding."

"Unless a hasty marriage would prevent a whipping," William leaned forward. "If Viney's desperate, she might do anything to save her life."

Charlie banged his fist against the small table, knocking his letters to the floor. There could be no wedding, not if he had his say. The envelope containing the dried roses burst open, and the faded pink petals scattered across the rug.

CHAPTER TWENTY-EIGHT

From our front porch, I watched the thunderheads crash against the mountain peaks, and wondered if James was in the barn comforting his animals or sitting with his sisters, telling stories. Here in the cove, sweat poured down my back as the evening shadows fell. Knowing how the creek would soon run brown from the mountain runoff, I had fetched two buckets of clear water, and because the cabin was so hot, I had made Pa a pallet on the porch. He lay on his side, shaking, muttering about Yankees and their cannons.

"It's just thunder, Pa." I plopped beside him, wishing I was privy to what those White Caps were up to, wondering if the Blue Bill guard could weather the coming downpour. "The storm will soon pass and send a breeze to cool things down. Try to sleep."

I leaned against the cabin's wall, scanning the valley for even a hint of white hoods and torches. Dr. Henderson had stopped by yesterday saying, how the White Caps' plans were so secretive that only the inner leaders knew what night they would attack. He had sighed and picked at his cracked thumbnail. "You'll have to trust that even if I cannot warn you, somehow, the Blue Bills will come."

"Yes, sir," I had said. His words had brought as much comfort as hugging a cottonmouth, but there wasn't anything I could do but wait. Every nightfall for the past week, I had slept only a few hours, fearing that I would hear the White Caps' horses and feel their whips. I was a rabbit, starving in my hole while the wolves circled my home. The memories of Katy's beating kept sneaking back, filling my mind with her screams.

Even now, I considered packing Pa on to Uncle Abe's horse and riding up to Uncle John's cabin. But my thoughts kept wandering to the Campbells losing their barn, and to Sissy, who wanted to sell baskets to Miss Dickinson, and to the men who had thanked me for being willing to help trap the White Caps. When Aunt Alta had been frustrated with folks judging each other, she had quoted a Psalm saying that the man who "'follows righteousness and mercy will find life'." She would also admit her own failings, and ask for the Lord's mercy, while reminding me to do the same. It appeared to me these vigilantes had forgotten the mercy part, and held twisted ideas about how to make folks righteous.

The line of black clouds hovered about the mountains, and twilight fell early. Back in Rugby, on such scorching nights, Charlie and I would sneak ice from the inn's supply and drop slivers of it into our water glasses. I longed to dangle my feet in the fast running rivers that circled around Rugby and jump into the lady's swimming hole. I rocked while Pa snored, watching the heat lightning shimmer, listening, hoping the storms would keep away the White Caps. At last, a screech owl's trembling call sang me to sleep.

• • • • •

A thunderclap slapped me awake. I straightened up in the rocker and smelled pine pitch and horses. Out of the darkness, flickering torches illuminated white hoods and guns. I jumped up and spun around, seeing how the clan had already spread into a menacing ring that squeezed the cabin. My tongue was glued to my teeth, and my legs shook. My heartbeat pounded in my ears as the white hoods dismounted and strode closer. How could I get Pa to the Blue Bills guarding me? Or perhaps because of the approaching storm, the hemlock trees didn't hide any men.

The men pointed their rifles at me. My ears strained to hear the rumble of the Blue Bills' horses, but only thunder growled. Pa whimpered, and half-opened his eyes. Fear nailed my feet to the porch floor. The torchlight swarmed around us. I was a moth, tapping against the glass lantern.

Three men in long white robes with hoods slunk towards me; the biggest carried a horse whip. Four other White Caps with ropes followed. Still, no far off sound from the Blue Bills. Mercy, I prayed, please spare Pa. I scanned the cluster of trees where the guards had waited, hoping someone would ride through the ring and snatch up Pa. One giant emerged from between the hemlock branches. I clutched the porch railing. Laws, Uncle

Abe stepped into the center of the torchlight and shouted:

"We've got you covered." Uncle Abe aimed his gun at the leader holding the whip. "An army of Blue Bills is sitting in these woods, with their guns pointed at you. You take your men and turn around. Best go home, get out of the storm, or this might be your last night on earth."

The men paused and lifted their torches higher. A few squinted at the trees and then at each other. Unless the Blue Bills had ridden in while I had slept, my uncle was bluffing, buying time so that the others could arrive.

"If'n your buddies come out of hiding, we might believe you." The leader stared up at the hills. "Any of you fools out there? Show yourselves."

Silence. Not even the screech owl called. Nor did I hear the rustle of the Blue Bills' horses. I tasted blood from my tongue.

The leader snorted. "You're lying. There ain't nobody with you. Put down your gun and let us do what we came to do. Even you, Abe, couldn't make this slut behave, but we will."

Uncle Abe fired, and gun smoke swirled around him. The leader screamed and clutched his shoulder. The mob howled as the man slumped against his friend and cursed. Behind me, Pa whimpered.

"Get him, boys!" Blood seeped across the leader's white robe. His hood fell back, revealing the storekeeper's face.

Like a blizzard, a dozen men with ropes rushed toward Uncle Abe. He swung one fist into a fellow's face, while slamming a fist into another man's shoulder. He kicked another man in the knees, and the man crumpled. A White Cap sprang on Uncle Abe's back and locked his hands around my uncle's throat. Uncle Abe twisted and shook like a dog, and flung the fellow off. But another man with a shotgun, walloped my uncle in the head, and another socked him in the gut. A man jumped in front of Uncle Abe and aimed a knife at his heart.

"Don't!" I shrieked. "He's got a family. And I'm the one you want!" How would I ever look at Sayward if they killed Uncle Abe?

"She's right," the man carrying the whip yelled. "He can't stop us, now. Tie him up, good."

Several men dragged my limp uncle to the chestnut, knotted ropes around his wrists and ankles, and fastened him to the tree. Uncle Abe moaned as blood oozed from a wound on his forehead. My ears ached from straining to hear any sign that the Blue Bills were coming. Pa stirred and sat up.

"Viney?" He squinted at the torches and the wavering white hoods.

"Pa, get inside the cabin. Crawl, quick-like, inside, and lock the door." Maybe if they didn't see Pa, they would leave him alone.

"Draw closer boys, time to teach this gal a lesson." The man waved his whip, and the white hoods slid toward me like vipers, poised to strike.

"Dear God, make Dr. Henderson hurry." I backed away, pulling my knife from my apron pocket and opening it. Even if it earned me more lashes, I'd cut into one of the devils and maybe give the Blue Bills a bit more time to arrive.

Two men pounded up the steps and grabbed me, but I slashed one's arms before he snatched my wrists. I kicked at the other fellow's ankles, but missed.

"You little vixen." His boots knocked the knife away, and he bent my elbows, twisting them behind my back. Shrieking, I doubled over as pain seared my joints.

"When we finish with you..." The leader lashed my wrists together. My jaw hurt from clenching my teeth, even my breath trembled as it left my lungs. The man's voice belonged to someone I knew, Johnny's brother.

Pa tottered as he tried to rise to his feet. His nightshirt billowed about him, and his white hair fell across his face. "Yankees! Run, daughter." He lifted a hand as if to protect me.

"Keep away, you old coot." The White Cap turned and shoved Pa across the porch.

"Pa!" I squirmed. How could these devils hurt an old man?

Pa cried out. He landed on his rear end and slid a few feet before bumping his head against the cabin wall. Blood trickled from a cut on his cheek. Groaning, he slumped to the floor.

"Have you no shame!"

"We'll teach you about shame." The leader slapped me, and I staggered backwards. "We warned you, but you think you're better than us. And cleverer. But you ain't."

The crowd parted, forming two lines like a ghostly gauntlet. Three hooded men pushed James through it as the ghouls spat on him. With his hands tied in front of him, James stumbled, but his guards booted him along until he reached the porch and mounted the stairs. Hunched over, his shirt torn, one eye swollen, black and blue, James stared at the floor like a small boy. Not a spark of resistance glowed in his hazel eyes.

Bile pooled in the back of my throat, as waves of terror crashed over me. I began to retch, but the man with the whip yanked my head up and through the slits in his hood, glared at me. Anger poured from his dark eyes, and scorched my soul. I fell on my knees. He laughed, high and thin, and a thousand shards of glass dug into my flesh.

CHAPTER TWENTY-NINE

"These are the three remaining horses." Charlie handed the reins to a quarter horse to William, and presented Lizzie with a dappled mare. A wagon rolled down the dusty street in Knoxville, lined with a mercantile, a lawyer's office, hotel, and a doctor's office. "Even if we start now, it'll be dark before we reach Sevierville." Charlie dragged his sleeve across his forehead. He had forgotten how hot it could be on a Tennessee afternoon.

"Yes." With her handkerchief, Lizzie wiped soot off her face. "I don't care. We must make haste. It's as if I can hear Viney calling for me."

William helped Lizzie into the saddle before mounting his horse, and Charlie climbed onto his black gelding. Without the sling, his wrist hurt, but Charlie couldn't be encumbered by a piece of cloth when riding into danger.

"That road there," Charlie said, "runs eastward and into the mountains."

They trotted out of the town and into the hills covered with oaks, maples and chestnut trees. Now and then an opening separated the woods, where a log cabin and barn stood. Barefoot children watched the travelers and a man hoeing corn waved. Ferns smothered the small springs flowing over the outcropping rocks. The trail rose around the hills and slid back down into valleys. When a small creek crossed the road, the trio rested their steeds.

"I could drink as much as my horse." Charlie cupped his hands and poured water into his mouth. "I didn't sleep much on the train. Too worried about Viney."

Lizzie removed a mug from her saddlebags and filled it. "I kept thinking about those White Caps. Wondering if they've come for Viney? If Dr. Henderson and his Blue Bills saved her?" She sipped and handed William the mug.

"Thank you. Five more minutes and the horses should be ready." William poured water down the back of his shirt. "If we had more time, I'd jump into the creek."

As their horses clip-clopped along, Charlie watched the cumulus clouds mounding higher and higher. The top of one flattened out to make an anvil shaped thunderhead. The sweep of rain brushed the peak of the mountain. The other clouds rolled over the ridges; their shadows gnawed the hills. From what the blacksmith had told him, they should reach Sevierville in an hour and from there must ride into the cove. Would he find a wedding or the White Caps?

Chapter Thirty

"That's more fitting." The leader's boot nudged my rear end. "Bring the Walker feller closer."

The men pulled James over to me. From the tangle of hair covering my face, I peered up the trail, but no pricks of light flickered. I had to stall these devils, but how?

Johnny's father shook James. "Remember, it's either her or we'll ride on up the mountain, and your sisters will feel our wrath. Do what you're told, and tonight will settle the blood between us."

No, James, don't listen to them, I wanted to beg. Make this nightmare end.

"Now, boys, we've gathered to show this gal and James that carnal pleasures such as they shared are wicked." The leader handed James two pieces of rope. "Bind her ankles good. Tight enough to cut her flesh."

As James knotted the rope, I winced, and bit the inside of my cheek. What if the Blue Bills didn't come? The torches tottered and swayed. The leader's fingernails bit into my shoulder.

"No fainting, dang it. Because this is the sweet part, ain't it, boys?" The leader nodded at James. "Haul her to the post. Let her dangle just a bit."

James stared at the rope coiled in his hands. His broad shoulders drooped as he chewed on his lower lip. His breathing came shallow and fast.

"Get moving, boy." The leader flicked his whip around James' ankles, and he jumped. The crowd laughed and taunted him. "Sissy! Sissy! Tame that kitty."

Holding my wrists, James pulled me to my feet and tied me to the post so that my toes just brushed the ground. I felt like a dead hog, soon to be gutted and butchered. Stretched by the ropes, my arms, shoulders and neck ached, but I refused to bow my head, and stared at James, hoping to see remorse in his soul. But he backed up and turned away as the leader stood behind me.

"You plotted to be the bait, so them Blue Bills could attack us, but honey, you stepped into our trap. You never dreamed that we'd use your handsome cousin to lead you into our hands. And seeing as how we love to hear women scream, we won't use no gag on you."

The leader's white hood brushed my face as he unbuttoned the top three buttons of my bodice, and rolled back the fabric. His fingertips seared my flesh, and I flinched.

"Well, now." The leader ran his rough fingers up and down my neck and along my collarbone. "I thought a slut like you would relish any man's touch."

I snapped at his fingers. He jerked away, and slapped me so hard that my head hit the post. The ring of white hoods rippled as the men shook their fists and shouted. Two of them dashed up the porch steps, but their leader waved them away.

"Didn't your daddy teach you any respect? Say you're sorry, *sir*." His fingers bit into my shoulder.

I yearned to spit at him, but gritted my teeth. "I'm sorry, sir."

"You try that again, and I'll order another ten lashes." He nodded at one of his henchman. "Grab her by the hair. Hold up her head."

Oh, Laws, Dr. Henderson, where are you? Behind me, Pa stirred. "Dirty Yankees," he muttered. "Let her go."

The leader raised his knife and cut off both of the dress's sleeves. "Take a look at those arms. My, my, she's got muscles, bet she can hoe five acres a day."

If'n Pa and I lived, we were leaving at first light, and I never wanted to see James or this cove, again. More thunder rolled, echoing between the mountains, and lightning illuminated the ridges. The leader's knife slowly slit the back of my bodice. I hated the smell of his sweat, and willed myself to believe that the Blue Bills would soon arrive.

"Not a mole or a freckle, but we'll give her stripes to last the rest of her days." Taking the flaps of the bodice in his hands, he yanked, ripping the dress in half. The fabric fell away, and the men howled. My thin chemise draped my bosom, and hugged my ribs where my petticoat cinched my waist. The torchlight accentuated my curves, and I hated the men as they pressed their ugly, half-shaved faces against the porch railing. Their hands grabbed my ankles, but the leader booted them away. Never again, could I walk through this cove and not feel defiled.

"Sorry, boys, but you know our clan teaches women to keep themselves pure. But after we ride away, if any of you should sneak back, well, I won't know a thing about it."

Lord have mercy on me. Left half dead like Katy, I'd have no way to fend off a mob. A White Cap offered the leader a jug, and he chugged on it, and passed it down to his men. The smell of whiskey spiked the air.

Pa stirred and mumbled. "Get away from her, you devils. Blasted Yankees."

The leader pinched my rear end. "Had a hankering to do that since I saw you necking with James. You'll be wishing that you had on more petticoats. My wife wears three, so that they'll hide what other men should never see." He fingered my chemise. "The first lash will shred this. Ready, James?"

No one was going to rescue me. I leaned my forehead against the post, and clenched my teeth as James unfurled the whip. My foolishness had brought me to this place. Every inch of me called out for mercy but these men's mouths had never tasted that word.

The leader gripped my chin in his fingers, and his breath heated my face. "I want to watch when the pain brings you to your knees. You know the afternoon you visited the fine Dr. Henderson? Well, that was the day we reckoned how you and him were planning something. Start with a dozen, James."

Chapter Thirty-One

In the sultry dusk, Charlie, Lizzie and William rode down the main street of Sevierville. Charlie dragged a sleeve across his brow, wiping away sweat. Heat lightning rippled over the village, illuminating the few houses. Outside the mercantile, a group of fifty men on horseback listened to another man speaking. He held a torch and gave orders as he pointed at fellows.

"They're not wearing white hoods." Charlie glanced at Lizzie and William. "But we have to find out who they are." He urged his horse towards the crowd. Although his wrist ached, Charlie ignored the pain, because a few of the men wore blue caps.

"Lizzie, you should stay here," William said. "There must be a place where we can find you a room." Thunder growled. "It's going to storm."

"Stop!" the leader called. "Who are you? It's late to be passing through."

"I will not stay." Lizzie kicked her heels and trotted up to the leader. "I'm Elizabeth Walker, and these are my friends. We're going to Wears Cove to see my father and sister."

"Good Lord." The leader shook his head. "No you're not. Jeb, keep them here and explain the situation. We've got to ride or we'll be too late."

"Yes, Doc." Coleman clucked to his horse. "Y'all come with me to the church, get out of the storm. You'll be safe there."

They might be safe, but what about Viney? Charlie studied the cluster of men, seeking away around them. He gasped as Lizzie leaned over her horse and plowed through a small gap in the crowd. The woman was mad! He squeezed his knees and followed her. Lizzie streaked ahead, Charlie caught up to her, and William came along beside him. No one was going to stop him from reaching Viney.

Behind them, hooves pounded the dirt. Like a pack of wolves, the Blue Bills enfolded them into the gang. They raced up and around the mountains, hugging the cliffs. Lightning stabbed the sky, and thunder echoed between the hills. Charlie dug in his heels, commanding his mount to fly. Rain soaked his clothing, but he hugged the gelding.

Riding six abreast, they roared into the cove. A flash of lightning illuminated the leader riding next to him, but Lizzie rode at the head of the gang. Thunder boomed. Lightning struck a tree, jagged splinters flew into the air. Far ahead, torchlight waved in and out of the trees. White hoods, white robes shimmered like moths. Bile filled Charlie's mouth. Sweat stung his eyes. A woman screamed. Viney! The brutes! He hammered his horse with his heels and pulled a pistol from his breeches.

Chapter Thirty-Two

The leather snapped and whined, slamming me against the post. I screamed, and writhed as millions of hornets stung me from my neck to my toes. Like an adder, the end of the lash curled around and bit my ankles as James yanked the whip backwards. They would kill me.

"Do it again! Come on, boy!" The White Caps cheered.

James thrust his arm forward and the whip screamed. I shrieked as the leather raked my back and shredded my chemise. Waves of fire consumed my flesh, my knees buckled, but the leader grabbed my arms.

"Please! Let me go, please, sir. I'll leave the cove." I choked on a sob. "Please, sir, let me take my pa and go home." I hated my pleas, knowing that I whimpered like a little girl.

"Mmm, I love to hear you beg." The leader mimicked my words. "Let me go, please, sir, let me go. Only two lashes and you're a heap more respectful. Can't wait to see what the next ten bring out of you."

The White Caps laughed, and waved their torches. A flash of lightning struck a tree, and thunder boomed. Through half-opened eyes, I saw one man shoot his gun in the air, and then another fellow fired his gun, and the smell of gunpowder stung my nose. A porch board squeaked. Behind me, Pa stumbled.

"Give it to her," a man yelled. A couple of other guns cracked; the smoke drifted through the crowd. The whip hissed as James swept back his arm.

From beside me, Pa stood straight and howled. His Rebel yell roared over us and ripped my heart. Pa's cry crashed upon the crowd, and they froze. His scream rose and bounced off the hills as it swirled in the treetops and through the cove. Pa fell across my back, and the lash sliced his shirt. He shrieked and fainted. His weight dragged me down, pulling at my arms. I screamed, unable to shrug his body off me. The leader released my chin, and fell backward

Like a river crested in flood, Blue Bills echoed Pa's yell as they exploded into the clearing. Through my screams, I heard horses galloping, guns blasting, and the voice of my sister calling my name. I squinted through the haze of gun smoke at Lizzie as her horse swept through the White Caps. She aimed her pistol at the leader. Crack. His high-pitched scream smothered me, as he stumbled and fell from the porch steps. His henchman grabbed him, pulling him away from Lizzie's horse's hooves.

Sheets of rain poured onto the men. Thunder drowned out the battle. A ball of lightning sizzled as it rolled across the clearing. My sister jumped onto the porch and hacked at my bindings. I slumped to the floor; pain consumed me, melting my bones. Lizzie pulled Daddy off my back. Boots stormed up the stairs, and I looked into Charlie's face.

Chapter Thirty-Three

Fire roasted the flesh on my back and seared my legs. My lungs ached, but I had to get Lizzie out of the Tabard. I yelled her name, grabbed her from the trunk, and dragged her along the hall. Flames swept up the walls and licked the floorboards as we stumbled to the stairway and fell, rolling and tumbling to the first floor. Smoke blackened the air, and I coughed, gasping as I squinted through the gloom. Where was the back door of the inn? The stairway collapsed behind us, and flying debris tossed me onto my belly. I crawled across the kitchen floor, pulling Lizzie next to me, aiming toward the dim light.

"Viney." A woman stroked my cheek. "You're safe. Daddy's alive. The beasts are gone. Sleep, sweet sister."

"Fire." We had to escape, but Lizzie's body was a rock. The floor burned my hands and knees as I rolled her in front of me. Shouts rippled above the roar of the conflagration. A sudden draft cleared the air, and the light grew brighter. I heaved Lizzie toward the opening.

"Charlie!" I reached for my beloved, as I rolled out of the inn's kitchen and onto grass. Timbers screamed as the roof collapsed, and the Tabard exploded.

The woman opened my lips, and dripped something bitter on my tongue. "There's no fire, Viney. Go back to sleep. I won't leave you. Nor will Charlie."

Pain pulsed through me. White light pierced my mind. Scores of White Caps grinned, as hundreds of fingers poked me, and pinched my calves. The leader screeched his thin laugh before covering my mouth with his. I shrieked, hearing the whip crack.

"Shhh, my brave sister," the woman said. "All is well. I'd hug you if it wouldn't hurt you."

Above me, Lizzie's blurred face wobbled and swayed as her hair brushed my cheek. She smelled like the roses around our cabin. My sister murmured soft words, wrapped her fingers around mine, and sang about a cuckoo. Her voice untangled the web of fear cast around me, and soothed me to sleep.

• • • • •

Sunlight prickled my eyelids. Every inch of me ached. Bruises blacked my swollen and cut wrists. My throat was raw from screaming, and fire burned in the sockets of my arms. I tried to roll over, but pain slammed my belly back against the mattress. Recalling how my father's body had shielded me from the whip, I inhaled the rank scent of Daddy's pee, and knew he lived. Like most mornings lately, he had wet himself. But the perfume of roses still floated from the pallet next to mine; Lizzie *had* slept next to me, but she wouldn't know to wash up our father.

Pressing my palms against the pallet, I pushed up until I knelt and leaned my forehead against my father. Daddy had fled our home in grief, just as Charlie had run from the hurt of losing George, from watching Rugby crumble. And I had thrown myself at James, imagining that he loved me, letting my lust for his touch fog my senses. Weeping, I laced my fingers through my father's.

"I'm so sorry, Daddy. For not wanting to come and care for you, for bringing the White Caps to your cabin." If he died, it would be my fault. "For being mad at you for too long. Please forgive me, Daddy. I love you. Thank you for protecting me."

The tips of his fingers were blue, but they pressed against mine. Not an eyelid fluttered, nor did his lips move, but his fingers released mine as I slid back down onto my pallet. Footsteps pattered across the floor, and Lizzie lay down next to me. I gazed into her lavender eyes, relishing the tenderness on her face, the love in her smile.

"Viney, Dr. Henderson says that Daddy doesn't have much time left. He will pass today."

"Then he'll never know that I love him." I snuffled. "He's hurting because of me." My pride and willfulness had brought such suffering. And not just to Daddy, but to the men who had been injured last night. Some might have even died. "My stupid plan failed." Pressing my face into the pillow, I sobbed.

Lizzie kissed the top of my head. "Daddy chose to protect you, like any good father would. I'm hoping he'll rally long enough so I can remind him of my love and introduce him to William. Now, there's someone who wants to talk with you." She pulled the coverlet over me. "I know you're not looking your best, but I don't think he'll mind."

"If'n it's Jamie, send that scum down the river." Pain flashed over me as my shoulders stiffened. Yet, another image from the battle tickled my mind, or had that been part of my dreams?

"I already did that. James rode out of here last night. Uncle Abe has several cracked ribs and some nasty cuts, but he will heal. Several men were injured, but thank God, no one was killed in the battle." Lizzie walked to the door. "I'll leave you two alone with Daddy to chaperone. And next you need to meet my William." She grinned and held up her left hand, where a gold ring set with a ruby and diamonds sparkled.

Charlie's scent of leather and beeswax floated toward me as his boots clomped across the floor. I clutched the hem of the sheet, and my heart thrummed. Oh Laws, and here I lay, bruised, scarred for life by bullies that weren't worth the powder to blow them to hell. At least, Lizzie could have combed my hair and washed the tears from my face. Thankfully, the coverlet hid my nakedness, but I couldn't face him.

Chapter Thirty-Four

Charlie hated the bruises on his beloved's arms, her swollen wrists, and the pink stain on the sheet from her weeping wounds. If he had stayed in Rugby, he could have prevented those injuries. He sat down next to Viney, stretching out his long legs beside the pallet. The sun shone on his auburn hair, and a fine stubble darkened his chin. His blue chambray shirt was slashed at the shoulder, and one pant leg was ripped.

Charlie's lips brushed her cheek. "My stubborn, courageous Viney. Always wanting justice and freedom. I suppose that's because you're an American."

He stroked her hair, untangling snarls with his fingers. How foolish he had been to think that he had stopped loving her. Viney lifted her head and stared with remorsefulness into his blue eyes.

"Welcome to Wears Cove, Charlie." Gasping, Viney rested the side of her face on the pillow.

Charlie laughed, and leaned back against the log wall. "What a welcome last night! I'd prefer a dance to a battle, but I'd fight the White Caps a thousand times, if need be. You are worth dodging bullets and risking my neck."

Charlie took her hand and kissed it. "I never wanted to kill a man before, but when I watched your cousin raise that whip I could have murdered him, and the rest of those White Caps. If any man ever tries to harm you again, I will. Why did you do it, Viney?" Charlie lay down on Lizzie's pallet.

Closing his eyes, Charlie listened to Viney's description of how revenge had driven her plan. He should have left Michigan sooner, and removed Viney from this evil place. Returned to Rugby and her farm, but his pride had shadowed his senses.

"I probably made the White Caps even madder than ever." With her palms, Viney wiped away tears.

"Here." Charlie handed her his handkerchief. "It's clean." He was silent, while she wept into it. How many handkerchiefs had he given this silly woman? He hoped she would let him provide her with many more.

"The passing of time will show if last night changed any of the White Caps. But your father's Rebel yell stirred in the Blue Bills a greater boldness that many hadn't felt since the war. One man told me how he had almost stayed home, but came at the last minute. Hearing your father's battle cry flamed his outrage. Now he wants to recruit more men into the Blue Bills. And he wants to run for sheriff to try to stop how the vigilantes control the law. The Blue Bills call you Queen Courage."

"Laws. I don't feel like a queen." Viney blew her nose on the handkerchief. "I wanted to stop the violence. No more killings or whippings."

"I agree, but the White Caps saw a fury that they had never experienced. Even though they outnumbered the Blue Bills, the White Caps fled from the howling banshees. Sometimes it takes a thrashing to squash bullies. Your courage and your father's sacrifice may still change more minds."

Chapter Thirty-Five

"My aunt Alta preached that the Good Lord won His battle over evil with love..." I clutched the edge of the sheet as a fresh tremor of pain flashed over me. Those men called me a queen, but I wanted no crown, just to be healed, to not hurt, to be free to love Charlie.

"Weren't you acting out of love for the women you met?" Charlie leaned over and kissed my forehead. "Perhaps the White Caps learned how bullying someone doesn't alter a person. My father used to ridicule me, telling me that I was wasting my talents by becoming a farmer."

"So you came to Rugby." I remembered Charlie's soft hands, and how hoeing my corn had raised blisters. Now calluses thickened his palms. "But you left for the north..."

"Yes. A mistake that I deeply regret." Charlie sat up and picked at the rip in his pants. "I wrote you, but Lizzie said, you told her not to forward the letters." Charlie pointed to where a stack of envelopes sat on the table. "I decided to deliver them, and talk with you. Maybe the best way to start is to read them to you..." He opened an envelope and cleared his throat.

His words of regret, his request for forgiveness, his love flowed through me as Charlie read the letters. His ache at missing me, his hopes to reclaim my love sifted around me like the mist floating between the mountains. Oh, what grief I could have spared both of us if'n I had let Lizzie send on those letters. From this day forward, I would leave behind my pride and my ornery ways.

"I'm sorry, please forgive me. I was being muleheaded, but I reckon what matters most is that you're here. And I still love you." I gripped his hand. Like pulling the tiny teeth on a set of cards over a lock of wool, the fibers of my soul straightened. I was ready to be spun into strong and beautiful yarn, to knit my life with Charlie's.

"Yes." He kissed my swollen wrists. "If you are willing, may I always remain by your side?"

I smiled. "Is that some queer English way to ask a girl to marry you? Aren't you forgetting something?" Oh, I might promise to be good, but it felt fine to tease my man.

Charlie knelt and kissed each of my fingertips. "I love you, my darling Viney, and would be honored if you would share the rest of my life as my wife."

"You may not feel so honored after a few months with me. Yes, I can't wait to be your wife." If'n not for my throbbing back, I'd have wrapped my arms around his neck and smacked him a long, hearty kiss. Thank goodness, we'd have a lifetime of loving.

"I can't afford a beautiful ring with gems, like William gave Lizzie." Charlie continued to caress my hand.

"Such a thing would catch on the wool when I'm spinning. I'd prefer a simple band."

Truth be told, I'd wed Charlie even without a ring. But I always liked the way our English neighbor's wedding ring shone while she dried dishes, and the music it made as the gold tapped against the china. And every day, I could look at my ring and remember this moment.

"Like this?" Charlie withdrew from his pocket a gold ring with a vine of leaves etched around it. The gold sparkled in the sunlight. "A leafy vine for a certain weaver."

"Yes, along with a preacher. As soon as I can walk." I smiled, knowing that Aunt Sayward and Sissy would still point out how marrying would solve my problems and bring new blessings.

"William and Lizzie plan to reserve Christ Church for the last Saturday of this month. They've invited us to join them in a double wedding, but first you need to heal enough so we can return to Rugby." Charlie glanced at Daddy. "I wish I could ask your father for your hand, but the doctor thinks that he won't speak again."

"Then we have to marry today. A church celebration would be fine, but we don't need it. Even if Daddy can't give me away, I want him to be with us when we wed. That's what's most important. I know he'd bless us, and say how thankful he was that the Lord sent you to protect his daughter."

Lizzie's feet pattered through the doorway. "I agree. Laws, Viney will finally have a husband to keep her out of trouble. Appears that William had better fetch the preacher, while I try to pretty you up a bit. I brought a nightgown that might work for a white dress. And you, Mr. Groom must leave until all is ready."

• • • • •

Dressed in Lizzie's white lawn gown with a lace collar and ruffled flounce, and with a garland of asters in my hair, I leaned on a chair next to Charlie. With my free hand, I gripped Daddy's gnarled fingers. Holding hands, William and Lizzie stood at the head of Daddy's cot, and my sister's sweet voice filled the room as she sang, "O Perfect Love". Goldenrod glowed in mugs set on the table by plates of molasses cookies baked by Aunt Sayward. She and her children ringed the room, while Uncle Abe sat; his chest wrapped in bandages and his right eye swollen. My Walker girl cousins, except for Polly and Margaret, stood on the porch.

Tears filled my eyes as Charlie and I repeated the sacred words spoken by the preacher. The late afternoon sun glinted on my ring as my beloved slid it onto my finger. After the preacher told Charlie to kiss me, he gently cupped my chin and our lips lingered. Like the morning dew on a mountain laurel blossom, his sweetness flowed into me. And from the desire in Charlie's eyes, I prayed that my back would heal quickly. Cheering surrounded us, rolling into the cabin.

"Hooray for Viney! Hooray for her pa!" Dr. Henderson called.

Someone shook a kettle full of pebbles while another clanked a cowbell. "Kiss her again!" a woman shouted. "Bless her heart, kiss her for us."

Sweat beaded my brow, and my legs quaked, but I had to see these friends. Charlie and William made their arms into a seat, and Lizzie eased me into it. We stepped out to the porch. Half the cove stood in our clearing; men wearing their Blue Bill caps, women holding bouquets of Black-Eyed Susans, and children in Sunday go-to-meeting clothes. Even the Campbells had left their hollow, and Mr. Campbell held a new fiddle and bow.

"We'll have to dance for you and your pa," Mr. Campbell said. "You can name us your favorites."

"Thank you, I will." My tears blurred their faces. Now, I knew who had fought with me, and I pitied the men who still wore White Caps. I prayed that something would soon release them from the bonds strangling their lives.

Sissy slipped next to me and kissed my cheek. "Thank you," she said above the racket of banging pots and shouting. "My friends and I thank you."

Charlie and I kissed again, to satisfy the shivaree crowd. Seeing the jubilee on their faces eased my throbbing back.

"Thank you! God bless y'all." I called, and waved as the children brought me bouquets.

Lizzie began to fuss, making clucking sounds like an old hen. "That's enough, Viney. You need to rest. Charlie, please take her inside."

Back at my pallet, William and Charlie slid me onto my stomach, and Lizzie made sure that I drank all of her nasty tea. Fiddling began outside. Charlie sat down next to me, placed a pillow on his lap, and slipped my head upon it. He leaned back against Daddy's cot where my father's chest still rose and fell.

"Heal swiftly, my darling wife, so we can return to Rugby." Charlie kissed my cheek. "It's high time that we get to work on our farm."

"Hmm, yes." While the dancers shouted and the fiddle sang *Blackberry Blossom*, the tea swirled a cloud of wool through my mind. Back home to my mountain.

EPILOGUE

A dome of periwinkle blue arched over Rugby as I knelt by Daddy's grave, and placed upon it a bouquet of white asters, red dogwood leaves, and goldenrod. In Knoxville, Charlie had bought a marble stone and had it engraved with Daddy's and Mama's names before hauling it to the ridge. Charlie squatted by me, and slipped our son in my arms. Sissy wiped away tears, and laid her own bouquet of late red roses near mine.

"We named him after you, Daddy, he's little Jessie. Lizzie called her firstborn after Mama, and by the time the dogwood blooms, she'll give you another grandchild." And our next baby would arrive a few months after Lizzie and William's wee one. While it saddened me that these youn' uns would never know their granddaddy, at least I could share stories with them. About how he had fought in the War Between the States, how he had traveled to where herds of buffalo grazed, and how his love and courage had saved my life.

Using a small spade, my handsome husband dug a hole and planted snowdrop bulbs. His mother had sent them, along with a poke of daffodil bulbs, from England. From my apron pocket, I withdrew a packet and sprinkled forget-me-not seeds. I guided my son's hands, and we patted down the dirt, dreaming of blue flowers shining beside golden trumpets.

AUTHOR'S NOTE

During the late nineteenth century, the vigilante group, the White Caps controlled much of Sevier County, Tennessee. Historians estimate that between six-hundred to fifteen-hundred men belonged to the group. Dressed in white hoods and sometime in full white robes, the vigilantes disciplined women for "lewd" behavior. Tennessee historian, Don Williams stated that the White Caps whipped about one-hundred women and murdered a dozen or more men. While most of the residents did not participate in the clan, they were too terrorized to fight back.

Eventually, a counter-vigilante band, the Blue Bills was organized, and they sought to prevent raids and destroy the White Caps' power. Their leader was Dr. Henderson, a shrewd warrior who for two years outmaneuvered the clan's attacks. Because of his wealth, the doctor hired a spy to invade the White Caps' camps, and made certain that his two-hundred men were well-armed. According to the historian, E. W. Crozier, either a law officer or someone who had been made a deputy rode with the Blue Bills. Although the White Caps claimed that they were morally motivated, most of the men from Sevier County had fought for the Union during the Civil War, while the Blue Bills had served the Confederacy, so in some ways, their feud continued the War Between the States. Even though the White Caps held their power in the 1890s, I set my story in 1883, the time period when the Rugby Settlement thrived.

High up in the Great Smoky Mountains near Wears Valley, dwelt the Walker family, composed of John and Margaret Jane Walker, their four sons and seven daughters. For some unknown reason, after their parents died, the sisters inherited the farm. Polly and Martha were engaged, but both of their fiancés perished in separate logging accidents. Only Caroline married, and moved to Knoxville, where she raised a family. In 1949, *The Saturday Evening Post* wrote a feature about the five single sisters who lived an early nineteenth century, primitive lifestyle that provided for most of their needs. The article brought visitors from around the world to the

Walker cabin, to whom the sisters sold their crafts.

When the Great Smoky National Park was established, the sisters refused to sell their land, and eventually, they were granted a life-long lease. A legend maintains that the sisters only agreed to the arrangement after a secret meeting with President Roosevelt who visited their home on the day he dedicated the National Park. The Walker Sisters' homestead still exists and can be reached by a trail that begins at the Metcalf Bottoms picnic area. In 2016, the Walker Sisters were cited as "Smokies Heroes" and were listed as one of the 100 Most Influential People in the history of the National Park.

About an hour west of Knoxville in the Cumberland Mountains sits the village of Historic Rugby. A nonprofit now maintains the agrarian utopian settlement founded by the Englishman, Thomas Hughes in 1881. During a recession in the English economy, Hughes created Rugby so that the second sons of the landed gentry would have a respectable institution where they could learn farming and other forms of manual labor such as working in the settlement's canning factory. English society frowned on young men from the gentry working with their hands, and they could only become doctors, lawyers, clergymen, or perhaps teach at a university or serve in the military. Hughes also invited women, including his niece, to partake in the experience and he encouraged equality between men and women. Hughes also hoped that at some future time, Rugby would be integrated with African American settlers.

What the Englishman neglected to foresee was how the Appalachian people didn't want their lives invaded by foreigners who believed their ways were better than the local culture. Eventually, the highlanders appreciated the inflow of cash from the summer visitors. They also enjoyed checking books out of the library and attending the school, but tensions continued over the years. Some of the young women, like Viney, became friends with the English settlers, and embraced Hughes's progressive ideas. Due to a severe drought, a cholera epidemic, and the burning of the Tabard Inn, Rugby lasted only ten years before the dream dwindled. The village remains, and today, Historic Rugby offers tours, and special events that show visitors what it would have been like to live in the Victorian oasis tucked in the Cumberland Mountains.

The character of Viney is based on a beloved weaver from Rugby, Dicey Fletcher. Some of her weavings are displayed at Rugby while others reside in the Cincinnati Art Museum. *On Viney's Mountain* tells the story of Viney's struggles with the English settlers and how she came to love Charlie. I changed Dicey's name to Viney and also gave her the last name of Walker, because of my respect for the Walker Sisters whose homestead I view as one of the most beautiful locations in the Great Smoky Mountains.

When I read about the White Caps ruling Sevier County, I knew Viney was the damsel who would pursue justice for the women of the cove. Still, I paused to ask questions. What would motivate her to interfere in the cove's culture? Why would men join a supremacy group that disciplined women? Again, historian, Don Williams cites numerous reasons for men joining the White Caps from "religion, racism, peer pressure, moonshine, male hormones, turf wars, and excess of women following the Civil War, and economic upheaval". While my characters express my thoughts, other folks may have better answers to these questions. Yet in the end, I knew that instead of revenge, a father's act of mercy would produce justice.

ACKNOWLEDGEMENTS

No author works alone. So with gratitude, I express thanks to those who helped me along the way: Vi Biehl, Carol Coleman, Robin Heald, Suzie Jenkins, Lisa Lenzo, Don Williams, and my best reader and husband, John. And especially to the friend who introduced me to Rugby, the late Eric Wilson. Thank you to the staff at Black Rose Writing, and to my beloved orange cat, Fergi, who sleeps by my computer while I create.

References and Bibliography:

Crozier, E. W. *The White-caps: A history of the organization in Sevier County*. Knoxville, Tennessee Bean, Warters and Gaut, 1899. This book is now available through Google Books.

Dykeman, Wilma, and Jim Stokely. *Mountain Home: A Pictorial History of the Great Smoky Mountains National Park*. Gatlinburg, Great Smoky Mountain Association.

Egerton, John. *Visions of Utopia*. Knoxville, University of Tennessee Press, 1977.

Goodrich, Frances. *Mountain Homespun*. Knoxville, University of Tennessee Press, 1989.

Houk, Rose. *Storied Stitches: Quilts and Coverlets of the Smokies*. Gatlinburg, Great Smoky Mountain Association, 2011.

Madden, Robert R. and T. Russell Jones. *Mountain Home: The Walker Family Farmstead, Great Smoky Mountains National Park*. Washington, DC. US Department of the Interior, National Park Service, 1977.

Miles, Emma Bell. *The Spirit of the Mountains*. Knoxville, University of Tennessee Press, 1988.

Myers, Bonnie. *The Walker Sisters: Spirited Women of the Smokies*. Myers and Myers Publishing. 2004.

Williams, Don. "Night Riders from Hell: White Caps in Sevier County." Smokies Life Magazine, 11, 1. 2017

Websites that offer more information are: http://www.historicrugby.org/ and their Facebook page: https://www.facebook.com/historicrugby/?fref=ts

The Tennessee State Library and Archives provides excellent services. They supplied both introductory information about the White Caps, and a microfilm of Rugby's newspaper. http://sos.tn.gov/tsla

For those interested in the Great Smoky National Park, consider joining the Great Smoky Mountains Association: http://www.smokiesinformation.org/

About the Author

Joan Donaldson is the author of two picture books, two young adult novels, and an essay collection. Her last novel, *On Viney's Mountain* won the 2010 Friends of American Writers Award, represented the State of Tennessee at the 2010 National Book Festival, and appeared on the Bank Street List of the Best Books of 2010. She received a Master of Fine Arts from Spalding University, and earns her living growing organic blueberries.

For more information, please visit:
http://www.joandonaldson.com

Made in the USA
Columbia, SC
10 May 2024

35532396R00124